Praise for *New York Times* bestselling author

SHARON
SALA

"Well-developed secondary characters and a surprising
ending spice up Sala's latest romantic intrigue."
—*Publishers Weekly* on *Snowfall*

"Spellbinding narrative...Sala lives up to her reputation
with this well-crafted thriller."
—*Publishers Weekly* on *Remember Me*

"Ms. Sala draws you in from the very beginning.
She delivers main characters who will touch your hearts
and quirky secondary characters who will intrigue you
as you try to figure out whodunit."
—*Romantic Times BOOKclub* on *Butterfly*

"*Whippoorwill* is a funny, heartwarming story, set in a
raw, untamed land and rich with indelible characters
that will stay with you long after the last page is turned.
I didn't want it to be over."
—Deborah Smith, *New York Times* bestselling author of
A Place to Call Home

"Once again, Sharon Sala does a first-rate job at
blending richly developed characters and inspired
plotting into an unforgettable read."
—*Romantic Times BOOKclub* on *Dark Water*

SHARON SALA

MISSING

MIRA

ISBN 0-7783-2403-6

MISSING

Copyright © 2004 by Sharon Sala.

www.MIRABooks.com

Printed in U.S.A.

Then God said, "Let the earth sprout vegetation, plants yielding seed, and fruit trees bearing fruit after their kind, with seed in them, on the earth," and it was so.

And the earth brought forth vegetation, plants yielding seed after their kind, and trees bearing fruit, with seed in them, after their kind, and God saw that it was good.

—*Genesis* 1:11, 12

It was never meant for man to try to improve upon God's perfection. I dedicate this book to my grandchildren, who are perfect in my eyes. To Chelsea, Logan, Leslie and Daniel.

One

That inner part of a soldier that tells him when he's being watched was going off big-time in Wes Holden's head. His face was hidden beneath a layer of menthol-scented shaving cream, which gave him a false sense of anonymity, yet, despite his disguise, they'd found him again.

As he looked up, his eyes narrowed to slits, staring first at his own reflection in the bathroom mirror, then into the room behind him. When his gaze centered on the woman standing in the shadows, he stifled a groan.

He should have known.

It was Margie.

The fear on her face was palpable. He knew he'd caused it, but unless he changed what he did and ignored who he was, he didn't know how to help her. He'd known her since childhood, had loved her since high school—and, for the last fifteen years, had called her his wife.

He started to acknowledge her presence but changed his mind. There was tension between them that had nothing to do with his most recent tour, which had sent him first to Afghanistan, in search of Osama bin Laden, then, after the president had declared war, into Iraq.

Like every soldier's wife, Margie knew that he served his country at the risk of his own life. But this time it had been different. This time they were at war. Every day she'd watched the news on CNN in silent desperation, partly hoping to see his face, partly praying, if the filming was in the midst of conflict, that he was nowhere around.

The day she'd answered the door to find two army officers and an army chaplain standing on her doorstep, she'd started to scream. It had taken valuable minutes of their visit to calm her down long enough to explain that her husband, Colonel John Wesley Holden, wasn't confirmed dead—only missing.

Missing in action.

Three words that had almost brought sanity to an end.

The next month of her life had been a blur of fear and numbness. She admitted to Wes later that, if not for the presence of their son, Michael, she would have gone mad.

At that point Wes quit thinking about the weeks he'd spent as a POW, not certain he would ever see his family again, and shifted his focus from her face to his own.

There were still whiskers that had to come off before his meeting with a base psychiatrist at 0900 hours, and while the pace of life might be slow and easy in Georgia, it was a different story at Fort Benning.

Before he could resume shaving, he heard the sound of running feet. Moments later, he heard Margie cautioning their son not to run in the house; then Mikey burst into the bathroom, landing with a none-too-gentle flop on the closed lid of the commode.

"Easy, buddy," Wes said. "You almost missed the landing pad."

Five-year-old Michael John Holden giggled, then shoved the hair out of his eyes as he gazed longingly at his father.

"Daddy?"

Wes pulled the razor through a patch of shaving cream and whiskers, twisting his chin to accommodate the blade.

"What?"

"Someday will I have whiskers like you?"

Wes hid a grin as he sluiced the razor beneath a steady flow of hot water.

"Yeah…someday, but not anytime soon. You have to grow up some more before you get whiskers."

"Is it as long as Christmas?" Michael asked.

Pain wrapped itself around Wes's heart as he looked down at the earnest expression on his little boy's face.

"Yeah, Mikey, it's at least as long as Christmas."

Satisfied with the answer, Michael settled back for his front-row seat for the ritual they shared, where Daddy shaved and Mikey watched, interspersing the moment with a constant barrage of comments and questions that soon had Wes laughing.

Mikey was so enthralled with the process that Wes finally caved in, took the blade out of an extra razor, handed it to his son as he stood him up on the lid of the toilet seat, then put some shaving cream on Mikey's face.

"This is just for practice, okay, son?"

"Okay," Mikey said, then took the razor with all the ceremony due a first shave and peered at himself in the mirror. "Look, Daddy, I'm 'most big as you."

"Yeah, buddy, you sure are," Wes said gently, then watched his son scraping the shaving cream off his face with the empty razor, twisting his chin as Wes did, and grimacing with great élan. A few minutes later, he pronounced himself done and settled back down on the toilet seat with a wet washcloth to his face while Wes finished his own shave.

Wes's thoughts wandered, trying to come to terms with the fact that when he'd left for Afghanistan, Michael had been barely four and his biggest interest was watching *Bob the Builder*. Now he'd come back to find him only months away from his sixth birthday and concerned about growing whiskers.

It was enough to stagger a normal man. For Wes, it enhanced his guilt about leaving his family, and reinforced his concern about the nightmares and flashbacks he'd been having.

Post-traumatic stress disorder.

PTSD.

A nice four-letter acronym for a bitch of a problem.

Fancy words for trying not to go crazy from the hell of war.

He'd accepted the diagnosis with little emotion. It was his opinion that army doctors, like all doctors, preferred to categorize their patients' health issues. It was easier to treat them if their symptoms fell within certain parameters, so they gave everything a name. Wes would like to give the name back, but he had yet to figure out how to shake it.

It should have been simple.

They had rescued him, sent him home to heal, and one day soon, when he was pronounced ready on all counts, they would send him back to Iraq. But it wasn't simple. There were days when he wasn't sure he would ever be healed. For now, he would make love to his wife, watch his son grow, and take all of the fierceness of their loving with him when he went.

He was almost finished when a trash truck backfired on the street outside. Wes's stomach lurched. His instinct for survival told him to duck and run, but reality surfaced. He could still see his son's face and smell the citrus scent of his own shampoo, which meant he was in a safe place.

Still, by the time he realized it was a false alarm, he had pulled the razor too close to his skin. When a tiny dribble of blood suddenly appeared on his neck, he cursed beneath his breath.

Mikey saw the blood and cried out in quick dismay. "Daddy! You're blooding!"

Wes studied the tiny droplets. Considering where he'd been and what he'd seen, they were nothing, but he couldn't seem to break his gaze, or stop the memories of bloody bodies and lifeless eyes from flooding back into his mind. A knot began to form at the back of his throat as a cold sweat beaded across his forehead. He knew where he was. He could feel the cold tile against the bottoms of his bare feet, but he couldn't seem to pull away from the dark.

Then, suddenly, Mikey's hand was on his forearm.

"Don't cry, Daddy," Mikey said. "I can fix it."

He bolted out of the bathroom as Margie came back into the bedroom with a stack of freshly laundered towels. Ever cautious that sometimes her son's swift exits were because he'd done something wrong, she hurried into the bathroom where Wes was still standing.

"What happened?" she asked.

He swallowed the bile at the back of his throat and then took a deep breath, willing his voice not to shake.

"I just nicked myself," he said, as he pressed a washcloth against the spot.

"Let me see," Margie said, and moved his hand aside. "It doesn't look bad," she said. "I think I have something that will stop the bleeding in the medicine cabinet."

Wes slid his arms around her waist and pulled her close before burying his face against the curve of her neck.

"You have everything I need right here," he murmured, then kissed the spot just below her right ear.

Margie moaned, then sighed, savoring the feel of

him in her arms. She'd loved him forever, and having him home—even for a short time—made her whole again. But before anything went further than a kiss, Mikey was back.

"Hold that thought," Wes whispered as Margie grinned.

"I got it, Daddy. I got it!" Mikey cried.

Wes knelt down on one knee and put his arms around his boy.

"Got what, my little man?"

"A Band-Aid. Mommy puts 'em on me when I get blood. This will be good, but you have to be still."

Wes nodded and sat down on the side of the tub, wondering how Barney the purple dinosaur was going to blend with his uniform. Now they were face-to-face and only inches apart. Wes could see his own reflection in Mikey's eyes and was slightly surprised he looked no different. He would have thought it would be evident that he seemed to be coming undone.

"Just a minute, Daddy," Mikey said as he peeled the wrapper from the small antiseptic bandage.

Wes looked at his son, taking strength from the tenderness of his little boy's touch. The mint from Mikey's toothpaste was still strong on his breath, and there was a tiny bit of scab just visible on the curve of his chin that his pseudo-shave had not disturbed. His hair was thick and black, with a swirl in the crown just like Wes's, and when he smiled, the gap left from his missing tooth was too heart-wrenching for Wes to take.

He took a slow, deep breath, swallowing past the

knot in his throat. His child was growing up without him. His commitment to serving his country and to the military was strong—as strong as it had been the day he had enlisted—but he had to find a way to honor his commitment to his family, as well.

"Sit still, Daddy," Mikey said. "Dis won't hurt."

Wes closed his eyes to hide tears and made himself smile as he felt small fingers pressing against his neck.

"You're a good little doctor," Wes said. "That feels great."

Mikey nodded but kept staring at his father's neck. Wes sensed there was more to come, and when his son slowly rubbed his own little neck, Wes suddenly got it.

"Better let me have a look there," Wes said. "Well, that's just what I was afraid of."

Mikey's eyes widened. "What, Daddy? What do you see?"

"Darned if it doesn't look like you need a Band-Aid, too, and right in the same spot."

Mikey sighed. "Yeah, that's what I was afraid of, too."

Margie quickly hid a smile.

"Since I'm the only one in the family who's not part of the walking wounded, I will get another Barney Band-Aid, ASAP."

As she left the room, Mikey scooted between Wes's knees and then slid an arm around his father's neck.

"ASAP means as soon as possible."

Wes nodded. "Yes, it does. Good job, buddy. You're learning fast."

Mikey beamed, and then, suddenly bashful, hid his face beneath his father's chin.

"I'm glad you're home," he said softly.

Wes wrapped his arms around his son and tried not to think of how small and fragile he felt.

"Yeah, buddy, I'm glad I'm home, too."

As soon as Margie returned, Wes returned his son's favor. With their heads so close together, Margie thought, it was like looking at the large and small editions of the same face. Then she put her hands on her hips and pretended to frown as Wes stuck the other bandage on his little boy's neck.

"Out now, please, before I have to start mopping up any more spilled blood," Margie teased.

Her words set Wes's stomach to turning, but, again, he hid the feeling.

"Come on, buddy. I think we're in Mommy's way."

A short while later, they were all in the car, on their way to the base.

Georgia was beautiful in the springtime. As they passed through their neighborhood, Wes glanced longingly at the lawns of new grass and thought of the endless miles of desert sand and heat to which he would soon be returning. The peach orchards they'd driven past yesterday, with their glorious acres of blooming trees, would set fruit, ripen, go through harvest and lose leaves before he would be back. Mikey was chattering in the back seat, keeping up a running commentary about what they would buy when they got to the base commissary, with peanut butter being at the top of his list.

Everything seemed so ordinary, and yet there was a measure of insanity within Wes that he couldn't seem to shake. As badly as he hated to admit he needed a shrink, if that would help him get a grip on reality, he would suffer it gladly.

Margie rode with her hand on Wes's leg, as if she needed the touch to assure herself that he was really here. Wes understood the emotion. For him, the ordinary act of driving in a car with his family seemed surreal, and he had to admire Margie's womanly skill of being able to answer all Mikey's questions and still carry on a conversation with him without losing her concentration.

Soon they were turning off the highway toward the main gate. Subconsciously, Wes sat up a little straighter and automatically returned the salute from the guard at the gate.

Wes glanced at his wristwatch. Five minutes to nine. He would be right on time.

"Margie, there's no need for you guys to wait on me. As soon as you drop me off at the hospital, go do what you need to do. If I'm done before you finish, I'll just wait outside. The day's too pretty to waste being indoors."

"Okay," she said as he pulled to a stop. He leaned over and gave her a quick kiss, then winked at Mikey before getting out of the car. "See you later, buddy. Be good for Mommy."

"Okay, Daddy."

He turned away and headed for the door, but a few steps away, he felt an overwhelming urge to call Margie back. He turned abruptly, lifting his arm to hail the car, but she was too far away. Shrugging off his uneasiness as nothing more than reluctance to spill his guts to a stranger, Wes opened the door and walked in.

A half hour later Wes was trying to find a way to answer Dr. Price's question without admitting how fragile his hold on reality had become, when a loud explosion suddenly rocked the building. A fraction of a second later, all the windows in the doctor's office shattered inward. Wes was belly down on the floor before the glass blew, but the doctor's reaction wasn't as sharp. He was running toward the door when the glass shrapnel began to fly, peppering the back of his head and piercing his clothing and flesh. He fell to the floor, writhing in pain and leaving a blood trail on the carpet.

Before he had time to look up, Wes went into survival mode. He glanced toward the gaping windows, making certain that no enemy was in sight, then got up in a crouch, grabbed the doctor beneath his armpits and dragged him out of the room.

Out in the hall, chaos reigned. People were shouting and running, and he could already hear the sounds of both fire and ambulance sirens. Still pulling the doctor with him as he ran, he was all the way into the lobby before he found help.

"What are his injuries?" one of them asked as Wes gave the doctor up to their care.

"The windows in the office blew inward. I think it's all glass, but I can't be sure."

The doctor moaned as a medic laid him facedown on a cot.

"Easy, sir. You're going to be all right."

Wes's heart was hammering against his ribs as if it were a wild bird trying to get out of a cage. He could already feel the cold sweat running down the middle of his back as he tried to pull himself into a rational state of mind.

"What happened?" he asked.

"Explosion at the commissary," one of them said as they wheeled the doctor toward an examination room.

The commissary? Oh, Lord.

At that point the room started to tilt and Wes felt himself losing control. In a panic, he hit the wall with his fist, knowing that the pain would force him to focus. He bolted out of the building and into the street just as an ambulance pulled away, heading for the site of the explosion.

At that point, he looked over the rooftops, saw an ominous plume of black smoke and started running. Two blocks later, a trio of non-coms in a jeep picked him up. When they arrived on the scene, a perimeter was being set up.

"I'm sorry, sir, but you can't go in there," a young M.P. said.

Wes tried to push past.

"My family… I need to see if—"

"I'm sorry, sir, but no one is allowed inside the perimeter until the fire chief says so."

Wes took a staggering step backward, then started walking down the line of onlookers without taking his gaze from the fire. The front of the commissary was gone. From what he could see, there appeared to be a very large hole in the pavement right at the loading zone. He didn't need anyone to tell him what had caused it. He'd seen this time and time again, only not on American soil. This was an American army base. Car bombings didn't happen here—and yet, from what he could see, it appeared that one had, just the same.

Suddenly he bumped into a car, then stumbled. He turned then, staring down the long rows of cars in parking spaces, and realized he was in the commissary parking lot.

He didn't see their car. What if their car wasn't even here? What if Margie was back at the hospital, trying to find him right now? God, please let that be so.

He laughed, and the sound seemed crazy, even to him, as he began walking past the cars on his way out of the lot, but his heart was lighter, his stride easier than it had been seconds earlier.

A secondary explosion suddenly sent fire and debris flying up in the air. Wes dropped, his fingers curling around a gun that wasn't there, as he rolled beneath a vehicle. It took him a few moments to realize that the vehicle was a red SUV, not military issue, and that he was flat on his belly in the parking lot of the Fort Benning commissary, not in Iraq.

"Damn it all to hell," he muttered, and crawled to his feet.

Wes was looking around for his hat when he suddenly stopped. The car in the row across from where he was standing… It was blue, but—there were lots of blue cars, lots of the same make and model of blue cars. That wasn't their car. That couldn't be their car.

Still, he began moving toward it. Then he saw the tiny ding on the right fender, and bile suddenly rose up the back of his throat. He wouldn't look at the sticker on the window, because it surely couldn't have the same number as the one on their car. Then he saw the booster seat in the back and shuddered. It didn't have to mean anything. This was a young people's army. Nearly everyone had kids.

He reached for the door handle, telling himself that the door would be locked. Everyone locked their cars when they got out.

But the door opened.

He moaned. Everyone locked their doors except Margie. She was forever forgetting. He looked back toward the commissary and swallowed a sob. This meant that they were in there. He had to go find them. They would share a laugh over the fact that she'd left the doors unlocked again; then he'd take them out to lunch. An early lunch was a good thing.

His legs were shaking as he began to retrace his steps. They appeared to have the fire under control, but that didn't surprise him. The army was made up of the best of the best.

He walked past a pair of M.P.s, then past a fire truck, unaware that he was walking in water. Heat seared his face, and without thinking, he took off the jacket of his uniform and handed it to a passing soldier.

"Sir! Sir! You can't go in there," the soldier called, but Wes kept moving.

The soldier ran after him, but Wes had disappeared into the smoke.

Inside, soldiers were everywhere, helping the firemen with the removal of victims, shoring up walls about to fall, digging under broken ones for survivors. He stumbled on a can of tuna and barely caught himself before he fell. Someone grabbed his arm, but he pulled free and kept moving.

He could hear people crying and someone moaning in obvious pain. Every time he saw survivors, he ran to their sides, pulling them free of debris while praying they would be Margie and his son, but each time his hopes were dashed.

He ran from corner to corner, past overturned displays, while his panic grew. His heart was pounding so hard now that he could hardly breathe. His belly was churning and his legs were weak. The place was big— so damn big. Whose...idea had it been to build a commissary this damned big?

Something loud banged behind him, and he dropped. He was belly down and crawling on the commissary floor when he realized something had just fallen from a shelf. He crawled to his feet, then covered his face with his hands, trying to block out the smell of blood and burning flesh.

Think. He had to think. There had to be something he was forgetting. Something that would tell him where to look.

Then he remembered the peanut butter. Mikey had wanted peanut butter. It was at the back of the store.

He started walking again, this time moving faster, trying to remember exactly where the peanut butter had been shelved. But the shelves were lying one on top of the other, toppled like a child's line of dominoes.

"Margie! Margie! Where are you, honey? It's me, Wes! Can you hear me? Just call out my name!"

But no one answered his call.

A few moments later, he turned a corner and saw several soldiers in the act of lifting up some shelves. When he saw a woman's leg and foot beneath the debris, he realized why. Then his gaze suddenly focused on the shoe, and he stumbled.

"Margie."

He didn't know that he'd spoken aloud until one of the soldiers looked up. Wes was bareheaded and without his jacket, so the soldier had no idea of his rank and spoke without thinking.

"Hey, soldier, give us a hand."

The urgency in the young man's voice pulled Wes forward, although his mind had gone blank. He stood where they put him, but when the shelf came up, he moaned. The finality of his wife's condition was impossible to ignore. Her body had been crushed, either from the shock waves of the blast or from the shelves that had pinned her to the floor. It hardly mattered what had dealt the lethal blow. He'd been unable to keep her safe.

He shoved the other soldiers aside as he dropped to his knees. When he started to slide a hand beneath her neck, her head lolled to one side. He wouldn't let himself think of what that meant, or if she'd suffered before she'd died. He just threw back his head and wailed.

Someone laid a hand on Wes's shoulder.

"Come on, soldier, you need to let us help."

But Wes's hell wasn't over. As soon as they moved his wife, he found his son.

"Please, God…please don't do this," he begged, as he felt just below the Barney Band-Aid in a desperate search for the faintest hint of a pulse.

Nothing.

Then he laid a hand on the middle of Mikey's chest, as if willing a tiny heart back to life.

With an agonizing cry, he prostrated himself upon their bodies, then pulled them close within his arms. The animal sound that came out of his mouth was like nothing the young soldiers had ever heard.

They tried, without success, to get him up, but he wouldn't let go. They didn't understand that he hadn't just lost his family. If he turned them loose, he would lose his last link with sanity, as well. Somehow, despite how careful he'd been, his worst fears had come to fruition.

The enemy had followed him home.

Two

It wasn't until more men from Search and Rescue arrived on the scene that they were able to pry Wes Holden's family from his arms.

"Come on, soldier, you need to let us help you," a medic said, then took Wes by the arm.

But Wes's voice was shaking as he pushed the man away.

"No, don't. I have to take care of them," he said.

When they went to lift Margie onto a stretcher, Wes jerked, then leapt forward.

"Watch out, goddamn it! You're about to bump her head!" Gently, he slid his hands under the back of her neck and didn't let go until they'd laid her down.

"There now," he said softly, then pulled loose a bloody lock of hair that was stuck to her cheek and smoothed it back from her face. "Don't worry, darling. I won't let them hurt you."

The medics looked at one another, then looked away. They'd seen stuff like this before, but it didn't make it any easier. Trauma did crazy things to people's minds, and this was a bad one. When they went to remove the child from the debris, Wes lost it. His face was expressionless, but his body was shaking. He kept shifting his weight from one foot to the other; then he started to moan.

The medic closest to Wes was sympathetic to his distress, but these weren't the only two victims he'd pulled out of the site, and he feared there were more to come.

"Sir, you need to let us do our job."

"No…no… I'd better do this," Wes whispered. "He's my son, and he's not very good with strangers."

Tears were running down the medic's face as he stopped and swiped at his nose.

"Christ almighty. I hate this shit."

Wes was oblivious to everything but his son as he bent down and picked him up. Then he walked toward the empty stretcher, stumbling through cans of green beans as he went. But when he got there, instead of laying Mikey down, he pulled him close against his chest, and in the midst of smoke and debris, with his cheek against that soft little face, he began to moan.

He couldn't believe this was happening. God was playing some horrible joke. Wes had sworn an oath to put himself in harm's way. He was the one who should have died. God knew he couldn't live in this world without his wife or his son, so if He'd wanted Wes dead, then He should have let him die in Iraq.

Wes rubbed his cheek gently against his little boy's face, and as he did, he caught a faint whiff of the menthol-scented shaving cream from that morning. Mikey would never grow whiskers, not even as long as a million Christmases from now. He would never learn to read or hit a home run. Every dream, every hope, every plan that they'd had for him, was gone. Within the space of one heartbeat, everything had ended.

The medic touched Wes's arm.

"Sir? Please. You have to put him down now."

Wes flinched, then looked up, as if surprised by the sound of someone else's voice.

The medic pointed to Mikey again.

"Sir?"

Wes tightened his grip.

By now, the medic was begging. "Please." He pointed to the stretcher.

Wes stared at the empty space on the stretcher and then looked down at the child in his arms. Something fell off a shelf behind them, while outside, someone was calling for help. He blinked, then, for the last time, kissed his little boy's cheek and put him to bed.

When the medics began to cover the body, Wes grabbed the plastic sheet.

"I'll do it. He likes to be tucked in."

Wes bent down and pulled the sheet up to Mikey's chin, then gently tucked it in around him.

"Night-night, buddy," Wes whispered, then traced the shape of the Barney Band-Aid on the little boy's neck, as if making sure it was still firmly in place.

A nearby paratrooper took Wes by the arm and led him away. He didn't know what to do with him, but he would find someone who would.

Outside, as they were walking past the fire trucks, an officer suddenly came out of the crowd and grabbed Wes by the arm.

"Wes! Are you all right?"

The paratrooper saluted quickly.

"Colonel! Sir!"

"At ease, soldier," the colonel said. "What's happened here?"

"You know this man, sir?"

Charlie Frame nodded. "He's Colonel Wesley Holden, Special Ops." He gripped Wes's forearm. "Wes…talk to me, man. Are you hurt?"

But Wes didn't acknowledge Charlie's presence, or, for that matter, anything around him. His smoke-streaked face, as well as his unblinking stare, suddenly gave Charlie the willies.

When the paratrooper led Wes to a stack of boxes and sat him down as if he were a child, Charlie followed. Then the soldier turned to Charlie.

"Sir, we just pulled the bodies of a woman and a little boy out from under some debris. From the way he reacted, I think he knew them."

"Dear God." Charlie looked around. Maybe it was a

mistake. It had to be a mistake. "The bodies…where are they? Where did you take them?"

The soldier pointed to a rapidly growing row of corpses on the nearby grass. Some were covered with plastic sheeting, others with whatever had been available at the time.

Charlie glanced back at Wes, then moved toward the makeshift morgue. Yet even after he got there, he hesitated. It was all he could do to make himself look. Finally he bent over and lifted the covers from the last two bodies on the end. Even while his mind was processing the information, he kept telling himself it had to be a mistake.

But it wasn't.

It was Margie, just as he'd feared. The last time he'd seen her, she'd been sitting by Wes's bedside in the hospital with a look of horror on her face. Now her face was barely recognizable. He glanced back at Wes, then looked down again, and this time his gaze slid from the woman's bloody face to the small boy lying next to her. It was Michael, and except for a tiny smear of blood on his cheek, he looked as if he'd just fallen asleep.

Charlie groaned. Quick tears blurred his vision as he reached out with trembling fingers and pulled the edge of the T-shirt back down over the little child's belly. The absence of mobility on a little boy who'd been a bundle of energy was almost obscene.

As he stood up, he silently cursed. They'd gone overseas to fight a war against people with a suicidal mindset so that their loved ones wouldn't suffer like this. But something had gone wrong. How could this have happened—and on a fucking military base?

He walked back to Wes, then sat down beside him.

"Wes, I'm so sorry, man."

Wes didn't answer.

Charlie put his hand on Wes's back.

"Wes, it's me, Charlie. I'm here for you, buddy."

There wasn't a shred of emotion on Wes's face. He'd gone to a place in his mind where this hell didn't exist, and Charlie didn't know how to get him back. He'd seen plenty of dead people, some he'd even killed himself. He often struggled with that, even knowing that what he'd done had been under orders and in time of war. But this was different. He wanted to lie down and weep.

There was a faint but constant spray of water blowing on Wes's face. He could feel the dampness but couldn't seem to focus on where it was coming from. The acrid scent of smoke was still in his nose, and he was only vaguely aware of his surroundings and not sure why he was there.

Added to that was a faint hint of anxiety, as if he needed to be someplace else but couldn't quite remember why or where it might be.

People were shouting, some even screaming, as they ran past him. Overhead, he could hear the familiar *whup-whup* sound of a chopper's rotor blades. It was a sound common in war, and he thought nothing of it. He was a soldier, well versed in the art of warfare, and for the past two years it was all he'd heard. But as he sat there, he felt something wasn't right. For some reason, his hands were empty. A soldier should never be without his weapon.

The driver of a nearby ambulance suddenly fired up a siren as he took off toward the hospital. At the sound, the muscles in Wes's legs began to jerk. His fingers curled into fists.

The sky was black. It shouldn't be black. And where the hell was his gun?

Mohammed El Faud was an imposter. For the past seventeen months, he'd been living in Columbus, Georgia, under the name of Frank Turner, while working for a civilian contractor at Fort Benning.

Five years ago, when he'd first come to the States, he'd had plastic surgery to disguise his appearance. Now he regularly frequented a beauty shop off base called Lighten Up, where a woman named Estralita applied chemicals to his hair to keep it blond. Then, to keep up the pretense of why he had such dark skin, he paid good money to a tanning salon for a tan that would never fade, and he wore sky-blue contacts to hide the near-black color of his own irises. He was a master at linguistics and had adopted a California surfer accent, but it was only after the American military had begun making inroads into the war in his home country that he'd been given a course of action.

Implementing it had been far easier than he could have imagined. After months of careful planning, he had pierced the infidels in the heart by striking out at the military in two ways. First by attacking them on their own strongly guarded military base, then by targeting not only the soldiers, but their families, as well.

The commissary had been the obvious choice. And it had been so easy. Today he'd driven right up to the loading zone, as he'd done a hundred times before. He'd spoken in jest to a groundskeeper named Jeter, then pretended great concern for a very pregnant woman by loading her groceries for her before calmly walking away. He was two blocks away and safely behind a concrete wall when he detonated the bomb in the truck he'd left behind.

While everyone else was running to assist in recovery, he'd run the other way, retrieved the last part of what he needed to complete his mission and set off toward the blast site.

He had slipped all the way inside the perimeter set up by the M.P.s and was almost on top of the survivors they'd been bringing out before he shed his poncho and let out a cry. It was a blood-curdling shriek, followed by a litany of curses in his native language. Even as he was shouting and waving the detonator that would set off the explosives strapped to his chest, he seemed to be standing outside himself, enjoying the growing looks of shock and horror on everyone else's faces. Search and Rescue came to a momentary halt as soldiers went into battle mode.

Mohammed el Faud was under no misconceptions about his fate. Today he would die. He would detonate the explosives strapped to his body and kill even more. It would be a first for his people. Many had sacrificed their own lives while driving a car bomb into a crowd or building, but none had come back to the scene to kill again, this time taking out the survivors and rescuers alike.

It was the man's sudden scream in Arabic that reset Wes's focus. He recognized the language. He understood the words. What didn't make sense was the fact that the man had a California tan with a pretty-boy face. Even more at odds with the situation was the man's short blond hair. But Wes could see the explosives and the detonator he was holding, and knew from past experiences that things were never as they seemed. All of a sudden, he knew what had happened to his family and who had done it. He knew, and while he was too late to save them, he wasn't too late to exact retribution.

He stood abruptly, shoved his way past soldiers, medical personnel and firefighters, all of them frozen in disbelief, ripped the rifle out of an M.P.'s hands and fired off one round. It went right between Mohammed el Faud's fake blue eyes and out the back of his head before anyone could react.

There was a collective gasp as the detonator fell from Mohammed's hands into the street. Mohammed quickly followed suit, landing with a splash, facedown in the water from the fire hoses.

There was a split second of complete silence where no one moved—no one spoke. Then everyone started shouting, talking and running at once. The M.P. grabbed his rifle out of Wes's hands and ordered him facedown on the ground. Hands pushed at him, then pulled at him. Shouts followed to hasten the orders being carried out. The retrieval of victims had dissipated into a hasty retreat for fear that more terrorism was yet to come.

Charlie Frame pushed his way through the crowd to the military police who were holding Wes down.

"Get him up. Now!" Charlie ordered.

"But Colonel, he—"

"He executed a terrorist. Nothing more. Nothing less."

They pulled Wes to his feet, then undid his restraints.

Charlie took Wes by the shoulders, carefully eyeing his demeanor. There was a scrape on Wes's chin from when they'd pushed him to the ground, and a small drop of blood was seeping out of his left nostril. But those were nothing compared to the look in his eyes.

"Wes—"

"It was them…it was them."

Wes spoke softly—more to himself than to Charlie—but Charlie heard him just the same.

"What are you talking about? Who is 'them'?"

Wes looked up at the sky to the thick and billowing pillar of smoke.

"The enemy followed me home."

Then his eyes rolled back in his head, and he went down with a thud.

Charlie panicked. Had Wes been injured and they'd missed the wound? Was he dying now, before their eyes, and it was all going to be too late?

"Medic! Medic! Get me a medic!" he shouted, then stepped aside as a pair of medics did a quick once-over before lifting Wes onto a gurney and rolling him toward an ambulance.

Charlie followed, running by Wes's side as they carried him away.

"Hang in there, buddy," he said. "We're gonna get you some help."

But it was too late to help Wesley Holden. For all intents and purposes, he was already gone.

Six weeks later

Every time Charlie Frame walked into the psych ward at Martin Army Hospital, the hair on the back of his neck stood on end. Even though the place was scrubbed spotless and the patients under perfect care, it always smelled like death, which didn't really make sense. This wasn't a ward with terminal patients, only people who'd lost touch with reality. He would not have believed that the death of sanity could putrefy like rotting flesh, but it was the only explanation he had for the way it made him feel.

The last six weeks had been chaotic. The media had had a field day with the commissary bombing. The civilian contractor who'd unknowingly hired a terrorist had been dragged over the coals by both the media and the military. He had responded by blaming the military for missing the fact that the man's identification papers were faked. The entire investigation had been a disaster without resolution. The hard truth was that a foreign terrorist had infiltrated an American army base and dealt a killing blow. The fact that he'd been killed before he detonated his suicide bomb was thanks to a man whose mind was now in a state of limbo. Not even the base doctors could promise that Wes Holden would recover. In fact, the more time that passed, the less optimistic they became.

Now, after talking to Wes's doctor a few minutes earlier, Charlie's hopes were dimmer than before. When he reached Wes's room, he hesitated. This was his third visit this week, and probably his last. He was shipping out in two days and had no idea when he would be back. It would be good to know that his friend was on the road to recovery before he left.

"God, please let this be okay," he said softly, then entered the room.

Wes was sitting in a chair with his back to the door. Charlie took a deep breath and then made himself smile as he moved closer.

"Hey, Wes, it's me, Charlie. How you doin', buddy?"

He pulled up another chair and sat down beside the window, then stared straight into Wes Holden's face. At that point, Charlie's last hopes died.

Without speaking, he scooted his chair forward even more and put his hand on Wes's forearm. The sunlight coming through the window made Wes's blue eyes appear transparent. The bone structure of his face was highlighted by a marked weight loss, and his lips were slightly parted, as if he was on the brink of speaking, although Charlie knew that was misleading. He hadn't heard a word out of Wes's mouth since his claim that the enemy had followed him home.

He gave Wes's arm a brief squeeze, then turned his chair so that he was sharing Wes's view. He sat quietly, believing that in some part of Wes Holden's mind, he had to know that Charlie was there. They'd lost so many good people as a result of the bombing. He didn't want to lose his best friend, as well.

Time passed. The sun had already begun its fall toward the western horizon when Charlie got up and moved his chair between Wes's gaze and the window. He watched for a few moments, hoping for a reaction, but got nothing. Still, for his own peace of mind, he had to say what he'd come to say.

"Wes…they tell me that you're in what amounts to a catatonic state. They're starting to hint that you might never recover, and you know what I think? I think that's bullshit. You're not lost, man, you're just sad, and God knows you have the right."

Charlie gritted his teeth, then moved his chair a bit closer.

"I need to tell you that in a couple of days I'm shipping out. I don't know how long I'll be gone, but I don't want you to think I'm abandoning you. So here's the deal. You deserve this state of grace. While I'm gone, I want you to grieve and hide from reality and whatever the hell else you feel the need to do, but when I get back, you better be standing on the tarmac to welcome me home."

Charlie took a deep breath and shoved the heels of his hands against his eyes to keep from crying, then stood abruptly.

"Goddamn it, Wesley, don't stay gone too long."

He walked out without looking back, crossed the parking lot and got into his car without remembering that part of Wes's view was of this very same lot. He didn't think to look, and even if he had, he would have been too far away to see the tears on Wes Holden's face.

Three

Ally Monroe was staring out the kitchen window with her hands in slowly cooling dishwater. Although she was looking toward the family garden, she wasn't really seeing it. Her gaze was caught in the sunlight reflecting off the standing water in the concrete birdbath. Wish dreaming, as her mother used to call it. Longing for something different was pushing at her soul, but she'd long ago accepted that the only way she was going to find it was through her imagination.

She had been born in this house twenty-eight years ago last March, and had never been out of the state of West Virginia. Despite being born with a crippled foot that left her with a limp, she was the baby of the family and had been her mother's pride and joy. Still, her life hadn't seemed all that stifling until a month after her sixteenth birthday, when her mother had died. Within days of her mother's passing, it became apparent that her father, Gideon Monroe, expected her to step into the breach left by his wife's death. Without any thought for his daughter's grief or plans for the future, he left her responsible for every household task her mother had been doing. At that point, whatever dreams Ally might have had for herself died, too.

With each passing year, burden after burden was added to her life until, twelve years later, she was still living at home, keeping house, doing laundry, and cooking for her father and two older brothers, Danny and Porter. Once in a while, she felt as if they were all caught in some time warp. Nothing changed in this house except the ages of its residents.

But there were times, like now, when she let herself wish dream, when she imagined a tall stranger walking right out of those woods at the back of the house. He wouldn't know her name, but there would be this instant magical connection between them, and then he would take her in his arms and spirit her away.

Water dripped from the faucet, landed in the dishwater with a plop and broke into her muse. She blinked, then looked back at the birdbath, trying to reconnect. It was no use. The sunlight had moved, taking the magic with it.

Frowning, she looked down at the dishes yet to be washed, then turned away in quick frustration. Without giving herself time to think about what her father would say about her leaving a task undone, she yanked off her apron, tossed it on the dining table and walked out of the house.

Her foot was dragging slightly as she came off the porch and walked onto the grass, but she was used to the gait, and compensated perfectly by swinging her hip just a bit more to pull the leg along.

Her father's old hound, Buddy, raised his head as she passed on her way to a bench beneath the trees, then, when it became apparent that she hadn't brought a bone for him to chew, calmly resumed his afternoon nap.

Ally plopped down in the glider, then pulled her hair over her shoulder, taking care not to sit on the honey-colored braid. She brushed a gnat from the front of her T-shirt, adjusted her blue jeans, then swung her legs up into the seat. Using the padded armrest for a pillow, she looked up briefly into the overhead branches, then closed her eyes.

A passing breeze lifted the loose baby hairs away from her forehead as it pushed at the fabric of her shirt. She had no idea how seductive she appeared, nor would she have tried to foster the image. All she wanted was a place to dream. And so she lay, sheltered beneath the spreading branches of an ancient oak, and wondered how she could have been so gutless as to let her life get this off track.

Single men in Blue Creek gave her a wide berth, though not because they thought she was ugly. She looked okay, and she knew it. But none of them wanted to take a chance on having a child with a cripple. What if she passed on the birth defect to her children? They didn't want sons or daughters with crooked feet and dragging steps. Life was hard enough on the mountain without adding a physical handicap to the mix.

Frustrated with herself for dwelling on something she couldn't change, she pushed off with her toe and set the glider in motion. For a few solitary moments, she could almost believe she was being rocked in her mother's arms.

Gideon Monroe's left hip was paining something fierce as he turned up his driveway. When he accidentally bounced through the dried ruts in the road, he groaned. He hated getting old. He'd been lonely for years, ever since his Dolly had passed, but he'd still had his health. Yet for the past five or six years, it seemed as if he'd been going downhill. There had been that prostate cancer scare, which had turned out to be false; then arthritis had set into his joints from all the heavy lifting at the logging mill where he'd worked all his adult life.

He would be sixty-five his next birthday. That was too close to seventy. He could file for social security. It didn't seem possible. Where had his life gone—and how could it have gone so fast? Danny and Porter would be okay when he was gone, but he worried about Ally. He knew what was said about her on the mountain, and unless he did something about it, she would be alone for the rest of her life.

Then, today, it had seemed an answer to a prayer when Freddie Joe Detweiller had approached him at the café and asked his permission to call on Ally. Gideon had alternated between uncertainty and relief. He knew Detweiller was desperate, which meant he was more willing to overlook Ally's handicap. Detweiller's wife had been dead almost a year, and he was trying to raise their three kids on his own. Still, he wasn't sure that what he'd done was right.

He continued up the driveway, parked, then sat for a minute before getting out, trying to figure out what would be the best way to introduce the subject of Freddie Joe to Ally without making it sound like an insult. He couldn't help but feel that if he pushed this relationship, he would be selling his daughter short. She deserved more than becoming a convenience in some man's bed, as well as an unpaid babysitter to his motherless children. But he felt the burden of his duty, as well as the uncertainty of how many years he had left. The least he could do was give them a chance. Who knew? Maybe they would hit it off. Stranger things had happened.

Having settled the uncertainty in his mind, he got out of the truck and headed into the house. But when he called out her name, she didn't answer. Frowning, he moved through the rooms, searching for her whereabouts. When he got to the kitchen and saw the stack of dirty dishes yet to be washed, he couldn't believe it. This wasn't like Ally.

He started to call her again when he glanced out the

window and saw her lying in the glider as if she didn't have a care in the world.

Surprise mingled with the guilt he'd been feeling. He stared at the dirty dishes, then back out at the sleeping woman, and it all came out in anger. She couldn't be like this. Her crippled foot was already enough to put off most men. She couldn't appear lazy, as well.

He hit the screen door with the flat of his hand, then stomped out into the yard in anger.

"Girl! What the hell do you think you're doing?"

Startled by the rude awakening, Ally woke with a start. Instead of landing on her feet, she fell out of the glider, catching herself on her hands and knees.

"Ow," she muttered; then she looked at her father in disbelief. "You yelled at me."

Ashamed that he'd inadvertently caused Ally pain, he reached down and pulled her to her feet.

"Get on in the house and put some medicine on them scratches," he muttered. "Don't want to go and get them infected."

Ally wasn't in the habit of being yelled at and told him so.

"You shouted at me, Daddy. I want to know why."

Unwilling to apologize, Gideon continued to push when he should have pulled back.

"What's a man to think, coming home and finding the woman of the house outside sleeping when there's work to be done?"

Ally felt as if she'd just been slapped. She moved

backward, unconsciously putting distance between herself and her father. On another day, she would have meekly taken his anger as her due. But today was different. She felt different—more empowered. And she knew that, more than anything else, she didn't deserve to be treated like this. Suddenly she was unloading twelve years of disappointment and frustration.

"What do you mean…the woman of the house? I'm *not* the woman of the house. I have never been the woman of the house. I'm the daughter. Somewhere during the past twelve years, we all forgot that. I have no life other than taking care of you and my brothers, and yet you begrudge me one small afternoon nap? I am not a child, and I don't deserve to be chastised like this. In fact, I will *not* be spoken to like this. Do you understand me?"

Gideon was stunned, both by her anger and the fact that she'd had the gumption to speak up.

"Now see here," he muttered. "You don't have any call to—"

"No, you're the one without any right. I'm going in the house, and I'll finish the dishes. But when Danny and Porter show up for supper tonight, you better be ready to take them out to eat or cook it yourself, 'cause I'm not going to be home."

If she'd just threatened to kill him, Gideon couldn't have been any more shocked. He stared in disbelief as she walked away in anger. All he'd intended to do was tell her that he'd given Detweiller permission to court her. Something told him that he'd just made that an insurmountable issue.

Disgusted with himself and the entire situation, he slapped his fist against the side of his leg and headed for the barn to do the evening chores. By the time he came back, Danny and Porter were pulling into the yard, and Ally was nowhere to be seen.

"Hey, Dad, where's Ally? There's no supper. What's the deal?" Porter asked.

"She's busy," Gideon muttered.

"Oh, fine," Porter grumbled. "I'm starved and she's busy. Hellsfire, she doesn't have anything to do but cook a simple meal. What's so busy about that, I'd like to know?"

Gideon heard his son and knew he was responsible for his attitude.

"She has plenty to do keeping us all comfortable and fed. If she needs a night off now and then, then we should honor that."

"You're right. I'll be happy to fry up some ham and potatoes," Danny said.

Gideon looked at his younger son and made no move to hide his appreciation.

"Then we thank you, son, don't we, Porter?"

Porter Monroe frowned. It wasn't often that his father ever called him down about anything, but something told him now was not the time to push the issue about being thirty-seven years old and his own man.

"Yeah, sure, Danny. That would be great. I'll go

down in the cellar and get a quart of green beans to go with it."

Gideon sighed. If only it was as easy to make peace with Ally as it had been his sons, he would be feeling much more relieved.

When he passed through the living room on his way to the bathroom to wash up, he noticed that his truck was gone. He sighed. At least she hadn't gone off on foot. He didn't like to think about her limping off down the road or up the mountain through the trees.

He washed up in haste, unwilling to look at his own reflection in the bathroom mirror, well aware he wouldn't like what he saw.

Ally drove without aim, her only intent to get as far away from home as possible. Still, less than three miles from home, she caught herself turning east on a narrow, one-lane road, instead of continuing down toward Blue Creek. Even while she was negotiating the road, her mind was already on the warmth and welcome that would be waiting for her at Granny Devon's.

Granny wasn't really her grandmother. She'd born no children, but in the mountains of West Virginia, being given the title of a family member, while being no blood kin, was an honor. In her younger days, she had garnered something of a reputation for being a seer, and it had held her in good stead, especially since she'd been blind since birth. But Ally hadn't come to get her fortune told. She just needed the comfort of another woman's voice and, hopefully, some of her wisdom.

An old gray tomcat missing one ear and two teeth came out to meet Ally as she parked beneath a stand of pines. His throaty greeting was somewhere between a cat's meow and a growl, compliments of a dog fight years ago that he almost hadn't survived. Ally bent down and gave him a good scratch between the ears.

"Well, hello to you, too, Mr. Biddle. Yes, I'm fine. Thank you for asking."

Then she moved toward the porch and the little old woman who awaited her there.

"Granny Devon, it's me, Ally Monroe."

"Law, girl, you got no need to identify yourself. I saw you drive up," she said, and motioned for her to sit down.

Ally laughed. It was Granny's idea of a joke, although everyone always played along.

"Nice-looking bowl of beans you have there," Ally said. "I'd be happy to finish them off for you."

"What a sweet child you are," Granny said, and relinquished the chore to Ally.

Ally sat down in the empty chair beside the old woman, smiled to herself at the rather youthful pink dress Granny was wearing, then began finishing the beans.

"These out of your garden, Granny?"

"No, honey. Didn't plant no garden this year. My hands are getting too achy to hold a hoe these days. Anson Tiller's boy, Duke, brung 'em over to me earlier."

Then she lifted both hands to her head, and with the

deftness of a woman who'd learned to see with her fingers, tucked a few flyaway strands into the bun she wore at the back of her neck and fluffed the ruffled collar framing her tiny face. Once satisfied that she looked presentable, she pushed off in her rocking chair as she turned her attention to Ally.

"Talk to me, sweet'en. How's that Gideon doin' these days?"

Ally sighed. "We had words, Granny."

Granny nodded while riding with the motion of the chair.

"Better than tradin' blows," Granny stated.

Ally snorted softly. "We came close."

Granny picked up on the sarcasm in the sound and frowned.

"You're too easy on your menfolk. They take you for granted."

Ally sighed, then let her hands go limp in the bowl.

"I know, but it's too late to change." She blinked back tears. "Oh, Granny, it's too late for everything."

The old woman reached out, took away the bowl of beans and set it aside.

"It's never too late," she said. "Now, give me your hands, girl."

Ally scooted closer, then laid her hands in Granny's lap. She knew what came next. She wouldn't admit it, but it was, after all, the real reason why she'd come.

Granny's hands were palms up, but the moment she felt Ally's hands, she grabbed them tight.

Ally knew what to expect, and still her heart rate accelerated. She stared into those pale, sightless eyes and tried not to shudder. Even though she knew Granny Devon had never seen a moment of light on this earth, she would have sworn she was seeing all the way to heaven.

The old woman's lips went slack, and she started to sway back and forth. Ally heard her moan, then exhale softly. At that point, she started murmuring in a high, singsong voice.

"Look to the family.
Look to the heart.
Danger around you.
Trouble will start."

Ally frowned. It was the last thing she'd expected to hear, and yet it wasn't enough to tell her how to prevent it, or save herself and her family from ruin.

"How, Granny? How will the trouble start?"

The old woman's eyelids were fluttering, and her gaze was fixed on a point far beyond Ally's mortal sight. Ally braced herself for the answer. "You are not your brothers' keeper."

Ally leaned forward until she was so close she could feel the old woman's breath upon her face.

"Which brother, Granny? What's happening to my brothers?"

But Granny Devon's moments of sight were gone.

She turned loose of Ally's hands and fell back in her chair. Her breathing was shallow, her body limp and shaking.

Ally sat without moving, waiting for Granny to recover herself. Even though she seemed close to apoplexy, Ally knew from experience that she would come to in her own time.

The old tomcat wandered up onto the porch, paused to look at Granny Devon as if he knew what was happening, then leapt up into her lap and curled himself into a ball. Ally could hear him purring from where she sat.

A few moments later, Granny inhaled deeply, then sat up, felt the cat in her lap and smiled.

"Well, hello there, Mr. Biddle. Real thoughty of you to come visit me like this," she said, then laughed out loud.

Ally smiled, but she couldn't laugh. Not after what she'd just heard. Her silence must have alerted Granny that all was not well.

"Girl…you still here?"

"Yes, ma'am."

Granny's hands stilled on the cat as her smile faded. "Was it bad?"

Ally sighed. Another thing about Granny that was somewhat unusual was that she never remembered what she said when she had her visions.

"Yes, ma'am."

Granny frowned. "I'm right sorry, girl."

"It's all right, Granny. You don't make stuff happen, you just give us a warning of what to expect, right?"

Granny nodded slowly. "Best I can figure. I don't rightly understand it myself." Then Granny dumped the cat from her lap and stood up. "Let's go inside. I'm right hungry for my supper. Have you et, girl?"

"No, ma'am."

"Then you can sit at the table with me. It's been a while since I had company for supper. It'll be a pleasure."

Ally shook off the anxiety of Granny's predictions and followed the little woman into the house. Soon the kitchen was filled with the homey scents of baking corn bread, frying chicken and fresh corn on the cob. Ally finished setting the table, then took a plate of sliced tomatoes from the refrigerator and put them on the table.

"The table is set, and the tomatoes are out, Granny. Is there something else I can do for you?"

"I reckon you can come look at this chicken and see if it's as brown as you like it."

Ally peered over Granny's shoulder and shook her head in disbelief. It was all she could do to time cooking a meal like that and make it work, and she could see.

"Granny, I don't know how you do it, but it looks amazing."

"Good, then fork up that yard bird and get it on the plate. My belly feels like it's gnawing on my backbone."

Ally grinned.

"Why don't you sit down and let me finish dishing up the food?"

Granny wiped her hands down the front of her apron.

"Well now, I believe that I will. Seems like my days just keep getting longer and longer."

Ally dished up the food as Granny took a seat at the table.

"Iced tea is already poured and to your right," Ally said.

Granny started to reach for the glass, then stopped and frowned.

"Reckon did you sweet it?" Granny asked.

Ally smiled. "Yes, ma'am. Is there any other kind?"

Granny laughed and nodded as her fingers curled around the glass and lifted it to her lips.

"Umm-hmm," she said, as she took a good long sip. "That's fine. Right fine."

"And so is this meal," Ally said as she sat the last of the bowls on the table. "It's very kind of you to invite me to stay."

"It's my pleasure, girl," Granny said. "'Sides, sometimes we women just need a break from the menfolks of this world."

"That's the truth," Ally muttered as she slid into her seat.

Granny reached for Ally's hand.

"Bow your head, girl. We bless the food before we put it in our bellies."

"Yes, ma'am," Ally said, and closed her eyes in quiet submission.

The prayer wrapped around her, comforting in its message and promising an ease to her worries that she sorely needed. When Granny ended with a hearty amen, Ally felt renewed and suddenly hungry.

"Since you're here, I'll take advantage of your kindness and ask you to fix my plate."

"It would be my pleasure," Ally said.

Granny nodded. "I like the back piece of chicken, my corn plain, and my corn bread buttered."

Ally stifled a chuckle. "Granny, you know what?"

"What's that?" Granny said, as she felt along the platter of chicken until she found some crumbles of the fried chicken batter and popped them in her mouth.

"I want to be just like you when I grow up."

Granny laughed and then slapped her leg as if Ally had made a good joke.

"First of all, you don't know what you're talkin' about. You're done grown up and we both know it. Your childhood ended when your mama died. As for wantin' to be like me, no, you don't. My womb was barren, and my eyes aren't nothin' but plugs for the holes in my head."

Ally covered Granny's hand with hers. "No, ma'am. You're wrong about some of that. You may not have born a child, but there's not a child on this mountain who doesn't love you as if they were your own blood. As for your eyes, I think you see more than anyone. You don't need eyes to see into our hearts. You are precious to all of us, Granny. Don't ever doubt that for a minute."

Ally could tell that her words had pleased the old woman, but she didn't comment other than to let go of a small smile.

"About that corn bread…" Granny said.

"What about it?" Ally asked.

"There's four corners in that pan and I'd like to have one of 'em. It's got more crust, and I like the crust best."

This time Ally giggled aloud. Granny sure did like her food.

"I'm cutting it now," Ally said.

"And the butter…don't forget the butter," Granny said.

"Who's doing this…me or you?" Ally said.

Granny slapped her leg and giggled.

"Danged if you ain't right. I'm sorry, girl. You fix it just like you like it, and I'll swear it's the best I ever had."

"Of course you will," Ally said. "You cooked it."

Granny was silent for a moment, then picked up her fork. "That I did. That I did."

Four

Nine months later

A short busybody of a nurse used her hip to shove the door to Wes Holden's room inward. Upon entering, she set a stack of fresh towels and washcloths on the end of the bed, then moved to the windows, pulled the curtains back and patted the mound of covers over Wes's feet as she headed for the sink with a washcloth. She noticed as she worked that Colonel Holden's eyes were open, but he neither acknowledged her nor behaved as if he even knew she was there.

"Good morning, Wesley. Did you sleep well last night? I didn't. My knee hurts like a big dog. I swear the weather is going to change. Mark my words. It'll rain before nightfall."

She dunked the washcloth beneath a stream of warm water, wet it good, then wrung it out and headed for the bed.

"Let's wash that sleep right out of your eyes, what do you say?"

She swiped the warm, damp cloth across Wesley's face as a quick wash and wake-up, ever aware of his blank, sightless stare.

"After breakfast, I'll give you a shave. It will make you feel like a new man."

She pushed buttons and plumped pillows, then readjusted Wes's posture until she finally had him sitting upright in bed. What was driving her crazy was that in all the time he'd been here, she had never seen one moment of life in his eyes.

He opened his mouth when she told him to, and chewed when food was put in his mouth. He was shaved and bathed and wheeled about as if he'd lost the use of his legs, when in reality it was his mind that was lost. She knew his story, but he wasn't the only soldier who had lost a loved one in the commissary bombing, and that had been almost a year ago. She figured this stemmed from something deeper. She knew what the doctors said about his PTSD, and she'd also heard the rumors that they were convinced he might never return to reality. But she was in the business of helping to save people's lives, and in her opinion, he was a man worth saving.

Once she was through washing his face, she pulled the guardrails down from the bed and swung his legs off the mattress, letting them dangle.

"Okay, mister. Bathroom for you. Get up."

Somewhere inside the shell of Wes Holden's mind, he was still able to respond to orders. He stood.

"Go do your business, soldier. When you come out, breakfast should be here."

She pushed gently, aiming Wes toward the bathroom. A short while later, he exited. She made him wash his hands, then sat him in a chair near the window, rather than back in his bed.

"Breakfast is served," she said, and pushed the small table with his tray of food in front of him. She put the fork in his hand. "All right, soldier, I'm too damn busy to sit here and feed you every day. Eat up."

But Wes didn't respond, and she was afraid to leave the food with him. Something told her that, if it was up to Wes, he would gladly starve and that death would be welcome. She patted his back and pulled up a chair.

"It's okay, honey. I'm not that busy, after all."

She took the fork out of his hand, scooped up a bite of scrambled eggs and aimed them at his mouth.

"Open wide."

To her undying relief, he not only chewed, but swallowed.

After months in the psych ward, the nurses had gotten used to Wes's inactivity, and for her, it was just another day.

When she'd finished feeding him, she got a basin of warm water, shaving soap and a razor, and began their morning routine. For a while, there was silence in the room, with only the occasional sound of the razor being swished through water and the soft notes of a song she was humming. Just as she was pulling the razor up the sharp angle of his right cheek, a loud clap of thunder suddenly rattled the windows. She jerked and flinched, and when she did, the razor nicked a spot on Wes's cheek.

"Oh, honey…oh, darn… I'm so sorry," she said, and grabbed the wet washcloth from the bed rail, pressing it firmly to his cheek. "It was the thunder. I told you it was going to rain, didn't I?"

She dabbed at the cut over and over until it began to clot, then dropped the washcloth into the shaving water.

"I'm going to get some antiseptic. I'll be right back."

Wes's unfocused gaze was turned toward the window as she left. Suddenly a shaft of lightning hit the parking lot just outside the window. The flash was violent and bright, and followed by another clap of thunder so loud that it sounded like a bomb.

Wes threw up his arms. As he turned to throw himself onto the floor, he saw the basin of bloody water. Then he froze, his gaze fixed as he stared at the red stain. It was only seconds, but for Wes, it seemed like an eternity. In the time it took for his breathing to resume, he was aware of everything. The sound of his heartbeat was so loud that the throb hurt his ears, and he was shaking from the inside out.

There was blood in the water.

There had been blood all over Margie.

It thundered again. He looked down at his hands, then up at the window. Wind was blowing the rain against the glass. The turmoil outside was as wild and violent as the feeling inside his chest. Kill or be killed. That was what a soldier was taught. Someone had killed his wife and little boy. He'd killed one of them, but there could be more. Trust no one. The enemy could be hiding anywhere.

"Here we are," the little nurse said, dabbing some antibiotic on the cut, then quickly applying a small circle-shaped plaster.

Wes shifted his gaze to a corner of the floor and willed himself not to scream. The way his heart was hammering, she was bound to hear.

"I'm really sorry about this," the nurse said, then gathered up the shaving utensils and wet towels, and quickly left the room. Thanks to this mess, she was already behind.

Wes exhaled slowly, then got out of the chair and crawled into bed, pulled the covers up over his shoulders and closed his eyes.

When the next nurse came in and found him in bed, she just assumed that the first nurse had put him there. Days passed, and as they did, Wes regained more and more cognizance, but with it came memories.

The fish on Wes's hook suddenly flopped out of the water, but before he could land it, it came off the hook and dropped back in the creek.

His daddy laughed. He wanted to cry. It had been a really big fish. But his daddy's laughter was contagious.

Before he knew it, they were both in stitches. Besides, he was ten years old—far too old to cry over losing a fish.

Suddenly, there was a bright flash of light in Wes's eyes, and that quickly, his daddy was gone.

Damn it.

The part of him that had learned how to live in the past had disappeared. It didn't matter that his father had been dead for years, because when his mind would cooperate, he knew where to find him.

Trouble was, it was becoming more and more difficult to stay gone. Once in the night he'd awakened, and when he opened his eyes, he had known immediately who he was and that he was in a strange place. But the worst of it came after he remembered why he was here.

The pain that had come with the knowledge was engulfing, and he leaned over the side of the bed and threw up. A passing night nurse had heard the commotion and hurried to his aid. In the business of cleaning up both him and the floor, she had completely missed the fact that Wes had come to himself enough not to throw up in bed.

Thinking that he was coming down with some stomach bug, they had given him a shot to stifle the nausea. It had served the purpose, but had also given Wes the necessary path to find his way back to limbo.

The next time his eyes had opened, he was safe at home with his six-year-old brother, Billy, asleep beside him.

There was frost on the windows, and he could smell gingerbread. It was Christmas morning!

"Billy! Wake up. It's Christmas!"

His younger brother rolled from his side of the bed while his eyes were still shut, stumbled, then fell. Wes threw back the covers and jumped down to help Billy up. Then they raced to the bathroom before heading down the stairs. They were halfway down when they heard their mother call up.

"You boys better not be coming down these stairs barefoot. You know how cold these floors are, and I don't want both of you sick."

They groaned in unison as they ran back for their robes and slippers. When they finally came down, they were wild.

"Oh, Mom! Dad! Bicycles! Santa left us bicycles!"

Patricia Holden threw up her hands in mock disbelief and then grabbed the camera, anxious to capture the expressions on their faces.

"Boys! Boys! Look this way!" Patricia called.

Seven-year-old Wesley was standing beside his bicycle. He turned toward the sound of his mother's voice and then laughed from the pure joy of the moment.

Someone was laughing. There was a yearning within Wes that almost made him turn and look, but he didn't. He was pretty sure there was a reason why he shouldn't laugh, but for the moment, he couldn't remember why. Within seconds, the notion passed and, with it, Wes's sense.

Some time later two men entered his room and stood on either side of his chair as he sat by the window. He'd known the moment they'd entered the room because he'd smelled them coming. One needed to change his deodorant, because what he was wearing had quit working. The other smelled of smoke and peppermints. Wes's heightened sensitivity to sounds and smells had come from Special Ops survival training—that same training that was urging him to drop, roll and shoot.

Only he didn't move. He wasn't armed, and he wasn't sure where he was, and running would be futile unless he knew the way out, so he settled within the silence of his mind, waiting for them to finish their foray, then get out.

Dr. Avery Benedict finished his physical examination of Wesley Holden, slipped his penlight into his pocket, shifted his stance to an "at ease" position, then clasped his hands behind his back.

Wes's psychiatrist, Dr. Marshall Milam, glanced down at Wes, then back to Benedict.

"Do you concur with my decision?" Milam asked.

Benedict hesitated. "I don't know. Physically, he's fine. In fact, damned fine."

"It's not the physical side of the man I'm concerned with. He's been here for nearly a year. I've been unable to connect with him on any level, and while I'm not willing to say he's incurable, I do think that another doctor, maybe one with a different approach, might be able to do what I can't."

Benedict glanced at Wes again. "Medical discharge?"

Milam sighed. "Other than the deceased wife and child, does he have any next of kin?"

Benedict flipped through Wes's chart. "Parents deceased. One brother, also deceased. Oh, wait…says here there's a stepbrother, Aaron Clancy, in Florida."

Milam nodded. "Notify the stepbrother. I'll start the paperwork."

Having made their decision, they walked away from Wes as if he were nothing more than a potted plant they'd stopped to view. It wasn't personal, it was just part of their process.

A part of Wes had heard, but none of it had soaked in. As soon as he'd heard the word *stepbrother,* he'd been gone.

Wes was sitting on the stoop at the back of his house. He hadn't felt this out of control since the day his father had died. Today it had been self-preservation that had sent him to the back porch in a sullen fit.

Mom was getting married again. He couldn't believe it. It was a betrayal of everything their family, or what was left of it, stood for. He swallowed back tears and swiped his hand beneath his nose. He would be damned before he would let anyone see him cry.

This wasn't fair. None of it was fair. Billy was dead. He'd died the spring after they'd gotten their first bicycles. Mom had warned them time and time again not to ride the bikes into the street, and the one time Billy broke the rule, he died for it.

After that, Wes had figured nothing bad could ever happen to their family again, because they'd already had their share of sadness. Then, a few years later, his father went to work one day and never came home. He died of a heart attack just after Wes's sixteenth birthday. The first time Wes used his new driver's license was to take his mother to the funeral home to make arrangements for his father's burial. That was the day he'd realized that nothing about life was fair, and that some people had more than their share of bad luck.

He'd thought nothing could ever top that until today. Hearing his mother say that she was marrying Aiden Clancy had been like being run over by a bus. Aiden Clancy was a bully, and his son, Aaron, was no different. On top of that, his father had disliked Aiden with a passion. He couldn't believe that his mom was unable to see through the man's smiles and lies.

Then he heard the hinges squeak on the screen door behind him and braced himself for the sound of his mother's voice. He knew he'd hurt her feelings. But she'd wiped out what was left of his world, and he didn't know if he would ever be able to forgive her for that.

"Wesley, would you please come inside? Aiden and Aaron will be here soon. I would like our first family dinner together to be one of congeniality."

Wes stood abruptly, and with all the displaced anger and pain a seventeen-year-old male could possess, he stared her down.

"I'll come in, and I'll sit down at our table with those people, but I will never consider them family. Dad didn't like Aiden Clancy, I don't like Aaron, and you've

known that my entire life. Still, you've chosen to ignore Dad's intuition and my feelings."

Patricia Holden stifled hot tears, channeling them instead into what she felt was justified betrayal.

"Your father is dead! I'm not. I am forty-two years old. I do not wish to live the rest of my life alone."

"You have me!" Wes shouted.

Patricia sighed. *"But for how long, Wesley? You're growing up. One day you'll move away and start a family of your own. Am I destined to be the old woman who gets a happy-birthday phone call once a year and a visit at Christmas?"*

Wes knew she was right, but he wasn't quite man enough yet to admit it.

"You're right about one thing," he said.

"What's that?"

"I turn eighteen two weeks after graduation. Rest assured that I will be moving my ass out of this house and as far away as I can get."

It was then that Patricia Holden knew she'd made a terrible mistake. Her promise to marry was causing her to lose the person she loved most on this earth.

"Wait! Wesley…Wes…no, please. Don't do this to me," she begged.

Wes looked at her as if he'd never seen her before. Then his chin quivered, and it was all he could do to speak.

"I didn't do anything, Mom. It was you who decided."

As promised, Wes had signed on with the United States army with a delayed induction to begin right after his high school graduation. He'd spent exactly three months and fourteen days under the same roof with Aiden and Aaron Clancy, and it had been three months and fourteen days too long.

Now the shock of hearing Aaron's name again had given him a mental shake he couldn't ignore. The last thing that flitted through his mind before letting go of reality was that he wasn't going anywhere with that man.

Aaron Clancy didn't know what to think about the phone call he'd received yesterday from Martin Army Hospital at Fort Benning. He'd hadn't seen or heard from Wes in years and, truthfully, had all but forgotten they'd ever had a fleeting familial connection. He'd been ready to tell that army doctor to kiss his ass, until he'd heard the word *benefits*. After that, he changed his attitude, as well as the tone of his voice. He didn't really give a damn whether Wes ever pulled out of the funk he was in, but he was willing to put him somewhere if he had power of attorney over Wes's finances. Mustering out of the army as a full-bird colonel, with all the perks that came with it, was bound to bring in more money than Aaron's job as shop foreman at a car dealership.

Having made his decision, he'd packed a bag and headed for Georgia. He'd landed an hour ago, caught a cab to the base, and had been waiting at the front gate for forty-five minutes for an okay to pass. Had it not been for the monthly tax-free money that came with

Wes Holden, he would have turned around and headed straight back to Miami.

Wes had yet to comment to anyone on the state of the nation, but over the past few days, he'd become aware of the state of his condition. There was a part of him that was ashamed he'd done such a cowardly thing as retreat and hide. But then there was the pain that would come with reality. If he started talking to anyone, then they were going to ask questions, which meant they would also expect answers, and he didn't have any. He'd come to the conclusion that his entire existence on this earth had been one big joke. Every time he let himself love someone, that someone died. There had been so many deaths now, and each time it had happened, he'd tried as hard as he knew to die with them, but it hadn't worked. Now he was faced with more than a virtual awakening. Either he got back into the human race, or—

"Good morning, Wesley."

It was the busybody nurse. He almost answered her, then caught himself. He wasn't ready to admit he was present.

"I'm going to miss you," she said, as she began packing his things into a duffel bag she pulled out of the closet.

Miss me? Where the hell am I going?

"I just know that this move is going to be what you need," she rattled on. "I just met your stepbrother. He seems like such a nice man…and so concerned about you. He's already seen to a power of an attorney and everything to make sure you don't want for a thing."

It was to Wes's credit that he didn't move or speak, but if anything might have caused him to, that would have been it. Aaron Clancy didn't give a rat's ass for Wes's welfare, but if he had already gotten power of attorney, then he was after money. It felt strange to feel anger. In fact, it felt strange to feel anything. He'd allowed himself to disintegrate for so long that the resurrection of emotions was almost frightening. If he got up from the chair and did what he felt like doing to Aaron Clancy, they would lock him up for sure. And there was the fact that if he left this place with Aaron, he could disappear again any time he wanted to—only this time for real.

The little nurse knelt down at his feet and began putting on his shoes and socks. He felt somewhat guilty for letting her do it, but he had a facade to maintain.

"I hear he lives in Florida," she said. "You'll love it down there…all that sun and water. If he lives near the ocean, of course. Anyway, you'll be with family, which is just what you need."

Sorrow filled Wesley so suddenly that he had to blink away tears, which, fortunately, she didn't see. It was the word *family* that had done it.

Dear sweet Lord…Margie…Michael. I hid like a coward and left someone else to bury them.

It hurt so much, it was all he could do to draw breath, yet the busybody of a nurse was wasting hers.

"There now," she said, and patted his knee as she stood. "Your brother will be here soon." Then she surprised Wes by looking straight in his face. "I'm so sorry," she said softly, then leaned over and gently hugged his neck. "I'm so very, very sorry for your loss."

She fussed with his hair a bit and then hurried out of the room before she broke down.

As soon as Wes heard the door swing shut, he started to shake. Tears burned the backs of his eyes as bile rose from his belly. He couldn't cry. It wasn't safe. If he started, he might never be able to stop, and then they might never let him leave. And he *had* to leave. He wanted as far away from the world of a soldier as he could get, and Aaron Clancy was going to be his ticket out.

Five

Aaron Clancy was finally in the waiting room, but more than a little uncomfortable. Too many uniforms, too many rules to suit him. He couldn't imagine military life, especially now. Having to go to some god-awful foreign country and get shot at on a daily basis was bogus. The only thing he'd been able to think as he was being driven to the hospital was, thank God the draft was no longer in effect.

He heard someone coming and looked up, expecting the officer from personnel whom he'd been told would take him to Wes's room. At first he was pleased by the appearance of a woman in uniform, but the look on her face wasn't friendly. She was long-legged and good-looking, but a little too stern for his liking. He immediately categorized her as Officer Tight-Ass. Still, if she'd given him any kind of a hint that she would be interested, he would have given flirting a shot. But the only hint she gave him was that she was busy and unwilling to waste time with chitchat.

"This way, Mr. Clancy."

Aaron followed Officer Tight-Ass onto the elevator, then onto the psych ward, where she turned him over to Wes's doctor.

"Mr. Clancy?"

Aaron found himself face-to-face with a man who looked like he could bench-press three hundred pounds with one hand.

"Yes?"

"I'm Dr. Milam, your brother's doctor."

"You mean shrink, don't you? They told me when they called that he'd flipped out."

Milam frowned. The man's flippant attitude left him with an uneasy feeling.

"'Flipped out' is hardly the term for a soldier like Wes Holden. I'm sure you were informed of the incident that led up to his current condition?"

Aaron knew immediately that he'd stepped off on the wrong foot, and that wasn't good. If he was going to get his hands on big brother's tax-free benefits, he was going to have to play nice. He swiped a hand across his face and then turned on "nice."

"Look…Dr. Milam…I didn't mean to sound so callous, it's just that the fear we all had when he was captured has weighed on our minds, then having Martha and Markie killed in that bombing here on base was just the last straw."

Dr. Milam's frown deepened.

"If you're referring to Colonel Holden's wife and son, their names were Margie and Michael."

Aaron shut his mouth and didn't open it again until a nurse appeared, pushing Wes in a wheelchair. At that point, Aaron turned it on again, pretending to appear emotionally wrought about Wes's gaunt appearance.

"Oh, my God," he said softly, then walked past the doctor and dropped to his knees beside Wes's chair.

"Wes? Brother? It's me, Aaron. I've come to take you home."

It was all Wes could do to stay still. He closed his mind's eye to everything except the scent of antiseptic permeating the hallway. He hadn't seen Aaron Clancy since his mother's funeral, but the smarmy little bastard didn't appear to have changed all that much. From the brief look Wes managed when no one was paying attention, Aaron appeared to have less hair and more gut than he remembered, but then, it had been years. He took a slow breath, then shifted mental gears, forcing all thought out of his mind for fear that his emotional disgust might be evident.

Aaron shuddered, then stood, for the first time realizing what he was taking on.

"Say…Dr. Milam, is he safe? I mean…he won't… uh, go psycho and hurt anyone if I put him on a plane?"

Marshall Milam felt sick. He didn't trust this man to see to Colonel Holden's best interests, and wished with everything he was that he could stop this from happening, but orders had been given and paperwork had been processed.

"He has given us no indication of any kind of violent behavior," Milam said. "In fact, it's been just the contrary. He does not communicate at all. However, I trust you will see to his continuing treatment as soon as possible."

Aaron looked nervously at Wes and then nodded.

"Absolutely," he said.

Milam sighed. There was little else he could do.

"I've taken the liberty of arranging a car to drive you and your brother directly to the airport."

Aaron looked relieved. "Thank you, Dr. Milam. I appreciate that." Then he looked at his watch. "I guess we'd better be going."

Wes felt a moment of panic as he was wheeled out of the hospital and into the sunshine. Still locked into the pretense of unawareness, it was all he could do not to lift his face to the sun and breathe in the fresh air. He let himself be led to the waiting car, then seated in the back seat. When his stepbrother shut the door and got in the front seat with the driver, he relaxed, but the relief was only momentary.

At Aaron's request, the driver took them right by the sight of where the commissary bombing had occurred. Unless he was willing to give himself away, Wes was helpless to do anything but ride. So he gritted his teeth, closed his eyes and refused to look as the car moved past. But as hard as he tried, he couldn't block out the sound of the driver's voice.

"Terrorist…car bomb…bodies everywhere…wearing a bomb."

His heart started pounding, and he broke out in a cold sweat. Every memory he had of the smells and the sounds came flooding back. He heard screams and sirens, felt the crunch of broken glass beneath his shoes as he stumbled through the debris inside the commissary, searching for his wife and child. He saw her foot, then her leg, then the damage that had been done to her face.

The blood. There had been so much blood.

And Mikey. So small. So still.

So far gone.

Then the driver added one last bit of info that, if Wes had known, he'd forgotten.

"Colonel Holden…one shot…right between the eyes. Saved us all."

He felt Aaron turn and stare at him, but he never acknowledged the motion. He never knew when they left the base, but the exodus was monumental, just the same, wiping out the last bit of his identity. After the bombing, his life as a husband and father had come to an end, and now he was no longer a soldier, either.

Colonel Wes Holden was finally dead, as he'd intended to be all along, but the shell of a man still existed. It remained to be seen if he would bother to refill the hollows.

* * *

Ally was already up and setting out the sausages and bacon she'd cooked for breakfast when her father and both brothers came into the kitchen.

"Something smells good," Porter said, and stole a piece of bacon.

"Are we having biscuits?" Danny asked.

"Isn't this Sunday?" Ally teased.

Danny grinned. "Yes, it's Sunday, and yes, I know, we always have biscuits on Sunday. Just thought I'd ask."

"Scrambled or fried?" Ally asked, referring to the eggs she had yet to cook.

"Scrambled works for me," her father said.

Ally gave him a cool glance, then nodded. They had yet to smooth over the rough patch they'd had when she'd gone to Granny Devon's, and she wasn't going to be the first one to say "I'm sorry," because she'd done nothing for which she needed to apologize.

She began breaking eggs in the bowl as the men poured coffee, got butter and jelly from the refrigerator, as well as the salt and pepper shakers out of the cabinet, and set them on the table.

Within minutes, they were seated with plates of fluffy yellow eggs, scrambled to perfection, at each place. Gideon looked at each of his children until he had their complete attention; then he bowed his head and blessed the food. He was on the verge of saying amen when he paused and added the words, "Bless the cook that prepared it, amen."

Ally looked up to find her father's gaze upon her. She sighed. It was all the apology she was going to get.

"Porter, pass Daddy the meat," she said, then took a biscuit and passed them on.

Gideon worried all through the meal, hoping he hadn't left his little bit of news too late. It would be horribly embarrassing to have company over after church and not have a meal to offer. He poured himself a second cup of coffee from the pot on the table, then took a third biscuit and buttered it up.

"Good bread, daughter," he said quietly.

"Thank you, Daddy," Ally said, then glanced at the clock and got up from the table. "I'm going to get a roast out of the freezer and put it on low heat in the oven so it can cook while we're at church."

Gideon nodded approvingly, then slapped his knee as if he just remembered something.

"Did I tell you we're having company at noon?"

Ally turned. "No, and please tell me it's not the preacher because I don't have anything special baked for dessert."

"No, no, nothing like that," he said. "It's just Freddie Joe."

She frowned. "Detweiller?"

"Yes."

"Is he bringing his children?"

"No, I think they're at their granny's for the weekend. He mentioned wanting one of my bull calves to raise for a new breeding bull. I told him he'd better come pick it out before I cut 'em all."

"I'll put extra vegetables in the roast. It will be fine."

Gideon breathed a quick sigh of relief. It was a lie, but it had served its purpose. The only stock on the Monroe property that Freddie Joe was interested in was his daughter.

Gideon had almost gotten over his guilt at deceiving his daughter when they pulled into the church parking lot. As soon as they got out of the truck, they joined other members of the congregation who were moving toward the doorway. The preacher was standing on the steps, greeting his parishioners, as well as paying special attention to the children who were accompanying their parents.

Ally's focus was on one of her old classmates, who was coming to church with a new baby. While she was happy for her friend's little family, it only enforced the lack of her own. She was halfway up the steps when someone suddenly grabbed her by the forearm.

"Ally Monroe, is this you?"

"Good morning, Granny Devon," she said.

There was a smile on the old woman's face as she started to answer, then her sightless eyes suddenly rolled back in her head. She moaned, then she spoke.

"There's a man who's done evil.
There's a man who's done bad.
There's a man who comes walkin'.
There's a man who's so sad."

* * *

The prediction gave Ally the chills. She remembered the previous warning that had come to her the night she'd had supper with Granny Devon. Now it seemed that evil still threatened her family. Before she could move, Gideon wrenched the old woman's hand from his daughter's arm and pushed Ally up the steps. When he got even with the preacher, he turned and pointed.

"You tell that old woman's family if she won't stop witchin', to keep her at home."

The preacher was taken aback by Gideon's anger, which embarrassed Ally to no end.

As they moved into the church, Ally pulled away and whispered angrily, "You had no right to talk to Preacher John like that. Granny Devon doesn't mean any harm, and you know it. Besides, nobody else is bothered by her predictions. I don't know why you're always so hateful about her. She's a sweet old lady."

"She's not right," Gideon muttered. "And I'm not discussing this with you again. Take your seat by your brothers."

Ally sat, but only because to do otherwise would have caused a bigger scene than what her father had done. She was in the house of God and knew how to behave, but she stayed angry with her father, just the same. When the services were over, she got up and walked out on her own, and was already seated in the truck with the motor running and the air conditioner on high when her father and brothers got in.

Gideon took one look at her face and resisted the urge to issue his normal set of orders about wasting fuel just to make cold air. He had bigger fish to fry than saving a few pennies and wisely drove them all home in silence.

Freddie Joe Detweiller was sitting on the front porch when they pulled up the driveway. Ally's mind was already on the things that needed to be done before dinner would be served, but to her surprise, Freddie Joe jumped up, took off his hat and opened the front door for her as she came up the steps.

"Good day, Ally. Something is sure smellin' fine inside this house," he said.

"Just roast," Ally said.

"I thank you highly for allowing me to your table."

Ally shrugged. "Thank Daddy. He invited you."

Freddie Joe had an odd expression on his face as he looked at Gideon. Gideon nodded formally, then quickly looked away.

Freddie Joe came to himself in time to jump in front of Ally. He opened the door, then stepped aside, bowing slightly as she passed.

As she stepped over the threshold and into the living room, she couldn't help but notice that his hair was thinning at the crown. Then he smiled at her, and it was all she could do not to recoil from his yellow, tobacco-stained teeth. Still oblivious to the true reason for his presence, she paused to speak to Gideon.

"Daddy, I'll need at least thirty minutes to finish up dinner."

Gideon smiled. "That's fine, daughter. We'll be in the sittin' room."

"I thought you were gonna look at—"

Gideon interrupted before she gave him away.

"Not until after we eat," he said. "Don't want to be trackin' in dirt from the barnyard."

"Oh. Well, yes, thank you," she said, and hurried to change her shoes.

Minutes later, she was in the kitchen, cooking vegetables and baking corn bread to go with their meal. She'd taken a pie out of the freezer before they'd gone to church, and she popped it into the oven after she removed the roast.

Her dinner was coming together just fine. It was her life that somehow felt as if it was spinning out of control.

There was a tiny droplet of roast gravy on the edge of Freddie Joe's bottom lip, and a smear of grease just below his nose. When he'd chosen to ignore the paper napkins she'd set at their places, she'd gotten up from the table, torn off a couple of paper towels and dropped them in his lap.

"Oh, yeah. Right," he said, and swiped them across his face, then tossed them on the table near a bowl of peas.

Ally resisted the urge to roll her eyes and instead refilled the glasses of iced tea all around the table.

"Hey, sis, good meat," Porter said.

"Just like always," Danny added.

"Ally is a fine cook," Gideon said, then added, "She's careful with money, too. That's a fine attribute in a woman, you know."

Ally was frowning slightly as she began cutting the pie. Her brothers never complimented her cooking. They just ate it. Sometimes her father thanked her for a meal, but today he was acting as if she was competing for a prize. What was even stranger was that with four men at the table, not one of them had talked about the cattle herd or the bull calf that Freddie Joe wanted to buy.

She served the pie without fuss, but when she slid Freddie Joe's pie in front of him, she was taken aback when he grabbed her hand and gave it a squeeze.

"Smells great!" he said. "Good thing you're used to cooking for lots of people."

Startled, she yanked her hand away, then looked to her father for intervention. To her dismay, he not only ignored her silent plea, but was smiling benevolently. Something was wrong—horribly wrong. It was like being the only person in the crowd who didn't get the joke.

"I don't know why it's a good thing that I can feed a thrashing crew without breaking a sweat, but I'd appreciate it if the conversation changed to something besides me and my skills in a kitchen."

Porter and Danny were stuffing pie in their mouths without looking at her, and her father's smile slipped a bit. Freddie Joe was frowning and looking from her to Gideon and back again, as if he was waiting for Gideon to put her in her place. When no one spoke, his tone of voice became belligerent as he pointed at Ally with his fork.

"Look here, missy, I came here willing to give you a chance to—"

Gideon stood abruptly.

"That was a fine meal, but we'd best be getting on to business. Freddie Joe, if you're done, let's go on out to the barn. I got some fine calves you'll be wanting to see."

Freddie Joe frowned.

"But I ain't finished my pie and your girl ain't—"

"Ally will pack you up a piece to go, won't you, girl?"

Then he grabbed Freddie Joe by the arm and all but dragged him out the door.

Frowning, Ally turned to her brothers.

"Danny, what's going on?"

He shrugged, stuffed the last bite of pie in his mouth and bolted from the room.

Ally frowned. "Porter?"

He shoved his chair back from the table and got up, then hesitated. He didn't like Detweiller and felt sorry for his sister, but he didn't want to get on the bad side of his father's plans. Still, he knew this wasn't fair. Ally wasn't some simple backwoods female. She had a fine mind and, except for the limp, was a good-looking woman.

"Please," Ally begged.

Finally, he sighed.

"Look, Detweiller's missing a wife, right?"

Ally's eyes widened as her lips went slack. Shock spread slowly, leaving her momentarily speechless.

Porter left before she could press him for further information, while silently cursing his father for putting
Ally in such a predicament.

"Oh, my God," Ally muttered. "He can't...he
wouldn't..." But she knew as soon as she'd said it that
he would.

Her father had always meddled in her life, and because
she felt obligated, she'd let him. But she would leave
Blue Creek forever before she would marry that creep.

Heartsick and feeling betrayed, she put away the leftover food, cleaned up the kitchen, then went to her
room. Even though the garden needed hoeing and she
had shirts to patch, she curled up on her bed and cried
herself to sleep.

And as she slept, she dreamed of a tall, dark-haired
man who came walking out of the trees. He asked for a
drink of water, then told her he'd been looking for her
all his life.

She cried again as she slept, but this time for joy.
When she woke, it was nearing sundown. She could
hear voices down the hall, and knew her father and
brothers were in the living room watching television.
She rolled over, then sat up on the side of the bed and
looked down at her crippled foot, absently wondering
how different her life might have been if she'd been born
without the deformity.

Then she thought of Granny Devon, who'd been born
blind, and told herself she was blessed. She had her
health, her sight and two strong legs on which to walk.

If she had a limp, then so what? As long as there was life, there was hope.

She put on her shoes, then slipped out the back door and walked to the garden. As she moved between the rows, she made mental note of the work that needed to be done tomorrow. There were green beans that needed picking, tomatoes that needed to be staked, and potatoes to dig. There was no need getting all bent out of shape about her father's stupidity. He could make her life miserable if he wanted to, but he couldn't make her marry Freddie Joe.

It wasn't the first time that Roland Storm had watched Ally Monroe from a distance, and it most likely wouldn't be the last. He'd stumbled upon her existence quite by accident nearly a year ago, and once he'd seen her, he'd become almost fixated on the fragile woman with the long blond braid. The fact that she limped had been noticed and then ignored.

This evening he'd walked out of his lab and down the road just to get some air. Or that's what he'd told himself until he'd gotten to the big curve in the road. At that point, he slipped into the trees and headed west, knowing he would come right up to the back yard of Ally's house.

His anticipation at seeing her had taken a direct hit when he'd stopped inside the tree line and she'd been nowhere in sight. He'd waited, watching while the old man finished chores in the barn and went to the house. He'd seen the two sons come back from the pasture where they'd been feeding cattle. They'd paused on the back steps to play with the family dog and then gone inside, as well.

Even then, he kept hoping he would see the girl. He didn't know why it mattered. He had far more important things to focus on besides some backwoods farmer's daughter.

And still he waited.

Just when he was ready to give up, the door opened. Breath caught in the back of his throat as Ally stepped out onto the porch. As he watched the sway of her hips, an ache spread in his groin. Despite her age, there was an innocence about her that reminded him of a girl. When she bent over a row of beans in the garden, he stifled a groan. No sooner had the sound come out of his voice than Ally straightened and turned toward the trees.

Roland froze. Now he'd done it. He'd been taking chances, and considering what he had in the works, that was crazy. He was jeopardizing his entire future by acting like some horny teenager.

He held his breath, watching the stillness in her posture, afraid to blink for fear she would see the motion, then his face. When she finally relaxed and turned away, he melted into the deepening shadows, and when he was far enough away to make sure she couldn't hear him, he ran the rest of the way home.

Six

Wes Holden was now a civilian without a plan, and Aaron Clancy was stuck with a situation he hadn't thought through. On the first day of their arrival, he'd put Wes in the extra bedroom of his apartment, turned down the bed and left him on his own. His focus was on getting to the bank and presenting his letter claiming power of attorney for his incapacitated stepbrother. He made sure they knew that Wes's monthly checks would be deposited directly into his personal account, took the praise as his due that he was being a Good Samaritan, and then went home a happy man. He checked into a facility to dump Wes in, then changed his mind at the cost and decided to pocket the money and care for Wes at home. It would all have been gravy, only brother Wes wasn't cooperating.

He wouldn't communicate. He didn't feed himself or bath himself, and Aaron hadn't planned on being a nursemaid. After four days, Wes's face was disappearing behind a rapid growth of black whiskers, which, to Aaron, made him look even more ominous than he had before.

Disgruntled and rapidly losing his patience with the situation, Aaron fed Wes a bowl of cold cereal in the morning, washed it down with a cup of warmed-over coffee, and left a bologna sandwich for him to eat at noon. Each night when he came home from work, the sandwich was right where he'd left it and so was Wes. Frustration was growing. He tried to hire a neighbor to come in and feed him, but the neighbor had taken one look at Wes and said no.

Now word had gotten out in Aaron's apartment building that he had a head case living with him. The news was not well received, and the few friends that he had in the area were starting to shun him. It was putting a crimp in his social life, and that couldn't go on much longer.

Meanwhile, Wes was in the same situation. He wasn't comfortable hiding behind a wall of silence and pretending he didn't know where he was, but there was nothing he had to say to Aaron. He'd wanted out of Fort Benning and away from anything that reminded him of war, and he'd used Aaron to make that happen. Now that he was out, his ambition seemed to have ended. He had no plan, and because he didn't, he felt caught by his own lies.

So each night and each morning until Aaron left for work, Wes hid behind a wall of silence. It was only after Aaron was gone that he would put his head in his hands and weep. Some days it seemed as if he would never quit. The sadness within him was total. He was certain that he would never know joy again. And there were also the dark days when he did nothing but curse God for taking his family and leaving him behind.

Each night he let Aaron put him to bed, ignoring the verbal insults and abuse Aaron heaped upon his head for being a useless bastard, then waited until Aaron turned out the light and closed the door before he could let himself relax, confident that he'd managed to maintain his lie for one more day.

And each night, as Aaron went to his own room, he had his own conscience to face. He had to consider where Wes had been and what he'd endured. He knew that Wes had been repeatedly tortured. He knew he'd found his own wife and child under the debris from the terrorist bombing, and that he'd killed the terrorist with one shot between the eyes. He also knew that directly after that, he had shut down as completely as if someone had turned out the lights in his mind.

Aaron then had to accept that the same man who'd killed without thought was lying just a few feet away, with only a wall and a door to separate them. At that point, he would turn around and lock himself in. If his crazy stepbrother woke up in a state of confusion and started trying to kill people again, he didn't want to be the first victim.

Aaron was reconsidering his plan to care for Wes and

thinking of taking him to the first nuthouse that would accept him and forget he was there. But he wouldn't make a dime if he did that. It would take all of those tax-free monthly checks just to keep him caged. That left Aaron uncertain as to how he was going to make this work, but either way, he knew he couldn't keep a crazy man in his house much longer.

It was the fifth night in Aaron's apartment, and Wes was beginning to make plans to leave. As soon as he heard Aaron go into his bedroom and lock the door, he rolled over onto his side and opened his eyes. A slow ache rolled through his heart as he thought of the home he and Margie had shared. It was nothing like the filth and drabness of the apartment that Aaron called home. Margie had loved plants, both green and flowering, and had some in every room of their house. He thought of the countless nights he'd lain with her wrapped in his arms, the faint fragrance of the roses growing outside their bedroom window wafting through the room.

There was nothing in this room but painful memories and a neon sign outside the window that created a garish slide show of green and yellow on the wall. He watched it flashing until his eyelids grew heavy. Finally he fell asleep, only to wake up some time later to the sound of rapid and repeated gunfire.

Wes's heart stuttered to a complete stop, then started again with a hard, solid thud as he hit the floor. His first instinct was to get into the bunker, and he began crawling toward it on his belly. Only the bunker turned out to be a shadow on the wall, and the gun he'd expected to find was missing, as well. He crawled straight into the corner before he realized he was not back in the Iraqi desert. Sweat was running out of his hair and down the middle of his back, and his hands were shaking. He looked up at the wall with the neon lights, then down at the grimy floor on which he was lying, and groaned.

"Son of a bitch," he said softly, then buried his face in the crook of his elbow.

Another round of gunshots rang out, then he heard the sound of a revving car engine and squealing tires. There were shouts, then more shouts, then a woman screaming. Within moments, he heard approaching sirens. When he was somewhat convinced that the gunshots were over, he got up off the floor and back into bed.

Oddly enough, the incident had given him a much-needed mental boost. It was the first time he'd considered the fact that he might not be ready to die, after all. And the drive-by had done something else for him. He'd already been in one war zone. He wasn't stupid enough to stay in another.

The next morning, Aaron was in a foul mood, cursing about the drive-by shooting, as well as his disturbed sleep. He managed to pour the cereal in the bowl for Wes, but he didn't take time to feed him. Instead, he shoved the bowl in front of him and slammed a cup of coffee on the table.

"Eat or starve, it's no matter to me. I'm gonna be late for work."

Without a backward glance, he left Wes at the table where he'd put him and walked out the door.

Wes sat without moving, staring down at the bowl of wilting cornflakes and listening for the sound of Aaron's truck driving away. Even after Aaron was long gone, Wes was still there.

A cockroach appeared at the edge of the table, then made a hesitating march toward the soggy cereal. The faucet at the sink was leaking. The repetitive drip into Aaron's empty bowl sounded loud in the silence of the room. The neighbor in the apartment next door was crying, and the one across the hall was fighting with her husband. Down the hall, a baby cried.

Wes's senses were on overload. The heat, the stench, the sounds—they all crowded in, pushing and pushing until he finally stood. For a few moments he stared around the room as if assessing his options, then moved to the cabinets, took down a coffee tin and pulled off the lid.

Every night he'd watched Aaron empty his pockets into this tin. Since Aaron had access to Wes's money, Wes felt no guilt in taking his. He moved to the bathroom, showered and dressed, and then began to pack.

With just under a hundred dollars in his pocket and a switchblade he took from Aaron's dresser, he stuffed his clothes in the olive-green duffel bag that had U.S. Army and W. Holden stamped on the side. As he started toward the door, he stopped and took Aaron's western-style hat from a coat stand and settled it on his head. But when he reached for the doorknob, he realized his hand was shaking. There was a knot in his belly and fear in his heart. He'd lost himself once out there, and there was a part of him that feared it could happen again.

He turned around, his gaze settling on the dreariness of Aaron's life, remembering the lies and deceit with which Aaron had claimed him from the hospital. Wes knew that if he didn't leave, something terrible would happen between them. There was enough left of the soldier he'd been to do what had to be done. He took a deep breath, gripped the doorknob firmly and turned it.

Minutes later, he was out on the street. He took his last look at his brother's shithole of a building, then turned his face to the north and started walking.

Aaron had a flat coming home from work and no spare. When he tried to call for road service, he realized his cell phone was dead. He spent all day working on other people's cars, but he couldn't fix his own. By the time he walked to a pay phone and back to his car, it was almost dark. He was still pissed as he pulled into his parking space at the apartment. To make matters worse, the elevator was out of service again. By the time he got to his fourth-floor apartment, he was cursing. He jammed the key in the lock and started to turn it when the door swung inward.

Unlocked? His apartment was unlocked?

His first inclination was that he'd been robbed; then

he remembered Wes. His demented stepbrother could be lying in a pool of blood. But when he moved farther into the room, he could tell that the clutter on the floor and tables was all his. A quick look into the bedrooms and the kitchen also failed to give up an intruder, although he was looking at the mess with new eyes. But the search did reveal one fact that made his heart skip a beat.

Wes was gone.

That didn't make sense. How could a man like Wes just get up and walk away when he hadn't even been able to feed himself? The best Aaron had been able to tell, Wes had never moved from where he'd put him each morning until he came home each night. Now he was gone. Aaron went back into Wes's bedroom, only this time he wasn't looking for a thief. He was looking for clues.

It didn't take long for him to realize that Wes's duffel bag was missing, as were the clothes he'd come home with. He stood in the middle of the room, growing angrier by the minute.

"The bastard! The sorry bastard! All this time he was playing me. He had to be."

He stomped out of the bedroom and into the kitchen. He got a beer from the fridge and was popping the top when he saw the coffee can on the table. At that point, he exploded. He threw the beer across the room, ignoring the fact that as it landed, it splattered beer all over the wall and floor.

"My money! He stole my money!" he screamed, and kicked over a chair.

He was on his way to the phone to call the police when he got a big reality check.

If he reported Wesley Holden as missing, and a thief, then how could he claim Wes's money?

"Fuck," he muttered, then plopped down on the sofa.

But the longer he sat there, the better his mood became. He had no reason to be angry. In fact, Wes had just done him a great big stinking favor. He was rid of the problem but not the dough.

He got himself another beer and then toasted the thin air.

"Thank you, brother dear. Thank you for your brief visit and your deep pockets. They were both a pleasure."

Then he downed the beer and picked up the phone. It was time to celebrate, and he knew just the little redhead to help him do it.

Wes's first night on the road was as close to a nightmare as anything could have been. Every large, unsettling noise threatened to trip him out of reality. Even after it got dark, he was afraid to stop walking. It wasn't until the sky had begun to change from black to gray that he finally stopped at an abandoned gas station on the outskirts of a small Florida suburb.

He stood for a few minutes, checking out the distant lights of Miami, then the area around the old building. Except for the traffic of passing cars and a bird perched on the sagging roof of the empty station, there was no movement in the area. Satisfied that he was alone, he crawled through a back window that was missing its glass and then paused for a quick reconnoiter. Instinctively, his hand went to the switchblade as he did a quick walk-through of the building. He found the remnants of a small campfire, which told him he wasn't the first person to find shelter here. Either someone was using it for storage or they'd just given up and left, because there were machine and engine parts scattered about the front of the building in varying stages of disrepair.

After checking to make sure he was alone, Wes kicked aside a stack of wooden pallets, dropped his duffel bag into a corner to use for a pillow, and lay down on the floor with his back to the wall and the knife in his hand. The last thing he remembered seeing was a small mouse coming out from under a stack of boxes and running from the room.

The downdraft from the rotors on the Black Hawk whipped sand into Wes Holden's face as he and a young G.I. covered the pair of soldiers who were dragging a wounded comrade toward the waiting chopper.

"Colonel Holden! Colonel Holden! You've both got to come now!"

The call came from the Black Hawk. Wes did a three-sixty, scanning the area with a practiced eye as he measured the distance between the sniper shelter and the open bay of the waiting chopper.

"Now! Colonel! We've got to go now!"

He heard the urgency in the gunner's voice and realized they knew something he did not. He turned abruptly to the G.I. and yelled.

"Go, soldier! Go now!"

"But, Colonel..."

"Now!" Wes shouted, and they both started running. It was just what the sniper had been waiting for.

More than a hundred yards from the chopper, the sniper opened up. The first bullet ripped through Wes's right shoulder. The numbness that came next caused him to drop his rifle. He didn't even know it was gone until he saw the expressions on the faces of his men, screaming at him from inside the chopper.

He saw the young G.I. ahead of him stop and turn back, intent on getting his commanding officer. The next bullet hit the man straight between the eyes. The wind from the downdraft caught the spray of blood and brains that came out the back of his head and blew it away, along with the scream on Wes's lips. Then a second bullet ripped through Wes's body, this time in the back of his left leg. Within seconds he was falling.

He heard the first of the antiaircraft guns firing as his elbows hit the sand. He tried to roll out of the line of fire, but the bullets in his shoulder and leg left him flopping like a fish out of water.

He turned toward the chopper and began frantically waving them off.

"Go! Go!" he shouted. "Goddamn it! Go!"

The Black Hawk was about ten feet off the ground and rising when a fireball exploded, flaring into a firestorm of boiling flames and flying shrapnel. Wes screamed out in rage. When the flames turned into a rising column of black smoke where the Black Hawk had been, he knew he was looking at a funeral pyre.

The devil had belched.

Days later, Wes woke up with a rat crouched on his chest, staring at him with tiny black eyes that glittered from the deprivation of its own life of hell. He slapped at it with his good hand, then missed as it darted from his chest into a small hole in the wall. The movement caused enough pain to make him want to weep, but his mouth was so dry he didn't dare waste the fluids. His shoulder was bandaged and in a sling, and there was another bloody, filthy bandage wrapped around his thigh.

He didn't know where he was, but the enemy had him—and he could hear them coming down the hall.

Wes woke up with a gasp, swatting at an invisible rat and looking for a place to hide from the soldiers of Saddam Hussein. Then he saw the pallets and the boxes and the greasy engine parts, and he said a quiet prayer of thanksgiving. He might be lost and homeless and hungry, but he was free.

He got up with a groan, brushed the dust off his clothes, picked up his duffel bag and crawled out of the building the same way he'd come in, only to realize it was sometime past noon and the sun was already on its way toward the western horizon. At that point, his belly growled. He shouldered his bag, slipped the switch-blade into his pocket and headed toward the light. He needed food. Beyond that, he couldn't plan.

Two weeks later, a trucker pulled into a truck stop on a highway in the mountains of West Virginia. He stopped for gas, food, and to drop off the hitchhiker he'd picked up outside Savannah. A veteran of Vietnam, he'd recognized the army bag on the tramp's back. With the United States back at war, he'd considered it his patriotic duty to give a buddy a ride. But when he'd seen the expression in Wes's eyes, he'd almost regretted stopping. The man looked like he had less than a fingernail's hold on sanity, and the cab of an eighteen-wheeler wasn't big enough for an all-out fight.

But then Wes had spoken softly, thanking the man for stopping, and the trucker had changed his mind. Now they'd come to the end of their road.

"Godspeed, soldier," the trucker said, and shook Wes's hand.

"Same to you," Wes said. "And thanks for the ride."

"Anytime," the trucker said, then added, "Stay safe."

Wes nodded, then went into the bathroom of the station as the trucker began fueling up. He washed up as best he could, then got himself a soft drink and a bag of chips, and began walking down the highway. The urge to keep moving was strong. He'd seen plenty of country in the past two weeks, and taken shelter from heat and storms beneath overpasses and inside culverts and bathed in ponds and ditches. With each passing day, he was growing stronger. Only now and then did he have a flashback, and when he did, he seemed able to come out of them in less and less time.

For the most part, he still shunned people, accepting rides only when he was too tired to walk. Once he'd come upon a man who'd lost a wheel off of a trailer he was pulling, and in doing so, had lost his load of sod. Wes had helped him put on the spare, then reload the heavy rolls of grass and dirt. The man had been so grateful for the help that he'd given Wes all the money he had in his pocket, which was just shy of sixty-five dollars. Wes still had most of it, but it wouldn't last forever.

What he needed was a place of his own—a place to live where he would not be bothered. He still wasn't sure of his ability to maintain composure in the face of adverse circumstances, so until he learned to trust himself again, he figured the best thing would be to stay as far away from people as he could. But to make that happen, he needed to find a place that felt right. So he continued in a rambling direction while telling himself that he would know the place when he saw it.

The mountains of West Virginia were lush with green and standing like sentinels along the highway. Now and then he would look up at the tall trees and thick underbrush and try to imagine the life up there. He heard birds calling, caught the occasional glimpse of a squirrel, and began to relax.

A dark sports car came flying past. Just as it drew even with Wes, the driver laid on the horn, pointing and laughing rudely as he went by.

For Wes, it was the end of his patience. Without thinking of the consequences, he moved from the highway into the trees. The shade alone was such a welcome relief that he just kept walking upward. He walked for what felt like hours, until his throat was dry, his belly was growling, and he was thinking about trying to find a road to a town. It was at that point that he heard someone singing. The sound was faint, but he could tell it was a woman.

He stopped, tilting his head until he had focused on the direction, then followed the lilting draw of her voice.

She was singing a hymn, humming parts of it, then skipping to words with no apparent rhyme nor reason.

He stopped.

The breeze in the trees was weak, but enough to rustle the leaves on the highest branches. The density of the forest felt sheltering. If he stayed here he would be safe, but the song drew him closer.

Ally didn't like to do laundry. It was the one chore she bore with little grace. Today she'd gotten a late start and was just now hanging out the last load. She could have used the dryer in the laundry shed and been done long ago, but then she would have had to listen to her father chastise her for wasting electricity, so it was easier to do some things his way.

She was humming to herself and hanging up one of Porter's shirts when she heard Buddy's deep, throaty grumble. It wasn't much, but it was all he could manage that passed for a bark. She turned around to see what he'd seen, then felt the breath leaving her lungs.

A tall man with broad shoulders and long legs was just walking out of the trees. Beneath the wide-brimmed Stetson he wore low on his forehead, she could see long black hair and a beard equally dark and long. He had a slight drag to his stride that didn't seem to slow his approach or hinder his ability to carry the duffel bag he had slung on one shoulder.

Her first instinct was defensive. The man was a stranger, and he'd come from the mountainside instead of the road. But when he seemed to sense her nervousness and stopped a good twenty yards away, she decided to stay put.

Then he took off his hat and bent down to pat Buddy, which she considered another good sign. Buddy's opinion of visitors was an unfailing test of their character. As he straightened, she got her first good look at his face. Even from this distance, she could see the expression in his eyes. It was the saddest, loneliest look she'd ever seen, and the thought crossed her mind to put her arms around him and never let him go.

Instead, she put one hand on her hip and shaded her eyes with the other as she spoke.

"Good day to you, mister."

Her voice was a slow, easy drawl that pushed at the man in him, but then he thought of Margie and frowned. He started to just walk away, but his thirst was stronger than his dread of confrontation.

"Good day, ma'am. I wonder if I might trouble you for a drink?"

When she hesitated, he realized she was afraid of him. Causing anyone more pain or fear was so horrifying to him that he took a couple of steps backward, just to reassure her that he meant her no harm.

Ally couldn't believe what she'd just heard. He was tall, dark and definitely a stranger, and he'd walked out of the trees and asked her for a drink of water—just like in her dreams.

"You want a drink of water?"

Wes shivered. Being around a woman was painful. Although she looked nothing like Margie, her gentle demeanor reminded him of what he'd lost.

"Yes, ma'am, that I would."

Ally motioned for him to follow her, then moved toward the porch.

It wasn't until she walked away that Wes realized she had a limp. But the hitch in her gait was nothing compared to the mangled bodies he'd seen. He shifted his bag to his other shoulder and followed a few yards behind her with the old hound sniffing at his heels.

Ally stopped at the kitchen door and pointed to a chair in the shade of the porch.

"Have yourself a seat, mister. I'll be bringing out the water."

"Thank you, ma'am." He did as she asked.

Then she paused at the door and turned around.

"My name is Ally Monroe."

The hinges on the screen door gave a homey little squeak as it swung shut behind her. The old hound sniffed a few more times at the heels of Wes's shoes, then dropped down beside him and closed his eyes.

Wes relaxed, then followed suit by closing his own eyes. He could hear the woman—Ally—moving around inside the house and a snuffling snore from the dog at his feet. But the sounds of what most people called civilization were missing. There were no horns or sirens, no choking fumes of gas and diesel thickening the air. It was so foreign to the life he'd been living that for a heartbeat he wondered if this was what Eden had been like before man messed it up.

A sudden and unexpected film of tears burned behind his eyelids. Man had messed up a hell of a lot more than Eden since then.

"Mister?"

His eyes flew open, and he sat up straight, automatically reaching for the switchblade until he remembered where he was. Embarrassed at being caught unawares, he took the water with a mumbled thank-you and began to drink.

Ally watched the Adam's apple bobbing in his throat as he drank and pretended she hadn't seen his tears. There was a small rip in his pants, and his shirt was stained with sweat. His hair was too long and his beard in need of a trim. But it was his hands that told her he might be more than he appeared to be.

His fingers were long and callused, but the nails were surprisingly clean.

She eyed the shape of his profile, mentally mapping the intelligent forehead, the faint line of an old scar across his nose and part of his cheek, and the wide cut of sensual lips barely visible behind the beard. As she was eyeing the formidable jut of his jaw and chin, he turned and caught her staring.

She took a sudden step backward, and as she did, she stumbled.

Before Wes thought, he grabbed her wrist. As soon as she was steady on her feet, he abruptly turned her loose.

"Sorry," he said softly. "Thought you were going to fall."

Unconsciously, Ally was rubbing the place where his fingers had been as she tried to steady her breath.

"Thank you," she said, then pointed. "My stupid foot."

Wes glanced briefly at the slight twist to the fragile ankle.

"Looks fine to me," he said, remembering the men he'd fought beside and the ones who'd come home with missing limbs. Then he handed her the empty glass.

"I sure appreciate the drink."

She took the glass. For a long silent moment they stared at each other without speaking. She watched him gathering himself up to stand. Now he would kill her.

The moment she thought it, she panicked. Where had that come from? What was it about this man that made her think he could kill? She backed away from the chair where he had been sitting and crossed her arms over her breasts.

Then he looked at her, and she thought she heard him sigh. Once again, the sheen of tears was evident in his eyes.

"Are you hungry?"

The moment she asked it, she wanted to slap her hand across her mouth in disbelief. What in the world was the matter with her? She wanted him to leave, yet she'd just offered him a reason to stay. She held her breath, fearing he would say yes—fearing he would say no.

Wes fingered his hair and beard, barely aware of its unruly length and style. Being around this woman was physically painful. All it did was remind him of his loss, and yet there was an emptiness inside of him that had nothing to do with food.

"Well, do you want something to eat or not?" Ally asked.

Wes took off his hat, then fiddled with the brim for a few seconds before he nodded.

"Yes, ma'am, I'm hungry."

"I have some food in the kitchen. Come sit at my table while I heat it up."

"No, ma'am. I'm too dirty to sit at anyone's table."

Once more Ally shocked herself by pointing to a small shed built onto the side of the house.

"In there's the laundry shed, but there's also a shower.

It's not much, but you're welcome to use it while I heat up your food."

Wes let the gentleness of her voice wash over him and thought of the luxury a shower would be. It had been days since he'd managed anything but quick wash-ups in farm ponds or public toilets in gas stations.

"I don't want to cause you any trouble," he said. "Some husbands wouldn't appreciate a strange man in their bathroom."

"I don't have a husband. Just a father who won't mind his own business and two brothers who don't care what I do as long as there's food on the table."

"I won't be long," Wes said, and headed for the shed before she changed her mind.

Ally waited until he'd closed the door on the shed, then bolted inside the house and began taking bowls of leftover food from the refrigerator.

Time passed, and the food was beginning to cool again when she heard him step up on the porch. She got up from the table and turned toward the door. He stopped outside, looking at her through the screen, as if waiting for permission to enter, even though he knew she could see him through the wire mesh.

"Come in," she called.

Wes left his duffel bag just outside the door and walked in. He had cleaned his boots and changed his clothes. They were wrinkled but clean, and there were tiny droplets of water still clinging to his hair and beard, giving them the sheen of polished ebony.

Blue. His eyes were blue.

She absorbed the fact as she motioned for him to sit.

"Do you take lemon in your tea?" she asked.

Wes looked at the plain white plate on the table, bordered by a set of cutlery in a style from a time long since past, and thought that it fit, like the hills and the woman.

"I'll drink it however you've fixed it, and thank you for the courtesy."

Ally liked the way he talked—like a gentleman.

"It's sweet," she said.

Wes was busy filling his plate and hardly noticed the tinkle of ice in the glass when she set the cold tea beside him, then took a seat across the table. For a while she watched him eat without speaking, giving him a chance to ease his hunger without having to answer questions. But finally curiosity got the better of her.

"Do you have a name?"

"Yes," Wes said, and looked away.

Ally felt an invisible wall come up between them.

"I'm sorry," she said. "I didn't mean to get personal. Do you want any more or are you finished?"

"I'm done, ma'am." Then he looked at her. "You're a good cook. I'm surprised some man hasn't already snatched you up."

"No one wants a cripple."

Wes felt an instant empathy.

"Lady, there are all kinds of ways to be crippled. Some wounds show. Some don't." Then he leaned back and looked her in the eyes. "My name is Wes Holden."

"Pleased to meet you, Wes Holden. Where are you from?"

"Nowhere."

"Never heard of it," Ally said. "Is it close to Nashville?"

Wes almost smiled, then caught himself.

"It's not close to anything."

"That doesn't tell me much," Ally said. "Never heard of that, either."

This time Wes actually grinned, unaware that the smile transformed his face.

"I was born and raised in Montana."

"You're either lost or a long way from home."

The smile on Wes's face went south.

"A little of both." Then he stood abruptly. "I'd best be on my way. You've been far too kind to a stranger."

"'Be not forgetful of strangers: for thereby ye may have entertained angels unaware.'"

Wes looked at her.

"It's from the Bible," she said softly.

He thought of where he'd been and the men he'd killed in the name of war.

"I'm no angel."

"No, sir, and I wouldn't take you for one, but you never can tell. My mother, God rest her soul, always said that God could appear in any shape or form." Then she smiled. "She also said that about the Devil, too."

Wes nodded. "Your mother sounds like she was a smart woman."

"She was."

"I'm sorry for your loss," he said quietly, while thinking about his own.

She saw the shadow of pain on his face and sensed it was time to change the subject.

"So your people are from Montana? What do they think about you being so far from home?"

"Everybody's dead," he said, and reached for his hat.

The tears that she'd seen before were back in his eyes.

"I'm sorry," Ally said.

Wes struggled to maintain his composure.

"So am I."

He started toward the door.

"Where are you headed now?"

He stopped, then turned around.

"Nowhere special."

"It's dangerous on the road."

"It's dangerous everywhere."

"If you were of a mind to rest a spell…maybe take some stock of things a little better without rambling… I know a place you could stay."

"I don't have the money for hotels," he said.

"No, no, it's nothing like that," Ally said. "Come with me."

He followed her outside and then off the porch. She stopped at the corner of the house.

"See that path to the left of the twin pines?"

He nodded.

"There's an empty cabin about two miles up through the trees. The power is still on. You're welcome to stay there for a while. People up here mind their own business."

Wes stared at the narrow, winding path for what seemed like forever. The thought of a roof over his head and all the solitude he wanted was tempting, but it was hard to trust her.

"The owner might not appreciate a squatter."

"My mother's oldest brother, Dooley Brown, lived there. When Uncle Doo died several months ago, he left it to me. It's mine to do with as I choose. I choose to offer you shelter. What's so bad about that?"

"But you don't know me," he finally said.

"That's right, I don't," Ally said.

"Then why are you being so…so…nice?"

Ally laid her hand on his forearm. She meant nothing by it, but when he flinched, she moved away.

"I don't think you're here by accident," she said.

Wes frowned. "What the hell do you mean?"

"I think God led you here to rest."

"There is no God," Wes said.

Ally's eyes widened in shock.

"Did you ever stop to think that maybe God isn't missing? That maybe you're the one who's lost?"

Wes groaned, and the pain that came with it scalded him raw. He stared at Ally as if she'd just grown horns.

"Who are you, woman? All I asked from you was a glass of water. It doesn't give you the right to play with my life."

His anger was sudden and frightening, and Ally

wanted to hide, yet an inner strength held her steadfast. She sensed this man was losing ground faster than he could gain it, and while it *was* none of her business, she couldn't seem to be able to step back.

"I'm sorry if I've offended you," she said. "Godspeed, Wes Holden. Whether you believe in Him or not, I can promise that He's the only one who's going to save you."

"I don't need saving," Wes said, and started walking, but Ally noticed that he took the path she'd pointed out, rather than going back the way he'd come.

She didn't know how she was feeling and wasn't brave enough to decipher her emotions.

For now, it was enough to know he hadn't gone too far.

Seven

Wes stayed angry all the way up the path and didn't know why. It took a while for him to realize that today was the first time he'd felt positive emotion of any kind since—

The moment his thoughts went to the day of the bombing, he shut them off.

"Focus," he muttered as he continued to put one foot in front of the other. "Focus on anything but that."

A few yards ahead, a small brown bird flew across his line of vision. He paused to watch as it landed on the branch of a nearby tree. A few hops led it straight to a nest of woven grasses and twigs, where it quickly disappeared.

A knot formed in his throat. Even that bird knew where it belonged. He wished he was as confident. Then he turned around and looked back the way he'd come. The world that he'd known was gone. If this path led to something—anything—it would be better than where he'd been. He didn't know what to make of that woman—what was her name—Alice? No, Ally. That was what she'd called herself. Ally Monroe. She'd offered him a place to stay, and despite his vocal objections, he'd known the moment he'd seen the leaf-covered path winding up this mountain that he was going to follow to see where it led.

He settled his hat a little more firmly on his head and once again turned around, only this time he was treading on new territory. Whatever lay ahead had to be better than where he'd been. He shifted the strap of his bag to a more comfortable position on his shoulder and continued walking.

A short while later he came upon a clearing, totally unprepared for what he saw. He'd imagined log walls and a ramshackle stoop, but certainly not this. It looked like a cross between a toadstool and a short, fat silo, and he wondered what kind of a man would choose to build a home like this.

As he moved closer, he caught glimpses of gray, mossy concrete among the tangle of ivy and wisteria blooming all over it. He wasn't sure if it was a house he'd come to or some kind of woodland hideaway abandoned by elves, although there was no such thing as elves. Still, the solitude of the place appealed to him. After a slow, careful scan of the area to make sure he was alone, he moved forward.

A few stray vines had fallen across the front door. As he drew near, he reached up, grabbing them with his fist and giving them a yank before tossing them aside. It occurred to him that the place might be locked, but when he turned the knob, the door opened.

The air inside was stale and the room was dark, but he remembered the woman had said the power was still on. He felt along the wall for a light switch, then gave it a flip. With illumination came an odd sense of déjà vu, which, to Wes, made no sense at all. He'd never been to West Virginia, never mind inside something like this. But still, the feeling remained, even growing stronger as he moved from room to room.

One side of the kitchen was round, following the contour of the outer wall. The cabinets were unique, with leaf-shaped cutouts on all the doors, while the counters were unusually low. When he checked the refrigerator, he saw it had been turned off, so he switched it on high for a quick cool-down, then moved toward a door on the opposite side of the room.

Inside was a small pantry, with a rather large assortment of canned goods still on the shelves. He wondered how far it was from here to a town and knew that if he stayed he would have to find some work.

He thought about his retirement checks, which were being deposited into Aaron Clancy's bank account, and frowned. If he pushed the issue to claim them, he would have to go to court to prove he was sound of mind. Not only did he not want to deal with the lawyers and the shrinks, he wasn't so sure he could prove he *was* sane. Life still rattled him on a daily basis, and he didn't want some do-gooder deciding he needed to be locked back up.

He closed the pantry door and moved back into the living room, found a set of keys on the mantel that fit the front door, and pocketed them before exploring the single hallway and the doors at the end of the hall.

When he opened the door to the room on the left and walked in, it felt as if he'd walked into a cave. Even though the ceiling was domed, it was low, and he had to duck his head to keep from bumping it against the light fixture. From there, he turned to the bed. It appeared to be of normal size, but was less than a foot off the floor.

This was getting weirder by the minute.

He set his duffel bag on the floor and then opened the closet. The rods where clothes would be hanging were so low that Wes knew his shirts would drag the floor. The other door led to the bathroom. He was almost afraid to look, for fear the bathroom fixtures would be minuscule, as well, but to his relief, the facilities were of normal size, although the showerhead was much lower than normal.

He walked back into the bedroom, and as he did, noticed a picture on the dresser. When he picked it up, the way the house had been built suddenly made sense.

It was a picture of the woman, Ally, and a small, older man, obviously her uncle Doo. He had long white hair with a beard to match, and was standing with one hand around Ally's waist and the other holding a cane. Wearing overalls and a blue, long-sleeved denim shirt, he looked no different from any man in this part of the country might look—except for the fact that he couldn't have been more than four feet tall.

Uncle Doo had been a dwarf.

Now he knew why the house had seemed so familiar. One of Mikey's favorite Disney videos had been *Snow White and the Seven Dwarfs,* and the little cottage in the movie was eerily similar to this. The realization hit him like a right to the chin. He didn't know whether to laugh or cry. Mikey would have been enchanted with this place, but could he live in something that reminded him of everything he'd lost?

The familiar tightening pain within his gut was growing with every breath when, suddenly, a flash of movement caught his eye. He turned just in time to see a small red squirrel silhouetted in the window and dangling from the vines outside. At the same moment he saw the squirrel, the squirrel saw Wes, and the expression of shock on the little furry face made Wes laugh.

But when the sound came out of Wes's mouth, he gasped.

"Have mercy," he whispered, then covered his face with both hands.

He'd laughed.

What the hell was wrong with him? How was that possible, when everything and everyone he'd ever cared about was gone? He started toward the door, intent on getting out of this crazy place as fast as he could before he lost what sense he had left, yet when he got there, he stopped.

The doorway framed an idyllic scene of tall trees and sunshine, with the rich, sweet scent of wisteria filling the air. Then his shoulders slumped. Instead of walking out, he swung the door shut, switched on the window unit air conditioner, then turned the lock and flicked off the lights. With an unerring sense of direction, he retraced his steps to the bedroom, turned that air conditioner on, as well, and crawled onto the bed. The covers smelled slightly of stale air and dust, but he didn't care. He reached for a pillow, pulled it out from under the spread, then hugged it to him as he rolled over onto his side.

He'd laughed. He'd gone and goddamned, fucking laughed—betraying his own grief, ignoring his pain.

Images of the faces of his wife and son washed through his mind. "I'm sorry," he whispered, then pulled the pillow up beneath his chin and wept.

And when he couldn't cry any longer, he closed his eyes and slept.

When night came, Ally could not sleep. All through supper, she'd had a knot in her stomach, remembering the man she'd let strip naked in the laundry room and then sit at their table. She'd fed him and given him shelter and knew only his name. Her father would be livid if he'd known the liberties she'd taken, but she didn't care. The shelter she'd offered the stranger belonged to her and her alone.

She thought of the pain she'd seen in his eyes and wondered what had happened to make him that way. He'd said his people were dead. She couldn't imagine what that might feel like, to lose everyone she loved. That olive-drab duffel bag he'd been carrying looked like something a soldier would have. She knew that such things were available at any army surplus store, but since the country was currently at war and there were thousands upon thousands of military still overseas, something told her he was the real thing.

When the digital clock beside her bed registered one-thirty in the morning, she was still awake. An owl hooted outside her window; then she heard Buddy's throaty grumble in response and she smiled. Buddy did not like to be disturbed.

These days, Buddy did little else but rest, but he was almost fourteen years old, which in dog years was the equivalent of a ninety-two-year-old man. Poor Buddy. He'd certainly earned his right to some peace. She just wished she could get some, too.

Despite the air-conditioning inside the house, the room felt stifling. Maybe if she got some fresh air, she would be able to sleep. She threw back the covers and got out of bed. The hardwood floors felt cool against her bare feet as she padded down the hallway to the tune of three men snoring.

Her daddy snored in long, gargling sounds as he

breathed in and out. Porter only snored when he was lying on his back, and Danny's snore was more of a faint whistling sound. But those were the sounds of her home, and the noise was oddly comforting rather than disturbing.

She took a cold can of pop from the refrigerator and let herself out the back door. Buddy heard the screen squeak and was up within seconds, sniffing at her bare toes with his big, wet nose.

"Hello to you, too," she said softly, then settled down in one of the wicker chairs and curled her feet up beneath her.

She popped the top on the can, taking her first drink while the soda still fizzed. She'd always liked that sip best—when the fizz was fresh enough to tickle her nose. She took a couple more sips, then leaned back in the chair, letting the silence of the night and the faint breeze wash over her.

The owl that had been bothering Buddy's rest must have flown away, because she didn't hear it anymore. But she did hear the crickets and tree frogs, and the mournful howl of someone's dog hunting on the mountains. The sounds were comforting and familiar to her, but she couldn't help wondering what the stranger might think; then she wondered why she cared. He was nothing to her but some poor lost soul needing shelter. She'd offered it. Whether he took it or not shouldn't matter to her.

Still, she made a mental note to bake extra biscuits in the morning when she was making breakfast—and maybe fry up an extra piece of ham. She'd been planning to take a walk up to Uncle Doo's place for a week now to check on things and hadn't gotten around to it. She would do it tomorrow and maybe take the extra food—just in case he had stayed. If he had not, then no matter. She would eat it later as a picnic lunch on her way back home.

She finished her cold drink, gave Buddy a brief hug and let herself back in the house. She trashed the empty can and washed dog off her hands before crawling back into bed. The caffeine in the pop should have kept her awake, but instead, as soon as her head hit the pillow, she fell fast asleep.

Gideon added a spoonful of sugar to his coffee then gave it a stir as Ally put the last of the food on the table.

"You made biscuits," he stated unnecessarily, since they were obviously there.

"We're almost out of light bread," Ally said. "Didn't have enough to make toast."

"I'll bring some home this evening when I come in from work," he said.

"I can get the groceries," she said.

"There's no need for you to go to town when I'll already be there. You just write the list, and I'll pick up whatever you need."

She shrugged. While she was perfectly capable of driving herself anywhere she wanted to go, her father always discouraged it. She was never quite sure if it was shame for her infirmity that made him want her at home, or if it was just another way of controlling their lives.

Porter and Danny used to have serious girlfriends. Now neither one of them did much dating. Her father had never liked any of the women they'd brought home. She wasn't sure if they still dated and just didn't bring them home, or if they'd simply given in to their father's disapproval to the point of not bothering to try at all. Gideon Monroe wasn't a man who liked change. She wondered what he would think about the stranger who'd come to the mountain.

And while she was stewing with her own little secrets, Gideon had one of his own. Freddie Joe Detweiller had been real put off by Ally's behavior at the Sunday dinner. But Gideon had smoothed it over by blaming it on Ally's inexperience with men, which had pleased Freddie Joe. Freddie Joe thought he would like a woman he could control.

Gideon knew Freddie Joe was desperate. He just didn't know how much. Freddie Joe already had three kids to feed and raise, and he needed a woman to help do it. Besides that, he missed having a woman in his bed. If she was flat on her back and under him while he was doing his business, it wouldn't matter that she walked with a limp.

Had Gideon known how little consideration Freddie Joe was willing to give another wife, he might not have pushed the issue so hard. But he'd become convinced that it was his duty to make sure that Ally would be taken care of when he was gone. It never occurred to him that she could, and had been, taking care of herself, her father and her brothers since she was sixteen.

And because of that, he'd invited Freddie Joe back again—this time, the invitation included the kids. He figured she might as well start getting used to their ways and them to hers. The older kids might have some resentment against another woman taking their mother's place, but the sooner they all got over it, the better.

Gideon forked a bite of cured ham into his mouth and gave it a couple of chews before he swallowed. Fortified with ham fat and coffee, he made his announcement.

"Company's coming for supper on Friday. That's days away, but I thought you might want to know now and give yourself a little time to do extra."

Ally looked up from her plate, unaware that she was frowning.

"Who?" she asked.

"The Detweiller family, which will make four more at the table. Porter will get the extra chairs out of the shed so's you can clean and polish them up before they come."

"Okay, Daddy," Porter said, and dropped some jelly onto his biscuit before taking a bite.

Ally listened to the men planning their day and her life. She knew what Gideon was doing, but she wasn't going to put up with it.

"I won't be courted by that man," she said.

Gideon frowned. "Now, daughter, I won't live forever, and you can't expect your brothers to take care of you their whole lives. One of these days they'll take wives, and most women don't like another woman in their kitchens."

Ally felt as if she'd been slapped.

"Take care of me?"

"Well, I didn't mean it—"

"And Porter and Danny are finally getting married? Are you going to pick their wives out for them, too?"

Gideon's face turned red. "Don't be rude."

"Then don't treat me like some idiot daughter who you have to sell to get rid of."

Gideon reeled. "I have never said you were missing your good sense."

"Just a straight leg and sure step, right, Daddy?"

He looked away.

She bit her lip to keep from crying as she scooted her chair away from the table and carried her plate to the sink.

"You didn't eat your food," Gideon said.

"I'm too full of that crow you insist on stuffing down my throat," Ally said.

Gideon knew he should apologize, but the only thing that came out of his mouth was a warning.

"There's still gonna be four extra for supper on Friday."

"I heard you the first time," Ally said.

Danny wished his father would stop. It embarrassed him to see his sister shamed in this way.

"Come on, Dad. Freddie Joe isn't much of a catch, and he's sure nothing to look at."

"They're invited. It's done, and I won't hear any

more about it," Gideon said, then shoved his chair away from the table and got up. He slapped his hat on his head and stomped out the back door, got in his truck and drove away.

Danny gave Ally a hug as Porter got up and left the room. "I'm sorry."

Ally shrugged. "It's not your fault he considers me the family burden. What he doesn't realize is that he can't make this happen, no matter how hard he tries. I won't marry any man I don't love." Then she made a face at him and grinned. "So, do you have a girlfriend?"

Danny's face turned as red as his hair. "Maybe."

Ally's smile softened. "Don't wait too long, Danny boy. We'll be old before you know it."

Danny grinned, then put a finger under her chin and tilted it up.

"Chin up, Ally. After Friday, it will all be over."

Ally rolled her eyes. "I'll tell you what's going to be over…Freddie Joe's dreams."

Danny laughed out loud.

"Atta girl. You tell 'em, sister." Then he yelled down the hallway at Porter. "Are you coming to town with me or not?"

"What for?" Porter yelled. "We got laid off."

"Yeah, but I heard the seed store's hiring down in Blue—"

"I don't care who's hiring where. I'm not in the mood," Porter said. "I'm going hunting."

"Whatever," Danny said. "See you later." He got in

his truck and drove away, while Porter got his hat and gun and headed out the back door.

Once they were gone, Ally hurried through the dishes, then packed up the extra biscuits and ham, changed into her walking shoes and hurried out the door.

Wes woke up in a cold sweat with his hands around an Iraqi soldier's neck, only to realize it was a pillow he was strangling. He groaned, then shoved it aside as he willed the dream into hell. He swung his legs off the side of the bed and grunted in surprise when he almost bumped his chin on his knees. He'd forgotten the bed was so low.

He turned on the light, then made his way into the bathroom. Despite the lack of hot water, it felt wonderful to be clean all over. He took his time in the shower, but when he began to dry off, he found that he didn't like the face in the mirror. He tied his hair back with a shoelace, then went through the drawers in the house until he found a pair of scissors. It took another thirty minutes to get rid of his beard.

First he cut until he couldn't cut any closer, then he picked up his razor to finish the task. As he was shaving, the memory of Mikey's first and last shave nearly sent him to his knees. He choked back a sob, then gritted his teeth to finish the job.

Later, as he was digging through his bag for clean clothes, his stomach began to grumble. Although he'd eaten snacks on the road, the meal he'd had yesterday at Ally Monroe's house had been his only real meal in two days. Now his belly was objecting to the sparse fare.

Once dressed, and feeling slightly light-headed at the lack of his beard, he started toward the kitchen. Even though he'd given the odd little house the once-over yesterday, in the light of day he saw dozens of things that he'd missed seeing before. There was a small shelf in the hallway with a carving of a dog. He thought he recognized it as the old hound from down the hill and marveled at the skill with which it had been carved. The shelves in the living room were stacked with books, including quite a few that identified flora and fauna native to the United States, as well as some bestsellers. It seemed that Uncle Doo had a fondness for Tom Clancy novels. But when Wes spied a stack of Spider-Man comic books stacked neatly beside them, he smiled. The old man must have been a treat.

His stomach rumbled again, so he abandoned the books for another time and headed into the kitchen. He was in the pantry looking for coffee when he heard a knock on the door. He started to panic, imagining some locals coming to accuse him of breaking and entering; then he heard a voice he recognized.

"Wes Holden? It's Ally Monroe."

His first instinct was that she had changed her mind and wanted him gone, and he was surprised by feeling regret. He backed out of the pantry and then hurried to the door.

The greeting Ally had planned died in her mind when

she saw his face. The beard was gone. Before, all she'd seen were those clear blue eyes; now she had a face to go with them. Then she found her voice and thrust a small woven basket into his hands.

"Breakfast," she said briefly, and walked past him without an invitation to come in. "I was hoping you'd stay. I'll show you how some of the things work here, then you're on your own."

Wes stood there with the basket in his hand, smelling fresh biscuits and fried ham and watching the slight sway of her walk as she went into the kitchen. She paused in the archway, then turned around.

"Well…come on."

He followed because intuition told him that her agenda for the day was probably better than his own—and because he suddenly couldn't wait to sink his teeth into this food.

"There's a small can of coffee in the basket," she said. "You'd better like it black, because I didn't cart any milk or cream."

"Black is good," he said, somewhat leery of her presence. Then he set the basket on the table. "I didn't expect this," he said.

Ally filled the carafe on the coffeemaker with water, poured it into the machine, then pushed the On button before turning around.

"I know that," she said. "Just like you never expected a meal and a place to stay when you asked me for a drink of water." Then she pointed to the basket. "Dig in. The coffee will be ready soon."

Wes Holden was a tall man, but in here he looked immense and somewhat distrusting of her presence.

"Don't think you're going to get this kind of treatment again," she said, and then grinned. "Consider it your welcome-to-the-neighborhood visit. One is expected, but one is all you get. After that, it's up to you whether or not you want to return the kindness."

Wes nodded, took out a biscuit and ate it in three bites.

"That was phenomenal," he said as he reached for another.

"Thank you. Mother always said I had a light hand with bread-making. I'm glad you enjoyed it."

"Still am enjoying it," he said, and bit into the second one.

"Coffee is ready," she said, and poured him a cup, then began prowling through the pantry. She poked her head out long enough to ask, "Can you cook?"

"Enough," he said, talking around the mouthful of biscuit and ham.

She nodded, then showed him where and how to light the gas pilot on the water heater, and how to operate the washer and dryer.

"There's enough laundry detergent left to do a couple of loads. After that, you'll need to get more. Do you have any money?"

Taken aback by her lack of pretense, he answered before he thought to hide the fact that he was more or less broke.

"Not enough to brag about."

"Are you hindered in any way?"

"What?"

She pointed to his body. "You know…weak back… hard of hearing…that sort of thing."

He wondered if being on the verge of insanity counted, then decided not to ask.

"No. Nothing like that," he said.

"I heard they're needing help at the feed store in Blue Creek."

"Blue Creek?"

She frowned. "Didn't you come through town on your way up the mountain?"

"No."

Her eyes widened. "Then how did you get here?"

"I don't know. I was on a highway, and I just walked off it and started up into the trees. Your house was the first place I'd come to."

"You came up the steep side."

"I guess," Wes said.

"Lord have mercy," Ally said softly.

"That would be a first," Wes countered, then turned his back on her and reached for his coffee.

Ally's heart went out to him, even as she frowned. That wasn't the first time that he'd indicated a huge lack of faith in a higher power.

"Anyway," she continued, as if the conversation hadn't taken a detour, "the feed store down in Blue Creek needs help. I heard Danny talking about it to Porter at breakfast, only Porter wasn't interested."

"Danny is your brother?"

"Yes. So's Porter. Gideon is my father. He works at a lumber mill."

"So don't you think Danny has already applied for the job?"

"No. He's worked there before. He and the owner didn't get along."

"Then what makes you think I would be any different?" Wes asked.

Ally shrugged. "Well, for starters, you're a whole lot bigger than Harold James, who owns the store. Harold is sort of bossy, and Danny is quick to anger, but you look like a man with a long fuse."

Her reference to not being quick-tempered almost made Wes laugh. He choked back what had started out as a chuckle, again shocked at himself for even entertaining joy.

"So you don't think I'm the type of man to fight back?"

Ally looked at his face, then down at his hands.

"I think if you wanted to, you could do a whole lot more than hit him," she said, and then headed for the door.

Wes followed her in spite of himself.

"Uh…hey…where are you going?" he asked.

"Home."

He stopped. "Just like that?"

She paused, then turned around.

"Did you have something else you wanted to say to me?" she asked.

Put on the spot, he immediately shook his head no.

"Okay, then. Neither do I. Have a nice day, Wes Holden."

"Yeah…uh…you, too…and, uh, thank you for the food."

"You're welcome," she said, and walked out onto the stoop.

Wes followed. "Hey…about Blue Creek."

"What?"

"How far is it from here?"

She pointed down the road from which she'd come.

"Five miles. Population eight hundred and forty-six until Georgia Lee gives birth to her seventh, at which time there will be eight hundred and forty-seven. Tell Harold I sent you."

"All right, and…thanks."

"You're welcome," she said, and kept on walking.

There was a moment when Wes thought about going with her, just following her down the mountain and into that sweet-smelling house. The way her mind worked was fascinating, and he thought he might like to just sit and listen to her talk.

Then reality surfaced. He went back into the toad-stool house and headed for the kitchen. There were four more biscuits and some ham that needed his undivided attention. After that, he was going to do a little garden-ing, then take a walk—maybe down to Blue Creek, maybe to see a man named Harold James about a job.

Eight

Roland Storm had known the day the lab rats tried to gnaw through the cages to get to the leaves on the other side of the wire that he was on to something big. That was six months ago. Today, when he'd come into the lab to run the tests, he'd realized that there might be a big drawback to his experiment. Eleven of twelve rats were belly-up in their cages.

Dead.

Odd injuries were also evident on the bodies, injuries that made no sense. The rat cages had been side-by-side along the wall, although none of the rats had been caged together. He stared intently at the bodies, trying to figure out why the two front paws of nearly every rat were bloody—some horribly mutilated and one missing a paw completely. When Roland found the paw in the adjoining cage, he inadvertently shuddered. What in hell had happened here?

His shock turned to horror as the twelfth rat suddenly fell over on its side, its body racked with spasms. A white froth appeared at its mouth, and a few agonizing seconds later, it was dead.

"Shit," Roland muttered. "What just happened?"

Roland had a master's degree in biology, a Ph.D. in genetic engineering and a Ph.D. in chemistry. He was no novice at research, but nothing about this particular project had prepared him for one-hundred-percent failure.

After years of experimentation and dead ends, he had been certain he had created the perfect hallucinogenic drug. More addictive than heroin, so as to keep users in need, easy to grow, harvest and ingest, and a genetic hybrid, which made it impossible to identify, since the plants grew in naturally irregular heights and shades of green, and could not be duplicated without his notes, which meant he would control the entire market.

From the air, the field would appear as one that had been left fallow by a farmer with more land than time and overgrown by weeds. On foot, a dozen DEA agents could come upon a field of the stuff and never see it as something other than grayish-green weeds with thick stalks. He called it Triple H for "heaven and hell of a high," because that was what a user would get, at least if his analyses were correct.

None of it might ever have happened if not for the unexpected inheritance of this house and land from a distant uncle. It had been a godsend in more ways than one. Not only did he now have a home, but also the perfect setup for his work. He had the isolation he needed to conduct experiments without interruptions, and once he'd developed the hybrid, he had the fifty acres of land on which to grow his genetically altered crops.

He lived alone, worked alone, slept alone, content to be the last house at the end of the road that began eight miles away down in Blue Creek. No one but the mailman ever came this far.

Watching the last test rat die, he wondered where the hell he'd gone wrong. Disappointment ran deep as he moved to the cages, took out a rat and laid it on an examining table. He needed to know what had happened, and the only way to do that was to conduct autopsies—twelve of them, to be exact.

With a muffled curse, he slipped on his lab coat, positioned the rat flat on its back and picked up a scalpel.

Three days and twelve autopsies later, Roland Storm had come to a rude awakening. There was a horrible problem with Triple H. One that he would never have envisioned, but the proof was in the tests—and the livers.

Triple H had been super-successful as a hallucinogenic, but the drawback was that it never dissipated. The build-up of the drug in the soft tissue samples was staggering. In fact, not only did it hook a user on the first try, it also turned out to be the drug that kept on giving. The build-up of Triple H in the rats' livers was astronomical. The livers had all but solidified, and the rats' brains looked as if they'd exploded. If he didn't know it was impossible, he would also have surmised that the nerve pathways in the body had tried to reroute themselves.

He stood for a few moments, trying to come to terms with what to do. Logically, he should destroy the crop and start over. While it was obvious that the first part of his experiment worked—one use and they were hooked forever—there still wasn't any market for something that would eventually kill everyone who used it.

The instant addiction had been the perfect marketing strategy, and would have insured a constant and growing market. But what the hell good did that do him when he was also killing off his customers as quickly as he made them?

He stared at the last of the dissected and dismembered rodents, then swept them into the garbage, yanked off his surgical gloves and tossed them in on top. Dropping his lab coat across the back of a chair, he headed up the stairs. He needed fresh air and a clear head to make a decision as monumental as this.

Once outside his house, he struggled to make sense of his failures. It just wasn't fair. All those years— wasted. He moved toward the path that led to his crop, then hesitated, went back to a shed, took a can of gasoline and resumed his trek.

As he neared the meadow, he could see the long, fernlike leaves of the mossy-colored plants dipping and swaying like exotic dancers flaunting their assets at paying clients.

His eyesight blurred as he contemplated destroying

so many years of work. It wasn't fair. His earlier work in cancer research at Lackey Laboratories outside Pittsburgh had been underappreciated and the credit for his work often taken by his superiors. He had resented it— and them—on a daily basis and let it be known. When they finally let him go, he was actually relieved, even though it had left him financially destitute. It was during that time, when he'd come so close to becoming homeless, that he realized there was big money to be made in creating designer drugs. He'd done a little of that on his own, while living in fear he would be caught. Roland was anything but a social animal, and the idea of doing time in a prison horrified him. Being in confinement with the dregs of society would destroy him, and he knew it, so when he learned of his West Virginia inheritance, he considered it a sign from God.

He'd retreated to the small home on the mountain above Blue Creek to lick his wounds. But the rage had still festered as he plotted the different ways he could enact revenge. He stewed about it so long that what had once been anger at one company and a specific set of individuals had become anger at the entire human race. Now he'd come to this.

As he stared at the crop, an idea began to evolve. He needed to look at what he had from a different angle. He had created a drug that was so addictive it could never be kicked. No amount of rehab, no drugs to help withdrawal, nothing—and it was lethal. So what if he unleashed it on the world, anyway? What if every drug user was dead? It would end the need for pushers, which would ultimately end the war on drugs. It would be the perfect proof that he was the smartest and best scientist in the world—and he would get rich in the process. But could he do it? It would amount to him becoming the largest mass murderer ever. But then he reminded himself that addicts didn't count. They were already useless to their families and to the world. He would be doing them a favor by ending an addiction they could not end on their own.

He stared at the field, well aware of the weight of the can of fuel he was holding. All he had to do was pour it at the edge of the field, then strike a match and watch it burn.

But the longer he stood there, the more convinced he became that he would be a fool to destroy this. He kept thinking that he could go down in history as the man who ended the war on drugs.

Once there was no longer a need for Triple H, he would destroy everything linking himself to it and follow the money he'd banked in Switzerland. Rampant drug use would be a thing of the past once people realized what had happened. They would be too afraid of another Triple H epidemic to take a chance on anything that gave them an unnatural high.

Having made his decision, he felt a huge weight of relief. He'd started his career trying to make the world a better place and had been somewhat conflicted over the fact that he was going to become involved in the drug trade. But this was different. He felt back on track.

He retraced his steps to the shed, replaced the can of fuel and then cleaned up the lab. It was time to begin the next phase of his plan—the harvest. But for that, he was going to need help, which immediately presented its own kind of problem. Who could he hire who would be trustworthy enough to keep quiet about what he was doing?

It occurred to him that isolating himself from the residents of Blue Creek might not have been in his best interests. Except for the occasional trip to the grocery store, he had no other associations. But with forty-some acres of Triple H nearly ready for harvest, it was time to switch tactics.

He changed his shirt and shoes and headed for his truck. Time to go shopping.

Wes was outside the house with a pair of garden clippers that he'd found in the barn, trimming back the overgrown vines from windows and doorways, when he heard the sound of an engine coming from up the road. His first instinct was to hide. He didn't want confrontation. But when the truck appeared and the driver showed no sign of interest in his presence, he relaxed, then resumed his task.

From the moment Ally Monroe had come knocking on the door with a basket full of ham biscuits, he'd known he was going to stay. She'd offered food, shelter and friendship, nothing more—which was good, because it was all he could handle. However, he couldn't stay anywhere without money, so as soon as he finished what he was doing, he was going to walk down into Blue Creek and see about getting a job.

Roland Storm couldn't believe it. Someone was living in Dooley Brown's old place. He'd seen the man out working when he'd driven by.

From the day he'd moved onto the mountain, he and Dooley Brown had been adversaries. It was as if the little man had seen right through everything Storm pretended to be. Still, Storm had chosen to ignore him until he'd caught Dooley Brown in the patch. He'd watched the little man picking leaves off a stalk and slipping them into a small plastic bag; then he'd followed him down the mountain and into the house.

To his credit, when Dooley Brown had turned around and seen Storm standing in his living room, he hadn't panicked. Instead, he had waved a hand toward the sofa.

"Have a seat, neighbor," Dooley said.

Taken aback, Storm had hesitated, then frowned.

"You have something of mine," he said, and pointed to the corner of a plastic bag sticking out of Dooley's pocket.

Before he thought, Dooley's hand went to the bag. Then he sighed.

"What? This?" He pulled it out and dangled it between his fingers. "It's just some herbs. I was going to boil them to make a tea."

Roland grinned. "Tea."

Dooley nodded, then pointed to his obviously crippled knees. "It's for my arthritis."

For a few moments Storm actually considered that he was telling the truth, but he couldn't take the chance.

"Sorry," he said, and snatched the bag out of Dooley's hand. "You've made a big mistake."

He stuffed the bag into his own pocket, but instead of leaving, he quietly shut the door. When he turned around, the old man was gone.

It only took a few moments to go through the house. When he didn't find him there, he ran down into the cellar beneath the house and found him trying to escape through an outer door. He'd killed him then and there, while taking great care to make sure it looked like an accident. It was easy to break his neck, less simple to break his arm. Who would have known such a genetic defect as Dooley Brown would have muscles like a bull? Still, he'd managed to do it, then positioned the body at the bottom of the cellar steps so as to make it appear that he'd tripped and fallen.

But that had been months ago, and now his gut was churning as he continued the drive into Blue Creek. While he hadn't associated with his neighbors, he had made it a point to know who they were and where they lived, and he knew for certain that the man living in Dooley Brown's house was a stranger. Storm couldn't afford to trust strangers to mind their own business. He would find his hired hands, then see what was up with his new neighbor.

Danny Monroe's face was as red as his hair as he stomped out of the local bar. He'd known Mac Friend all of his life. They'd been Boy Scouts together, then on the same baseball team in high school. Four years ago, when Mac's father suddenly up and died, Mac became the sole owner of the only bar and grill in Blue Creek. Now he lived in a three-bedroom brick house, drove a brand-new Dodge four-by-four, and wore fancy cowboy boots made out of python and ostrich. The fact that he could have any girl he wanted was less irritating to Danny than the fact that he'd just turned him down for a job.

Danny still couldn't believe it. Mac had advertised for a bouncer. Danny had been so sure he would get hired. But Mac had told him flat-out that he was too short and sent him packing, as if he was some nobody begging for a handout.

Danny was furious, and it showed. He slammed himself into the seat of his truck and drove away, leaving skid marks on the road as he did.

Roland Storm had been having lunch at the grill when Danny Monroe had come in, then had become an inadvertent bystander to the entire proceedings. As soon as Danny was gone, Roland paid for his food and left. He wasn't certain, but he just might have found himself a hired hand.

* * *

Wes's step was light as he returned to the little house he was beginning to think of as home. It hadn't taken him nearly as long to walk the five miles down the mountain as it was taking to go up, but the weeks he'd spent on the road had gone a long way to getting him back into the fighting shape he'd been in before his world had come tumbling down.

As he came around a turn he saw the Monroe house, then convinced himself it was just curiosity that made him look, when in truth, he was hoping to catch a glimpse of his landlady. When he saw her sitting on the porch, he slowed down.

Buddy was lying near the mailbox at the road. Wes caught himself smiling as the old dog opened his eyes, although he didn't bother to lift his head.

"Hey there, fellow, looks like you've got the best job in town."

Buddy managed a greeting that was somewhere between a gargle and a woof, but it was enough to make Ally look up. Wes lifted a hand in greeting.

Ally laid aside the bowl of beans she was snapping, then got to her feet and started toward the road.

"Hello!" she called.

Wes waited, telling himself it was out of courtesy, but the truth was, there was something about her that left a man with a good feeling, and since he was sadly lacking in that department, he couldn't afford to pass it up.

"Hello, yourself," he said.

Ally stopped just short of throwing her arms around him and settled for leaning on the fence instead.

"I see you've been shopping," she said, pointing to the sack of groceries he was carrying.

He nodded, wondering why he found it so difficult to carry on a conversation with this woman, when he'd thought nothing of giving orders to, and being in charge of, any number of soldiers.

"I got that job," he said.

Ally's smile widened. "That's wonderful," she said. "Congratulations."

"I probably have you to thank for it," he added.

"Why is that?" Ally asked.

"Because he wasn't giving me the time of day until I mentioned your name. When he found out I was staying in your uncle's house, it was a done deal."

"It's a small world up here. People tend to stay to themselves a bit, probably a holdover from the early days of prohibition. Anyway, I'm happy for you."

Wes nodded, while wondering if he would ever be happy again.

Ally sensed his discomfort and immediately backed away.

"I'll let you get on home, but if you need anything, will you promise to let me know?"

"Yes, sure," Wes said, then added, "Thank you."

"For what?" Ally asked.

"For helping me help myself. And just so you know, as soon as I get paid, I'll start paying you rent."

"That's not necessary," she said.

"It is for me," he said, and waved goodbye.

Ally held the gentle sound of his voice close to her heart long after he had disappeared.

Wes was less than a mile from home when he heard a car approaching from behind. Without turning around, he moved off the road into the grass along the shoulder, expecting the driver to go on by. But when he realized that not only was the car not passing him, but that the driver had slowed down, his instinct for survival kicked in. He turned in a motion so fluid that it startled Roland Storm into hitting the brakes even harder. In that moment, time seemed to stand still.

Wes knew he was looking at the enemy, he just didn't know why, and at the same time, Roland realized he'd more than met his match. And when he saw the stranger set down his sack of groceries and reach into his pocket, he realized he was also armed. Startled by the defiance in the stranger's stature, Roland quickly took his foot off the brake and stomped the accelerator, leaving Wes in the dust.

It wasn't until after the man was gone that Wes realized Aaron's switchblade was in his hand. He looked down at the deadly edge on the ten-inch blade, then calmly flipped it back in its sheath, picked up his groceries and headed for home.

The incident had been startling, but, strangely enough, it had also awakened Wes's instinct for survival.

When he'd looked into that man's eyes and seen the enemy, he'd known for sure he wasn't ready to die.

As he neared the little house, instead of approaching from the front, he slipped into the woods and slowly circled the property until he was certain there was no one lying in wait. Then he entered the house and did a quick search inside before locking the doors.

It occurred to him as he was putting away his things that there was danger on this mountain. A part of him wanted to walk away right now, but he didn't like the feeling that gave him. It would be as good as admitting he was not only a failure but a quitter, and since that wasn't part of who he'd been, he refused to give in to the urge.

What he needed was some intel. He needed to find out what that man was all about and why he'd targeted Wes. That would come after dark. For now, he was going to make a meal, maybe read one of Dooley Brown's books and relax.

As he opened up a can of stew and turned on the stove, his thoughts slipped to the woman down below. Most likely she would be in the kitchen about now, preparing food for her family, probably laughing and talking, catching up on the events of the day. He thought of Margie and tried to recall similar memories, but nothing came to mind, which only served to remind him of how far their lives had separated. He'd loved her. They'd made a baby together. He'd given her his heart, but he'd given his time and his soul to Uncle Sam. It had been a mistake, but one that was impossible to retract. Instead, all he could do was promise himself that it was a mistake he would never repeat.

Danny's mood was high as he pulled into the driveway and parked in the shade. Ally was sitting on the porch drinking a glass of lemonade.

"Hey, Ally…where's Porter?"

"He hasn't come back from hunting," she said. "What's up?"

"I found us a job."

"Porter, too?"

"Yes, Porter, too," Danny said. "It's supposed to rain tonight, so on the first sunny day after, we start work."

"Who for?" Ally asked.

Danny's smile shifted just enough to make Ally think he was hiding something, but then she discarded the thought as he answered.

"You know that man who lives on the old Harmon place?"

"Are you talking about that odd skinny man who wears his hair in a ponytail?"

"Yeah, that's him. Name's Roland Storm. He's a bit of an oddball all right, but he's willing to pay big money for some help."

Ally didn't have a good feeling about this, but she had no logical reason to question Danny's decision.

"What does he want you to do?" Ally asked.

"He's been growing some kind of Chinese herb, and he wants me and Porter to harvest it for him."

This time Ally made no attempt to hide a frown.

"Chinese herbs in West Virginia?"

"It's what he said."

"What's he paying you?"

"Five thousand dollars apiece."

Ally gasped. "That's ten thousand dollars! Just to harvest a crop? Danny! You've got to know that's suspicious! For that kind of money, it's bound to be something illegal."

Danny was getting angry, Ally could tell. Still, she couldn't stop.

"Don't do it, Danny. Something bad will happen. I just know it."

"Hellsfire, Ally, I thought you would be happy for me. You know how hard jobs are to come by up here. I haven't seen the crop yet, and truth be known, I don't know if I'd recognize it if it *was* some kind of drug. All I know is, it's good money for a job well done, and I'm taking it."

He started into the house, then paused and turned.

"And I'd appreciate it if you wouldn't say anything negative about this to Dad."

Ally glared. "You act like I'm going to tattle on you, which is childish. I didn't do that when we were kids, and I'm not going to do it now. However, you know Dad will find out, and if I were you, I'd make sure I was the one who told him."

Danny glared back.

"I'm going to find Porter."

Ally shrugged. "I've said all I'm going to say."

"You've already said enough," Danny muttered, then let the door slam shut behind him as he went inside.

The sound was like a slap in the face. Ally's shoulders slumped, and her hands went limp. The words of Granny Devon's prophecy, about her being her brother's keeper, kept repeating in her head. But Granny had also said something about a man who had done evil. A man who was bad. Could Roland Storm be that man? Or was it the stranger she'd let into their world?

Roland had come to the conclusion that it was fate that had led him to hire Danny and Porter Monroe. His fascination with their sister, Ally, was the only thing besides Triple H that he cared about. Maybe hiring them had just given him the link he needed to meet her face-to-face. He was disturbed, although, by the presence of the man living at Dooley Brown's place.

Roland was nervous—very nervous. He'd come too far and gone through too many disappointments to let the unexpected arrival of the enemy stop him now. The man had to go, but Roland needed time to decide how to go about it. It was obvious that he couldn't overpower him as he had Dooley Brown.

He made himself a sandwich, reached for the newspaper that he'd purchased in town and settled down at the dining table for a relaxing meal. There would be plenty of time later to decide what to do about his new neighbor.

* * *

That night, the only thing to be said for the mood around the Monroe dinner table was that it was cautious. Ally felt guilty, knowing something her father didn't—something she felt could cause problems for her brothers. And there was the fact that there was a stranger living—by her invitation—in her uncle Doo's house. Confused as to what she should do, she did nothing.

Danny had filled Porter in on his news and they kept giving each other nervous glances and quick half smiles.

Thankfully, Gideon was blessedly oblivious to the undercurrents and completely focused on his own agenda. Come Friday, Freddie Joe and his children would be sitting at this very table. Ally would realize how much she was needed in the Detweiller family and accept Freddie Joe's advances. After that, it was only a matter of time before she was married. When that happened, Gideon would have fulfilled his last promise to his wife, to see their only girl-child happily settled.

Nine

It was fifteen minutes after one in the morning when Wes rolled out of bed. He was getting the hang of Dooley Brown's world and hadn't bumped his chin on his knees in nearly two days. He was, however, still stumped as to how to take a shower without having to stoop over, but that was a small price to pay for the shelter of this house.

As he went about the business of gathering up clothes, he knew he couldn't be late for his first day of work tomorrow, but he was still unsettled about that man in the truck. He didn't know who he was or where he lived, but since he'd been coming down from above Dooley's house, it seemed simple enough to Wes he needed to follow the road upward and see where it led.

He pulled his darkest clothes out of the closet and dressed quickly, taking care to pocket the switchblade as he slipped out of the house. After locking the doors, he stood near the wall of the vine-covered cottage, waiting until his eyesight had adjusted to the spare moonlight and shadows, while absorbing the smells of the night. There was a faint smell of polecat, as well as moisture in the air, which made him wonder if it was going to rain. He could hear the faint, faraway sound of traffic on the highway below—a distant reminder of the world from which he had come. Still, it was what that world and the army had taught him that was holding him in good stead now.

He circled the house, then started walking upward, taking care to stay away from the road. As he walked, he became aware that the higher up he went, the fewer trees there were. Following the faint outline of the light from a quarter moon, Wes moved without leaving a trail. Something large and feathered glided silently past his head and disappeared into the darkness—most likely an owl. It reminded him of hunting with his daddy when he was a kid—the quiet times when they'd been sitting in a tree in a deer stand and watching the first fingers of daylight tearing strips out of the dark sky. Feeling the chill of frost settling on fingers and the end of a nose, seeing breath forming small white puffs of condensation and knowing that nothing would ever be better than this. It was a camaraderie that only another man could ever understand.

Suddenly a twig snapped behind him, and by the time he turned around, the switchblade was out of his pocket, the blade bared. It wasn't until he saw a raccoon waddle out of a thicket that he let himself relax. Still, the incident was a reminder for him to keep his focus on the business at hand and save the reminiscences for later.

The soldier in him was back.

A few yards later, he found the first dead animal—a small doe.

Puzzled by the fact that no predators had eaten it, he gave it a wide berth and kept walking. Just before he got to the house he found another dead animal—this time a squirrel. It was lying beneath a bush, and if the moonlight hadn't been shining down on the spot, he would have missed it completely.

Again, nothing had fed on it.

Something felt wrong, but he couldn't say what.

When he got to the house, he knew it belonged to the man he was looking for when he recognized the two-tone brown truck parked next to the porch.

He stood for several minutes, taking in the entrances and exits while looking for a dog or any other animal that might sound an alarm. As he waited, a small opossum walked out from under the truck and headed for the back of the house. Still, there was no sign of a dog.

Convinced that there were none at the place, he moved closer to check the truck, but it was locked. He circled the house, checking for signs of a security device. The only thing he found was a single line for electricity. There were shades pulled down on every window, which Wes found strange. It was hot outside, and very still. The house was at the end of a road, at the top of a mountain, yet every window was covered so that no one could see in. Either the man inside was some kind of recluse, or he had something to hide. Wes's gut instinct told him it was the latter, only he had no way of finding out what it was unless he looked.

Without hesitation, he moved around to the rear of the house, quietly picked the lock on the back door and walked into the kitchen.

The room smelled of fried food and cold coffee, but the countertops were clean, and there were no dirty dishes in the sink.

So the man wasn't a slob. That didn't tell him anything. There was a door on his left that was slightly ajar. He opened it enough to look in and realized that it must lead to the basement. He slipped inside, then shut the door before descending the stairs. It wasn't until he was all the way down that he took out a small flashlight and turned it on. There was a scent of decay in the air, although the room seemed scoured and clean.

The moment he saw the lab equipment and the empty cages, his curiosity rose. He checked for some notes or papers, anything to tell him what had been going on down here, but he found nothing specific—until he started back up the stairs and noticed the huge trash container that had been pushed beneath the steps. He dug through it, searching for a name. He found a bill and looked at the address.

Roland Storm. So the man's name was Roland Storm. He started to drop the papers back in the trash, then stopped and frowned. What he'd first taken as spilled ink now appeared to be blood. He pushed aside the top layer of papers, and saw the blood and the gore and the dismembered rodents.

Now he knew what had been causing the stink. But…why?

Crap. Is the man a nutcase who likes to cut up small animals…or is there something more going on?

On closer look, he realized there had been a purpose to the violence. The rats had been dissected. With a shudder, he pushed the trash can back under the stairs, crept up the steps, turned off his flashlight, then slipped back into the kitchen. He listened again, and when he was satisfied his presence was still undetected, he moved into the hall. It was long and narrow, with a number of doors along the way. He thought about the risks involved in taking this further, then shoved them to the back of his mind. Although it would solve nothing, he needed to see the enemy's face up close.

He kept close to the wall as he went, knowing that the boards there were less likely to creak, until finally he'd reached the first door. It was slightly ajar, and he stopped, barely breathing, listening intently for the sounds of habitation. When he heard a soft snore, he tensed. It was now or never.

He put a hand on the door, applying just enough pressure to move it while hoping the hinges didn't squeak. When it swung silently inward, he breathed a sigh of relief and followed it, stopping a couple of steps inside the doorway.

The light inside the room was faint, but Wes could see the man's outline beneath the covers. A window-unit air conditioner had been positioned so that it blew directly across the bed. Its busy little hum masked any number of small sounds, which gave Wes time to study his prey.

Storm was tall—very tall. The angular planes of his face gave him a skeletal appearance, but with his eyes shut, it was difficult to judge his personality. What Wes could see was a long, grayish-brown ponytail lying over his right shoulder and down across his chest.

The urge to wake him up was strong. Wes knew how to get information from people who were unwilling to divulge it, but at least as yet, this wasn't war, and he wasn't a cold-blooded killer, so he had to be satisfied with what he'd learned so far.

Suddenly Storm snored and then choked. Wes froze. Within seconds, Storm would be awake. He took a silent step backward, pulling the door with him as he went and leaving it slightly ajar, just as he'd found it.

Then, moving quickly along the wall, he retraced his steps through the kitchen and out the door, taking care to lock it behind him. Once outside, he ran into the woods, then stopped and looked back at the house.

As he watched, a light came on in what appeared to be the bedroom, then, a few seconds later, another in the kitchen. When the kitchen door opened, Wes took another step back, although he knew that, given where he was standing, he could not be seen.

Storm was naked except for a pair of briefs, but Wes could see that his hands were curled into fists.

"So…you felt me in there, did you?" Wes muttered.

Roland Storm stepped off the porch into the dust.

"Who's there?" he called, but he heard nothing except the faint echo of his own voice.

He focused his gaze on the darkened forest surrounding the house, and for the first time since he'd come here, felt imprisoned by the isolation, rather than hidden. He shifted his focus from the trees to the meadow, wondering if someone was out there now, stealing that which did not belong to them. Then he smiled. If they were, they would have a rude awakening.

"You're going to be sorry!" he shouted, then turned on his heel and stalked back into the house. Moments later, the lights went out.

Wes's eyes narrowed as he thought about what he'd seen down in that basement lab. He felt threatened by the man, though he didn't know why. He wasn't going to find out anything more tonight. Satisfied that, for now, he'd done all he could do, Wes began to retrace his steps.

He'd been moving at a pretty rapid clip down the mountain when suddenly he heard the sound of an engine on the road behind him. In that moment, he realized he'd underestimated Roland Storm. The skin crawled on the back of his neck as he judged the distance he had yet to go to get home. He didn't know how he was going to do it, but he had to be inside his house before Roland Storm came knocking.

He leapt forward into an all-out dash. As he ran, the sound of Storm's truck out on the road suddenly seemed fainter; then he remembered the big curve, knowing it would slow Roland down. It wasn't much, but it might just be the edge Wes needed.

Rocks rolled beneath Wes's feet as he ran; branches slapped him in the face. Rabbits spooked and dashed for cover, as owls startled from feeding abandoned their prey and took to the sky. Twice Wes tripped and fell, and each time he quickly scrambled to his feet.

He was running almost parallel to the truck he could hear off to his right. His heart was hammering in rhythm to the pounding of his feet against the earth. This mad dash through unmarked territory was against everything he'd been taught in Special Ops, but there was no time for caution. Either he got there first or he was found out.

Just when he thought it was over, he was out of the trees. He was running across the backyard toward Dooley's house just as the headlights of Roland Storm's truck appeared up the drive. Earlier, Wes had used the front door, but he couldn't go back the same way without being seen. The back door didn't have a key, only an inside bolt, which he knew was locked. His only chance was through the root cellar. Thankful that it had no lock, he yanked the door open and then let it fall shut as he flew down. Stumbling on the bottom step, he tripped and fell, but again he picked himself up and flew up the other set of steps on his hands and feet. He burst into the kitchen just as he heard Roland pulling into the yard.

His heart was thumping, his chest heaving. Without taking time to think, he ripped off his shirt, tore off his pants and shoes, and kicked them under the kitchen table as he dashed to the sink.

He turned on the water, then leaned down, frantically washing the blood from his scratches as a knock sounded on the door. Drying quickly, he started into the living room, then did a quick one-eighty, grabbed the switchblade out of his pants pocket and moved toward the door as another knock came—this time louder and longer.

He took several deep breaths to calm the sound of his voice, then made noise, as if he was just coming down the hall.

"Who the hell is it?" he shouted.

There was a long, startled moment of silence, and Wes knew that his presence had taken Storm aback. Storm obviously believed he'd had an intruder and believed it was Wes. The last thing Storm had expected to hear was the sound of Wes's voice. Wes popped the switchblade, then opened the door.

Roland Storm hadn't expected the stranger to be home, let alone meet him at the door, nearly naked—with a switchblade in his hand.

"Uh…I am—"

"I know who you are." Wes peered past him to the

truck beyond, then frowned. "You're that crazy bastard who almost ran me off the road this afternoon. What's wrong now? Was I snoring too loud?"

Roland didn't know what to say. The man was standing in the shadows, but he could see the shimmer of the blade.

"Someone broke into my house tonight. I thought…"

Wes cursed rudely. "Mister…if someone broke into my house, I'd be calling the local authorities, not calling on my neighbors."

"Yes, well…I just wanted to make sure it wasn't—"

Wes slammed the door in his face, then held his breath, waiting to see if Roland Storm left. Within seconds, he heard the sound of footsteps moving away from the door, then the sound of a car door slamming shut. Moments later, an engine fired. When Storm backed up to turn the truck around, the glare from his headlights swept through the windows.

Only then did Wes turn the lock on the door. When he heard Storm leaving, he slid to the floor with his back against the door and started to shake.

He'd done it.

It took long, agonizing minutes before Wes was able to move. Even then, the muscles in his legs were still cramping. He staggered into the bathroom, then into the shower, letting the warm water soothe the aches and pains. Finally, when the water began to run cold, he got out and dried, then crawled into his bed. Just before he fell asleep, he rolled over and set the alarm.

In what seemed like only minutes later, it was buzzing rudely, waking him from a deep and restless sleep. He shut it off and rolled out of bed. Considering it was his first day of work, he didn't want to be late.

Harold James still didn't know what had possessed him to hire a perfect stranger to work in his store, and once the man who'd identified himself as Wes Holden was gone, he hadn't really expected to see him again. Yet there he was, coming in the front door of the feed store before the clock had struck 8:00 a.m. Harold studied the width of Holden's shoulders and the leanness of his physique, as well as that head full of dark hair that he wore tied back at his nape. He was a fine figure of a man, all right, but there was something guarded in his expression. Then Harold shrugged. If Ally Monroe vouched for him, and as long as he did what he was told, Harold wouldn't have a quarrel.

"'Morning, Holden," Harold said.

Wes nodded as he came through the door.

"Where did you park? I meant to tell you that employees park in back."

"Don't have a car," Wes said. "What do you want me to do first?"

Harold stared. "No car?"

Wes shook his head.

"Then how did you get here?"

"Walked."

Harold's eyes widened.

"Dang, man, that's a good five miles."

"Don't know how good it is, but yes, it's every bit of five miles."

Suddenly Harold had a new respect for the man he'd hired. If he wanted to work bad enough to walk five miles to get to the job, then he figured he'd just hired himself a good man.

"Got a load of chicken feed coming in around nine. Why don't you go clean up around those empty pallets before we fill 'em up again? Oh…and one of your jobs will be to feed Scooby first thing every morning."

"Who's Scooby?" Wes asked.

"A damn good mouser, and in a place like this, you got to have yourself a good mouser. However, he likes his tuna. I always feed him a tin of tuna before he starts his day. You'll find Scooby and the cat food in the back room near the loading dock."

So Scooby was a cat.

"Tuna it is," Wes said, and headed for the hallway that linked the front of the store to the warehouse.

And so the morning passed. Wes soon discovered that Scooby did not discriminate. Whoever held the key to opening the can of tuna also held the key to Scooby's heart. The big gray tom entwined himself between Wes's feet, rubbing against the legs of Wes's pants until the tuna was on the plate. After that, Wes was on his own.

The semi arrived from the warehouse in Charleston promptly at nine, and Wes began to earn his pay. After unloading four tons of chicken feed that came packaged in twenty-five-pound sacks, the muscles in Wes's arms were beginning to burn. But it felt good to be tired, and even better to know that, once again, he was earning his way.

Wes spent the rest of the morning loading the occasional sacks for the customers Harold sent his way. He expected their curiosity but was unexpectedly touched by their genuine friendliness and welcome to Blue Creek.

It was nearing noon when Harold walked into the warehouse.

"It's going on twelve," Harold said. "You get an hour for lunch. Kathy's Café across the street is your only option, unless you're in the market for pop and candy, in which case, you got the fillin' station on the corner or the grocery store down the block."

All too aware of his dwindling funds and uncertain of when he would get paid, Wes decided against spending the money.

"Thanks, but I'll pass," Wes said.

Harold frowned. "Listen, Wes. You hauled a lot of weight around this morning. I don't want you foldin' up on me before quittin' time."

"I don't fold," Wes said shortly.

Harold's attention shifted. Once again, he suspected there was a whole lot more to this man than met the eye.

"Suit yourself," Harold said, and started to walk off, then something occurred to him. He pulled a couple of twenties out of his pocket and handed them to Wes. "Thought you might need an advance on your pay."

It took swallowing some pride, but Wes accepted the money with a nod.

"I appreciate it," he said.

"I pay weekly, remember."

"Yes," Wes said as he pocketed the money. Then he took off his gloves and combed his fingers through his hair. "See you in an hour," he said, and headed for the bathroom to wash up.

Once again, he'd unintentionally given Harold another view into the man he was. He would willingly go hungry rather than ask for money he had yet to earn. Harold wondered what had driven a man like Wes Holden to the road. He'd done a little wandering himself in his early days, but he'd had the good sense to stop and put down some roots. Then he heard the bell jingle over the front door and hurried back to the store.

It was nearing quitting time when the sky started to darken. Harold frowned as a faint grumble of thunder sounded on the other side of the ridge.

"Looks like we're gonna get a little rain," he said.

Wes glanced out the window, then kept sweeping. He'd been wet before. At least it was summer. Winter rain was what sucked. After the haircut he'd gotten during his noon hour, it wouldn't take long for his hair to dry.

Harold thought about the five miles up that mountain that lay ahead of Wes Holden before he got home, then watched Wes hang up the push broom and dust off his hands.

"I'm done with the sweeping," Wes said. "Anything else you want done?"

"No. You did good today," Harold said. "Real good. Why don't you head on home? Maybe get a jump start on the rain before it gets here."

"I've been wet before," Wes said. "I don't melt."

Harold grinned. "Hell, man…if you get any tougher, I'll have to get myself some new teeth just to talk to you."

Wes grinned, then shrugged.

"Sorry, but I'm not in the habit of making excuses for myself."

Harold chuckled. "Yeah, you've proved that, so go home already."

"Thanks," Wes said. "I'll see you tomorrow."

"Yeah, tomorrow," Harold echoed.

Wes stepped out onto the sidewalk, then took a deep breath. He was hot and tired, and the muscles in his back and arms ached, but he couldn't remember the last time he'd felt this good. He looked up at the sky again. Harold was right. It was going to rain.

He rubbed the back of his neck, unconsciously massaging sore muscles and cognizant of the missing hair. He was stepping off the sidewalk and into the street when he heard the sound of screeching brakes, then a woman's scream. Seconds later there was a loud crunch of metal against metal, then a quick rush of escaping steam.

He was running toward the accident before the logging truck had stopped skidding. The driver of the car was pinned into the seat by a log that had plowed through his window, while another three logs from the load that had been en route to the lumber mill had slammed into the back of the truck cab, then slid over the hood, trapping the truck driver inside the cab. A large pool of fuel was running out from under the car, increasing the risk of fire and explosion.

Wes vaulted over a log to get to the car, then leaned through the broken window on the passenger side to check the driver's condition. All he could tell for sure was that he was still alive.

"Mister, help is on the way," Wes said quickly, and when the driver moaned and tried to push at the log against his chest, Wes stopped him with a touch. "Don't move. Don't move, okay?"

Wes couldn't tell if the driver understood, but at least he stopped moving. As he started away from the car, a half-dozen other bystanders were arriving on the scene.

"Ambulance is on the way!" someone shouted, then Wes heard another man shouting, "Get a fire extinguisher! The truck engine is on fire!"

Wes crawled over the car to get to the truck. The top of the cab had been flattened from the impact of the logs, but the driver didn't seem to be injured, only pinned.

Wes looked down into the cab through a broken window and found himself staring straight into the driver's face. He looked young—barely in his twenties.

"Help me!" the young man yelled. "Help! Don't let me burn!"

For a split second the man's face appeared to be covered in blood. Wes shook his head and then rubbed his eyes. He felt reality slipping and slammed a fist against the cab, using pain to retain his hold on reality.

"We'll get you out," Wes said. "Help is coming."

He reached into the cab and pulled back on the crumpled steering wheel, trying to give the man room to crawl out, but it wouldn't give.

The young man was begging now, but Wes couldn't look at him. Instead, he began pulling at the crumpled door, willing it to open.

As Wes struggled, he could see tiny fingers of fire through a crack in the dash. That bystander was right. The engine was on fire, and with the puddle of fuel from the car spreading by the second, they were caught in the middle of what would probably be their funeral pyre. The driver had begun to cry. Wes wanted to cry with him.

Just when he feared help was going to come too late, an old red fire truck came speeding around the corner. Wes thought about the high-tech equipment in big cities and stifled a groan. If this little fire department even had a Jaws of Life, it would be a miracle, and that was exactly what it would take to get this man out.

Suddenly Wes heard someone calling his name. He looked up as Harold James arrived on the scene. Giving Wes only a split second to prepare for the catch, Harold tossed a fire extinguisher into Wes's hands. Wes grabbed it and then dropped to his knees on top of the truck cab, popped the trigger on the extinguisher and aimed it into the engine just as the firemen spilled out of the truck.

Within seconds, someone had produced a chain saw and was sawing the protruding end of the log away from the man pinned in the car, while another sprayed water on the fire inside the truck. When the imminent danger was gone, the firemen immediately began adding fire retardant onto the spilled fuel.

With paramedics and firemen now on the scene, Wes began walking away from the accident. There was a small cut on the side of his face and a burn on his forearm, but he felt nothing. Logically, he knew he was in the middle of the street in Blue Creek, West Virginia, but emotionally, he was struggling.

In his mind, the smoke and chaos surrounding the wrecked vehicles were coming from the downed belly of a Black Hawk, and the shouts and cries of the firemen and paramedics had morphed into screams for mercy from dying soldiers trapped in the blaze.

Wes put his hands over his eyes, but the images were still there. He groaned, then staggered as a wave of panic sent him to his knees. The siren squall of an approaching police car turned into the whine of a warning siren, signaling incoming missiles.

Suddenly someone grabbed him under the arms and pulled him to his feet.

"Wes. *Wes!* Look at me, man!"

Wes heard the voice—knew he'd heard it before—

and tried to focus. He could see a face—a man's face. The large jaw and long nose looked familiar.

"Wes! It's me, Harold."

Wes shuddered. Harold. He knew a man named Harold, only Harold didn't belong in Iraq. Slowly he reached out and touched Harold's face, expecting it to disappear. When he felt solid flesh, he actually flinched.

"Harold?"

Harold James shivered. He'd seen men like Wes before, after he'd come home from Vietnam.

"Come on, man. Let's go back into the store and wash the smoke off your face, okay?"

Wes shook his head, like a dog shedding water, then covered his face with his hands. A long, silent moment passed, during which Harold James wanted to cry. Instead, he waited for Wes to pull himself together. Finally Wes dropped his hands and looked up.

"I lost it, didn't I?"

Harold grimaced, then pointed to the wreck.

"Naw, man, you helped save those men's lives."

Wes turned and looked, and as he did, felt the ground shift again, but this time only slightly.

"It was the smoke…maybe the fire…or the screams. Who knows," he mumbled.

Harold put a hand on Wes's shoulder.

"What branch were you in?"

Wes sighed. "Army. Special Ops."

"What got you sent Stateside?"

Wes tried to form the words, but to his dismay, he couldn't say them.

Harold thumped Wes on the back, then cleared his throat to steady his voice.

"It don't matter none," Harold said. "You'll get better. It happened to all of us in one way or another."

As they stood, a drop of rain landed on the toe of Wes's shoe.

"See, I told you it was gonna rain," Harold said. "Come with me."

Wes felt disoriented. He could hear Harold's voice, but it sounded as if he were at the other end of a long tunnel.

"Where are we going?" he finally asked.

"I'm taking you home," Harold said. "I think you've earned the ride."

Ten

Before they were halfway home, the rain began to fall in earnest. Harold glanced nervously at the man in the passenger seat, then kept his gaze on the road. Even in the best of weather, the two-lane dirt road wasn't easy to navigate. Driving it in a thunderstorm took some nerve and a lot of attention.

"You wanna talk about it?" Harold asked.

Wes shivered. It hurt to breathe. It hurt to swallow. How in hell was he supposed to talk? He shook his head.

But Harold wasn't ready to quit. He eyed Wes again, this time taking into account his age and bearing.

"You were an officer, weren't you?"

Wes managed a nod.

"Get yourself a Purple Heart?" It was Harold's way of asking if Wes had been wounded.

Wes leaned his head against the back of the seat and closed his eyes.

Harold knew he'd said enough.

Wes never knew when they passed the Monroe house and only realized they'd arrived at Dooley's house when the motion of Harold's truck stopped.

"We're home," Harold said.

Wes sat up, then opened his eyes. Home? This little toadstool of a house wasn't his home. He didn't belong here. Truth was, he didn't know where he belonged.

"Thank you for the ride," he said, and got out of the truck.

"Don't come to work tomorrow if it's still raining," Harold called. "No need to walk all that way in the mud and rain."

Wes gave no indication that he'd heard as he kept moving toward the house. The rain was hammering against his face and body. He thought about running but knew he would fall. He heard Harold turning around. Politeness would require at least a wave of thank-you, but he couldn't manage anything more than just getting to the house. When he finally reached the front door, it took three tries to get the key in the lock. When he stepped inside, the sudden absence of rain was a blessing.

He shivered as he closed the door. The little house was just as he'd left it this morning. If only he could say the same about himself. There was a faint scent of coffee and cold grease from the eggs that he'd fried, but the sound of rain on the roof was muffled by the presence of the overgrowth of vines.

He turned on the lights, stripping his wet clothes off

as he went and dropping them in a pile in the kitchen. His legs were starting to shake, and he felt his belly roll. He made it to the bathroom in time to throw up and was sweating profusely by the time he was done. A cleansing shower would be welcome, but he wasn't sure he could stand up long enough to get clean. Instead, he gave himself up to the memories he'd been fighting, letting the same old sick feeling of loss flow through him, pulling him deeper and deeper into the darkness of his mind.

He wanted to die, but would settle for the blessed forgetfulness of sleep. He thought of the bed across the hall, but his legs wouldn't move. Slowly, he slid downward with his back to the wall. By the time he reached the floor, the darkness had come, shadowing reality and pulling him under.

Harold felt guilty driving away. He could see that Wes was in a bad way, but they were strangers. Wes needed help Harold wasn't capable of giving. Still, Harold's conscience continued to prick until he came upon the driveway leading to the Monroe property. That was when it hit him. Ally Monroe had recommended Wes. Maybe she could help.

Harold wasn't the type of man who got involved in people's business, but there was something about Wes Holden that touched his heart. He hit the brakes and turned up the driveway before he could change his mind.

Ally was taking a cherry pie out of the oven when she heard the sound of a car coming down the driveway.

She glanced up at the clock and then frowned. It was too early for her father, and because of the weather, Danny and Porter couldn't start work and had gone into Charleston for the night. She set the pie down on a cooling rack and was wiping her hands when someone knocked at the door.

She hurried into the living room as a knock sounded again.

"I'm coming," she called, and then opened the door. "Why, hello, Mr. James. Come in. Come in. The rain is really coming down."

Harold took off his hat but stayed where he was.

"Thanks, Ally, but I need to be getting on home." At this point, he wished he'd just kept on driving and minding his own business. "Look, I may be out of line here, but I was thinking that maybe since you rented your uncle's house to that Holden fellow, you two might be friends."

Ally felt the blood running out of her face, but for the life of her, she couldn't speak. She reached for the door-frame to steady herself as Harold continued to speak.

"There was a real bad wreck in town today and—"

Ally swayed on her feet. She had to ask. She had to know now.

"How badly was he hurt?"

Harold frowned. "Oh, no, no… I didn't mean to make you think it was him. He wasn't in the wreck, but he helped save the drivers who were."

Ally's legs went weak.

"Thank goodness. You scared me."

Harold fidgeted with his hat. He wasn't good at this.

"Sorry. I didn't mean to do that."

"Then he's okay?" Ally asked.

Harold's frown deepened.

"That's just it. I don't think so. What do you know about him, anyway?"

"Not much," Ally said. "I don't think he has any family. I asked once, and all he said was that they were dead."

"He was a Special Ops officer in the army. It showed when he jumped right in the middle of the fire and smoke at the wreck as if he knew what he was doing. Afterward, I asked and he admitted it. The deal is, he put out a fire and kept the logging truck from blowing up and killing both drivers, but right afterward, he sort of had a meltdown."

Ally felt sick. "What do you mean?"

Harold eyed Ally carefully. "Ever hear of PTSD?"

"Post-traumatic stress disorder?"

Harold nodded. "I'm no doctor, but I saw a lot of it after Vietnam. I don't know what's happened to him, but I'd bet money that the wreck triggered some kind of flashback."

Ally felt sick. "What should I do?"

Harold shrugged. "I'm not saying you should do anything. He's not your responsibility, but I figured if you were friends, you'd want to know."

Ally nodded. "Thank you, Mr. James."

"Don't thank me," Harold said. "That's not news I'd want to hear."

"No…no…I appreciate it, I do," Ally said. "Be careful driving home."

"Yeah, that I will."

Ally watched until he'd driven away; then she rushed into the kitchen and turned off the stove. The stew was on the back burner and warming. The pie was cooling. She didn't know when her father would be coming home.

When the phone suddenly rang, she flinched, then hurried to answer.

"Hello?"

"Ally, it's me."

Her father's voice was oddly reassuring.

"I was just wondering when you were coming home."

"That's why I called. I'm staying in town for a while. One of my lodge buddies was in a bad wreck."

"Oh, no, who?" she asked.

"Pete Randall. Brakes went out on a loggin' truck, then it slid right into Pete's car. Happened right in the middle of town. I'm goin' to the hospital and sit with the family 'til we know more about his condition."

"All right," Ally said.

"It will probably be late. Oh…uh, don't hold supper. I'll eat in town."

Thank goodness. "Give my regards to the Randall family."

"I'll do that," Gideon said, and hung up.

Ally needed a vehicle, but both of them were gone. She knew that with her leg like it was, it would take forever for her to walk up the mountain in the mud and rain.

Then she remembered Porter's four-wheeler ATV. It wouldn't keep her dry, but it would get her where she needed to go.

Without thinking of the consequences, she ran to her bedroom to change her clothes and shoes, pulled one of Danny's hunting ponchos over her jeans and shirt, and hurried to the barn. Within minutes, she was wheeling up the road, slinging mud and water behind her as she went.

She didn't think of what disaster she might find, or if her appearance would make Wes Holden angry. All she could remember was the lost, lonely look in his eyes.

Despite the wind and rain, she made it up to her uncle Doo's house in just under fifteen minutes. She stopped the ATV near the porch and pocketed the key as she ducked under the small stoop. It wasn't until she started knocking on the door that she realized she might have made the trip for nothing. If she was locked out and he wouldn't answer, she wouldn't be able to get in. She had an extra key to this house, but she hadn't thought to bring it.

With a prayer on her lips, Ally knocked on the door. She waited and waited for what seemed like forever, then knocked again, and still no one came. But to her relief, when she tried the doorknob, it turned. She stepped inside, pausing in the doorway, and called out, "Mr. Holden! Are you home?"

No one answered.

She called again.

"Mr. Holden?" Then, finally… "Wes?"

Still no answer.

She took off her muddy boots and poncho, and dropped them at the door, then started through the house, calling Wes's name as she went.

The first place she looked was the kitchen. She saw a pile of wet clothes near the back door and stopped. He'd been here. But where was he now? She turned around and started down the hall.

"Wes...it's me, Ally. Mr. James was worried about you. He stopped and asked me to—"

The bathroom door was open. Words ended when she saw him naked and curled up on the floor with his arms over his head in a gesture of defeat. She ran to him, then knelt.

Although the house was stuffy, almost hot, his skin was cold to the touch. She laid a hand at the back of his neck.

"Wes, it's me, Ally Monroe. I've come to help."

He didn't answer, but she'd felt a muscle jump beneath his skin where she'd touched him. Quickly, she got up and ran across the hall, turning on lights as she went. She yanked the bedspread off the bed before rushing back to Wes.

The new and healing scars on his back and legs were horrifying when she thought about how they'd come to be there, but there was an even uglier one that ran from his right shoulder to the middle of his spine. He'd been so terribly hurt. It didn't seem right that he should still be suffering.

She draped the spread around him, then rocked back on her heels. She needed to get him up and in bed, and for the first time, she wished she'd told her father, even though it would have made him furious to know she'd let the place to a stranger. At least she would have had help. But since that hadn't happened, she was going to have to deal with it herself. She braced herself firmly as she took hold of his arms.

"Wes, you have to get up. Do you hear me? You have to get up now!"

Something in the tone of her voice registered. Wes shuddered.

"You can do it," Ally urged as she pulled with all her might.

He rolled onto his hands and knees, taking the cover with him.

Ally shifted her hold again and braced her feet on the floor.

"Come on!" she said. "Get up. You can do it!"

Wes was trying to focus. The voice was louder now—telling him to move, to get up. Concentrating all his efforts toward obeying the command, he pushed himself up as hard as he could.

Ally saw the muscles bunching in his shoulders and knew he was trying. She tightened her grip and gave him one more pull. Moments later, he came up, but the bedspread went down.

She made a frantic grab and once again pulled it close around him. Once she was sure he was covered, she slipped under his shoulder and put her arm around his waist, steadying him on his feet.

"Good job. You did it! Now just a few more feet and you'll be in bed. Lean on me. It will be all right."

Wes felt her strength first, then heard the promise. *Lean on me.* He didn't think he knew how.

Despite her fragility, Ally managed to get him into bed. With each passing minute, Wes was regaining his sense of self, and being naked in front of a woman who was little more than a stranger was making him uneasy. He pulled the bedspread tighter, then sat up.

"Do you think you should be getting up just yet?" Ally asked.

"What I think is that you shouldn't be in here."

Ally felt as if she'd been slapped. She straightened, then turned away.

"I apologize for the intrusion. I meant no harm."

The moment she turned away, Wes knew he'd hurt her. It was the last thing he'd meant to do.

"Miss Monroe... Ally...wait."

Ally stopped, but she wouldn't look at him.

"Would you wait in the living room...please?"

She walked out of the room without answering, but when he didn't hear the front door open or close, he took it as a good sign, and quickly dressed in clean jeans and a shirt.

His legs felt weak, as if he'd been running for miles, but the worst of the flashback was gone. He shoved his fingers through his hair to comb it away from his face, then headed for the living room.

She was standing near the window. She looked up

when she heard him come into the room. There were tears on her cheeks. Just the sight of them made him sick.

"Oh, hell…please don't cry."

It was the only thing he could think to say.

Ally swiped at her cheeks. He saw her hands trembling as she bit her lip to keep the rest of the tears at bay.

"I didn't mean to be rude," Wes said. "It's just that I'm… I, uh, don't know how to cope with this… It's difficult for me to—"

"Stop," Ally said. "You have nothing to apologize for. Mr. James obviously cares about you. He felt concern, mentioned it to me, and I jumped to conclusions. I'm the one who must apologize. I promise I will leave you alone." She ducked her head and looked away, then made herself face him again. "It won't happen again."

Wes sighed. Even as she was saying it, he knew he didn't want to be left alone.

"Does this mean no more ham biscuits?"

Ally blinked. Was he kidding with her? Did this mean it was okay?

Despite the fact that he was the one who'd demanded distance between them, Wes was the one who moved toward her. When he was close enough to see his reflection in her eyes, he stopped, then held out his hand.

"Truce?"

Ally stared, first at his hand, then at him.

"You aren't mad at me?"

Wes heard the question. He would have answered right then, but he'd seen a slight tremble in her chin and felt sick that he was the one who'd caused it. Finally he realized she was waiting for an answer.

"No. Not at you. I guess I'm more mad at myself. It's difficult for a man like me to admit…even to himself…that he's weak."

"You were a soldier, weren't you?" Ally asked.

"Yes."

"Are you…do you…?"

"I'm not dangerous…to anyone but myself," Wes said. "But if I make you uneasy, I'll leave."

Ally frowned, and grabbed his arm before she thought.

"I'm afraid of a lot of things in this world, but you're not one of them," she said fiercely. "You don't leave this house…not until you're good and ready. Do you hear me?"

Wes almost smiled. "Yes, ma'am. I hear you just fine."

Embarrassed by her own ferocity, Ally blushed. "All right," she muttered, then suddenly turned on him, fixing him with a hard, studied look.

"You sure you're going to be all right?"

He nodded.

"I'm going home, then. Please forgive the intrusion."

She was reaching for the doorknob when Wes stopped her again.

"Ally?"

"Yes?"

"Thank you for caring."

"Yes…well…it's what we do up here. If you're going to stay, you'd just better get used to it."

This time the smile made its way all the way to Wes's lips.

"Yes, ma'am."

Ally began to put her boots back on. She was pulling the poncho over her head when she realized he was helping.

"Thank you," she said as he gave the poncho a final tug.

"You're welcome," Wes said softly.

She opened the door. Rain was still coming down.

It was the first time Wes realized exactly what she'd faced by coming alone in a storm.

"I didn't know," he said.

"Know what?" Ally asked.

He shook his head without answering, but he felt as if he were seeing her anew. Her hair was still damp from the ride up, but there was a jut to her chin he hadn't noticed before.

"You're tougher than you look, aren't you, girl?"

Taken aback by his observation, Ally didn't know how to respond.

"I'm thinking that you're quite a little soldier. Ride safe," Wes said.

Ally nodded. Moments later she was out the door and walking through the rain, dragging her leg as she went.

As Wes watched, she straddled the ATV, fired up the engine and threw it in gear. She left him without a backward glance, and yet he stood in the doorway, watching until she'd been swallowed up by the trees and the rain.

He was on his way into the house when the hair on

the back of his neck suddenly rose. He turned abruptly, scanning the area. Nothing was visible, but his instincts for survival had rarely been wrong. Someone was watching him. He thought of Ally on that mountain road alone, and for the first time wished he had a phone, just so he could make sure she reached the safety of home.

He backed into the house, locked the front door, then hurried into the kitchen to make sure that door was locked, too. He stood for a moment, then remembered the root cellar. After a quick trip down into the cellar to bar the door from the inside, he began to relax. If whoever was out there was persistent enough, he could get in—but not without making a whole lot of noise. It would be all the warning Wes needed.

At that point his stomach began to grumble, reminding him that it had been a long time since he'd eaten. He headed for the kitchen to see the pantry about a can of soup.

Roland Storm was so angry he was shaking. When he'd seen Ally Monroe coming up the mountain on that ATV, he'd let himself toy with the fantasy that she was coming to him. Then, when she'd turned off the road and ridden up to where the stranger was staying, he hadn't been able to believe his eyes. He'd staked out the stranger's home, never imagining that Ally would appear.

But she'd walked in as if she'd been expected, and immediately, his imagination had taken root in carnal thoughts. After all, the stranger was well built and good-looking. He'd let himself believe that Ally Monroe was different from other women—that she'd held herself to a higher morality than the norm. But he'd been wrong—horribly wrong. And the longer he stood across the road in the rain, the more certain he'd become. She'd been in there for a long time—long enough to give herself to the stranger three times over.

He cursed. If she was giving it away, he wanted some.

Eleven

The can of soup was open and Wes was pouring it into a pan when a gust of wind blew rain against the kitchen window. He stopped, set it aside, then bowed his head. He couldn't ignore his gut. Someone was out there. It remained to be seen whether the threat he sensed was to him, or to anyone in general, but until he saw Ally Monroe walk safely into her home, he wasn't going to be able to rest.

With a sigh, he turned off the burner, stripped off his dry clothes and quickly re-dressed in the wet clothes he'd come home in. If he was going back out in this weather, there was no need getting two sets of clothes soaked.

The clothes were clammy against his skin, but in a few seconds they were going to be even wetter. He felt in his pocket for the switchblade, thought about a hat and discarded the idea. He was going to be moving fast.

He locked the door from the inside, then grabbed the house key. He locked the back door, as well, then went out through the cellar and began to circle the area. If there were footprints, the rain would have washed them away, but there were other ways to track a predator. He struck a trail into the trees, then began to veer to the left in order to come out on the other side of the road.

A loud rumble of thunder shifted the air. The sound settled between Wes's shoulder blades like a blow to the back. He shook off the crawl of nerves in his belly and made himself focus on Ally.

Lean on me, she'd said. Lean on me. And he'd pushed her away. She had come out in this because of him. Because she had a gentle heart.

Wes had an enemy here. He didn't know why, but he knew who it was. He could handle his own enemies, but he didn't want them taking revenge on someone else. If Ally's innocent visit had given Roland Storm the idea that hurting Ally would be a way to get to him, Wes had to stop him before the thought became deed.

Rain peppered down through the leaves, pelting him as he went. The sound brought back the memory of distant gunshots from an automatic weapon. Frustrated with himself for relating everything to a distant and ongoing war, he made himself focus. He kept his eyes to the ground, the trees and the brush through which he was passing, looking for broken limbs, a footprint protected by undergrowth—anything to prove his instincts had been right—but it was impossible to tell if anyone had been here. He was just about to give up when he saw a glint of metal half buried in the mud and leaves.

It was a key ring with car keys on it. He fiddled with it a couple of times and then dropped it in his pocket. Just because he found car keys across the road from his house, that wasn't proof someone had been watching his place. There was no way to tell how long the keys had been here, or who they belonged to. Still, the keys were too shiny to have lain there long.

Then his focus shifted to Ally, and he began moving downhill, following the road while staying within the trees. Several times he thought he could hear the ATV in the distance, but there was too much wind and rain to be sure.

Just when he was at the point of believing he'd imagined the whole thing, he caught a flash of something dark moving through the trees ahead of him. He dropped into a crouching position and moved deeper into the trees.

From where he was standing, he could see the back of someone in a dark green parka with a hood attached. He couldn't see a face, but he could tell it was a man, and from the way he was behaving, his presence was due to anything but an innocent stroll in the rain.

The man moved with an ungainly gait—his shoulders stooped, while his arms swung loosely at his sides. What made it even more obvious that he was up to no good was the way he kept moving from bush to bush, taking great care not to be seen.

Suddenly Wes heard the sound of an engine accelerating and knew it was Ally. Was she stuck? Had she driven that ATV into the ditch? Was she hurt? Forgetting about the stalker, he ran to the road for a better look. Then he saw her. Despite all she was doing to correct the motion, the ATV was sliding sideways in the mud. She was fighting for control while struggling to stay upright, and Wes mentally cursed himself a thousand times over for chasing her out of the house. A sane man would have insisted she wait until the storm had passed, but he hadn't been sane in so long he'd forgotten how it went. He started to run after Ally just as the stalker suddenly appeared at the edge of the road about fifty yards ahead of him.

Wes saw him lift his hand, as if hailing Ally's attention. When he began to run toward her, Wes panicked. He couldn't tell if the man was intent on saving her or attacking her.

A loud crash of thunder was followed by a shaft of lightning struck nearby. Wes winced, and had to fight the urge to throw himself to the ground and take cover.

"It's not a bomb. It's not a bomb," he kept mumbling, while his teeth chattered and his fingers curled into fists.

The man was running all out now, drawing closer and closer to Ally, and Wes couldn't seem to make himself move.

Then suddenly Ally had ridden out the slide and had the ATV under control. Steering it carefully around a deep set of ruts, she gave it some gas and sped down the hill at a steady pace.

As the distance between Ally and the man began to lengthen, Wes saw him trying to run faster; then he slipped and went facedown in the mud. By the time the man got up, Ally was nowhere in sight.

Satisfied that Ally was, for the moment, out of danger, Wes centered his attention on the man. He was getting up now, and even though Wes was too far away to hear what he was saying, he finally saw his face.

Just as he'd feared, it was Storm, and he was furious. Storm's features were contorted in anger as words spewed from his lips. He was waving a fist in the air and then slapping it against his leg as he stumbled from the road into the trees. When Wes realized Storm was coming his way, he started to hide, then changed his mind.

Water squished in Roland's socks and up the backs of his shoes with every step that he took. He was mud from head to toe, while, once again, he'd missed his chance with Ally. But he wasn't giving up. He'd seen her first, and now that he'd discovered her true nature, he was through playing nice and waiting for a proper introduction.

Angrily, he wiped his muddy hands on the front of his jacket and, bowing his head against the rain, began the trek back to where he'd left his truck. He didn't see the other man until he was directly in front of him. He stifled a gasp and wished he had a gun.

"You were following me," Roland accused.

"You were following her."

Roland frowned. He wasn't a man who liked being on the defensive.

"Following who?" he said.

Suddenly there was a knife in the man's hand, the same knife he remembered from their meeting the other night, and Roland was grateful for the rain soaking his clothes. It successfully hid the trail of warm urine running down his leg.

"Leave her alone," Wes said.

It was the lack of emotion in the man's voice that made Roland shiver.

"I wasn't doing anything," he spluttered, and took a slow step backward. "It's a free country and—"

Wes shifted the switchblade from his left hand to his right, then back again.

"Stay away from her."

Roland could hear the man talking, but his gaze was fixed on the water dripping off the end of the blade. Finally he made himself look into Holden's face.

"Who are you?" Roland asked.

"If you so much as harm a hair on her head, I will make you disappear."

Roland felt the warning as physically as if the words had been blows. He grunted in reflex and started moving backward.

"Who sent you up here to spy on me?"

"You heard what I said," Wes said softly, then stepped aside and pointed up the hill. "Now get, before I change my mind."

Roland started running and never looked back. Even after he'd reached his truck and locked himself inside the cab, he was still shaking. But when he reached in his pocket for the keys, he felt nothing but fabric.

"Shit, shit, shit."

Frantically, he dug through every pocket in the raincoat, as well as his pants, but still came up empty.

He looked back the way he'd come, thought about that crazy man with a knife, and knew there was no way he was going looking for his keys, so he got out of the truck and started to run. When he finally got home, he took the extra key from under a rock near the door and locked himself in, then began to pace, trying to make sense of what had just happened.

The stranger's presence was a threat to everything he held dear. The longer he paced, the angrier he became. He thought of the years of abuse he'd suffered at Lackey Laboratories, and then the years of frustration and failure before he'd perfected Triple H. Dooley Brown had been the first to threaten his discovery, and he'd had to deal with him accordingly. Now the stranger had come, threatening more than the crop. He was threatening Roland himself. The next time they met, Roland would be prepared.

As for Ally Monroe, Roland would deal with her, too, but all in good time. For now, Triple H had to take priority. On the next sunny day, Danny and Porter Monroe were to report for work. While they were harvesting, Roland was going to reconnect with the contacts he'd made from his days on the street. Once Triple H hit the pipeline, nothing would ever be the same.

When Ally finally pulled into the barn and parked the ATV, she was shaking. The ride down had been harrowing, but not as harrowing as coming face-to-face with Wes Holden in his home and being rebuffed. Her steps were dragging even more than usual as she walked to the end of the barn, unrolled the garden hose at the spigot and turned on the water. It seemed odd to be sheltered from rain and still be standing in water, but she needed to clean the mud from the four-wheeler before it dried. Porter wouldn't mind that she'd used it, but he wouldn't appreciate it being left in a filthy condition.

Once she finished, she covered it with a tarp, just as Porter always did, then turned the water on her feet and sluiced the worst of the mud from her jeans and shoes. After everything was finished and the hose rolled back up, she was reluctant to go back to the house.

When she'd been small, the barn had been her refuge. She'd played in the loft with the barn cats and made playhouses among the bales of hay. Her brothers would sneak cookies and cold bottles of pop up to her, despite her mother's warnings that it would ruin her appetite. Back then, her world had been perfect.

Ally glanced up at the loft, then looked away. Like her dreams, those years were gone. The reality of life was that here in the mountains, she was a woman past her prime. It was likely she would never marry, but that didn't seem quite as devastating as it once had. She'd grown accustomed to being alone. When a gust of wind blew rain in on her face, instead of stepping back, she walked out into the storm.

Wes watched Ally coming out of the barn. She walked with her head bowed and her steps dragging. Water was ankle-deep in the puddles, but she didn't seem to notice. There was a defeated slump to her shoulders that he'd never seen before, and he hated himself for putting it there.

But there was a more urgent problem than her hurt feelings. He didn't know what Roland Storm would have done if he'd caught up with Ally today, but he didn't think it would have been good. He'd looked into Storm's eyes. He'd seen the twitch at the corner of his mouth. The man was unstable.

Then Wes sighed. That was a case of the pot calling the kettle black. He wasn't exactly Cool Hand Luke himself. Besides that, when he'd walked away from his stepbrother's apartment, the last thing he had wanted was to get involved. He didn't want to care. He didn't want responsibility. Most of the time he hadn't even been too crazy about taking his next breath. But all of that had changed because of a woman who had given him shelter.

Wes saw her stumble, but then she caught herself before she fell. When she got to the back door, she left her poncho and her shoes on the porch. It wasn't until she shut the door that Wes finally breathed easy.

When he saw the lights come on, he knew she was

safe, but only for the moment. He couldn't just walk away in good conscience without warning her about Storm. He wouldn't always be around as he had been this time, and from what he could tell, Ally was usually alone all day. It made her a perfect target for a man with no good on his mind.

Bracing himself for the confrontation, he headed for the back door, then knocked.

Ally was stripping out of her wet clothes when she heard footsteps on the back porch. Startled, she reached for one of her father's clean shirts from the laundry she'd folded earlier and was putting it on when someone knocked. The hem of the shirt brushed the tops of her knees, leaving her legs bare, but she was covered, and that was all that mattered.

When she peeked around the corner and saw Wes standing on the porch, her heart skipped a beat. She pulled the shirt a little tighter across her breasts, then called out through the door, "What do you want?"

"It's me, Wes. I need to talk to you," he said.

"You shouldn't have come out in this weather in your condition," Ally said.

"I'm suffering from a lack of good sense, not a fever," he fired back.

Ally grinned in spite of herself and opened the door.

Taken aback by her bare legs and feet, Wes found himself staring, unwilling to remove the only obstacle between them, which was the screen door.

"Well…are you coming in or not?" Ally asked.

Wes gritted his teeth and opened the door.

"I'm getting water on your floor."

She looked down at the growing puddle in which he was standing, and smiled.

"Yes, you are."

Wes almost smiled back.

"Sorry."

"I should hope so," Ally said. "So I am assuming you have a good reason for coming down to my house in this rain…since you pretty much ran me out of yours."

Water was dripping from the heavy braid in her hair, dampening the shirt just enough that it was molding itself to her body. The faint hint of soft, womanly curves made him ache—made him yearn to get lost in a sweet woman's arms. But as soon as he thought it, he felt guilty again, as if he'd betrayed Margie—or, at the least, her memory. Because he was pissed off at himself, he blurted out the reason why he'd come without pretext.

"Do you know Roland Storm?"

The change of subject was abrupt, but she went along with it just the same.

"Yes…well, not really, but I know who he is. My brothers are going to work for him soon."

Wes thought of the lab, the dead animals in the woods and the dissected rodents, and frowned.

"Doing what?"

"He hired them to harvest a herb crop."

"What kind of herbs?" Wes asked.

Ally was already concerned, and his question hit a nerve.

"He told them they were Chinese herbs. He's also supposed to be paying them five thousand dollars apiece for the job."

Wes had suspected all along that the man was involved in something criminal, and her information confirmed his suspicions.

Ally frowned. "Why the interest in Roland Storm?"

"I just caught him following you. From the way it looked, he's done it before. Were you aware of that?"

All expression disappeared from her face, and Wes immediately regretted his abruptness.

"What do you mean? Like stalking me?"

He nodded.

"When?"

Her face was pale, her hands shaking, but Wes had to give her credit for guts.

"Just now. As you were leaving, I sensed we were being watched. I snuck out the back of the house and found him following you. I think he'd been watching my house, but when you left, he followed you, which led me to believe it's you and not me he was tailing."

Ally swayed where she stood. Wes caught her just before she went down. At that point, he realized the shirt was all she was wearing, and again felt guilty that he'd noticed.

Ally started to weep, but she was angry, as well.

"This is so pathetic," she muttered.

Wes frowned. "What do you mean?"

She pulled from of his arms, needing distance between them.

"I can't believe this is happening. Although you have made your feelings clear, you're the first man I've ever let get under my skin, so I have no one to blame but myself. I'm just mad as hell for letting it happen."

When she saw Wes's expression, she hastened to add, "Oh, don't panic. I'm not going to jump your bones or beg you for something you don't feel. But it sucks. As if that's not enough, my father has been pushing me to marry this loser, because he thinks no one else will have me. Freddie Joe is mean and lazy and bullied his first wife repeatedly. She died last year—probably just to get away from him—but her death left Freddie Joe with no wife and three kids to take care of. And, since I'm such a charity case, everyone is assuming I'd be stupid not to accept his attention." She swiped angrily at her tears and threw her hands up in the air. "Now you're telling me that I have another loser dogging my heels, which proves my father was wrong. There *is* another man interested in me. Although he's a stalker. Maybe I should be grateful that he's choosing to keep his interest in me all to himself. Anyway, what's one stalker, compared to marrying and sleeping with a degenerate like Freddie Joe?"

Wes felt as if he'd been sideswiped. He couldn't decide which made him angrier—her sleeping with some bullying bastard, being dogged by a creep like Storm, or the fact that she had admitted her feelings for him and he didn't have the guts to respond. What he did know was that her tears made him sick.

"I'm sorry," he said.

"Don't be," Ally said, then lifted her head, unaware that she'd angled her chin as if bracing herself for some unseen blow. "Pity disgusts me."

Wes's eyes narrowed angrily. "I don't pity you," he snapped. "I just wanted you to be aware so you could be careful."

Ally sighed. "Of course, and I should thank you for the warning, which I will take seriously. I apologize for being angry. It wasn't directed at you, just the circumstances of my miserable life."

"You're beautiful," Wes said softly. "The men around here must be both stupid and blind not to have seen that in you."

Ally was simultaneously startled and angry. She didn't want to hear platitudes when her heart was breaking.

"Yes, well, thank you so much for the compliment, but the men up here are too gutless to take a chance on marrying a woman who might give them flawed children."

The word *children* hit Wes like a fist to the belly. He tried to draw breath, but it sounded more like a sob. He looked at Ally, then turned away.

Immediately, Ally knew she'd said something wrong. She ran to his side.

"What? What did I say? Whatever it is, I'm sorry. I'm so sorry."

Wes shuddered.

Impulsively, Ally wrapped her arms around his waist and laid her head against the middle of his back.

"Please forgive me. I didn't mean to hurt you."

There was a long moment of silence in which Wes selfishly let himself be comforted, but he had to accept that he wasn't the only one in pain. His was new and fresh and as devastating as anything could be, but hers came from a lifetime of disappointment and shame, neither of which she deserved.

He turned around, and when she would have turned loose of him, he pulled her close, savoring the softness of a woman against his body.

"I was married. We had a son."

Ally stilled. She had let herself get too close to a man she didn't know, and it was all her fault. She wanted—no, needed—to know what made him so sad, but she was afraid of the answers. Still, she waited.

Wes rested the side of his cheek against the crown of her head and closed his eyes, letting himself remember.

"Margaret…Margie…was my childhood sweetheart. We got married after I'd finished basic training."

Ally felt his arms tightening around her and knew he was remembering another woman, another time and place. It hurt to know she was a substitute, but she'd asked for it just the same.

Wes continued. "She made it fine as a military wife—until we went to war. She was so damned scared and tried not to show it, but I knew. Our son was so small. I think she feared I would die and he would grow up without a memory of the man who was his father. Only I wasn't the one who died. If there is a God, he has a horrible sense of humor."

"God doesn't kill people," Ally said. "People kill people."

Wes felt as if he'd been punched. He'd needed to place blame ever since the day it had happened but had never thought of it that way.

"Where were you when I needed you?" he muttered, more to himself than to her, but Ally heard him.

She leaned back until she could see his face.

"I was here, waiting for you to come," she said.

He groaned, then pulled her off her feet and up against him so tightly that she could barely breathe. When his head lowered and his mouth centered on her lips, Ally thought she would die. It was everything she'd ever dreamed a kiss could be, and at the same time, the saddest she'd ever felt. He was kissing *her* but remembering the woman who was his wife. It wasn't what she would have wished for, but she wouldn't turn him down.

When he finally pulled away, they were both breathless and shaking. It would have been easy to let the kiss be the start to something more. But not even Ally was desperate enough to let the ghost of another woman into her bed. She cupped his face with her hands, then rubbed a thumb across his lower lip, feeling the strength, but remembering the tenderness.

"What happened to them, Wes?"

He drew a deep breath, then closed his eyes.

"Remember the bombing at Fort Benning last year?"

"Yes. It was awful. The news was full of it for months." Then she realized what he was trying to say. "They were there?"

When he opened his eyes, they were swimming with tears. He nodded.

Her expression crumpled. "Oh, Wes, I'm so sorry."

"Yeah, so am I."

She held him again, but this time there was nothing but comfort in the touch. Finally he pulled away.

"Don't take Roland Storm's attention lightly."

"I won't," she said. "I promise."

He nodded. "If there's anything I can do for you, just ask."

At that moment, a thought occurred.

"Do you mean that?" she asked.

Wes didn't hesitate. "Yes."

"Come to supper Friday night."

"Okay…but why?"

"Other than another chance to eat my wonderful cooking, I would appreciate a buffer between me and Freddie Joe."

Wes's eyes widened.

"He's coming to eat with you Friday night?"

"Despite my objections and at my father's insistence, and with all three of his children."

Wes hadn't been around children since the day Mikey had died. He didn't know how he would handle it, but it was the least he could do for her after all she'd done for him.

"Are you sure you want to do this?" he asked.

"Yes, I want you here. No, I don't want to deal with Freddie Joe, but Daddy has given me no choice."

"I'll come," Wes said. "But now I'd better be going before your father comes home and finds you with me and wearing that shirt."

Ally blushed.

Wes allowed himself one last look, then opened the door.

"Lock this behind me," he said, and then he was gone.

As soon as he had left, Ally picked up her wet clothes and ran out to the laundry shed, tossed them in the washing machine, adding her father's now-wet shirt to the mix, then went back in the house and locked the door. The stew was still on the back of the stove, and the pie she'd taken out of the oven had long gone cold. The sight of both turned her stomach. She continued through the rooms, turning on lights as she went. The air-conditioning in the house brought out goose bumps on her skin and made her nipples pointy and hard. Both sensations made her ache in an empty, lonely way, and it occurred to her that she'd never been naked in this house before. There had always been a sense of urgency within her when she undressed, whether for a shower or to change her clothes, that she must hurry and cover herself with clothes. But things were changing—*she* was changing. Her father had started it by trying to force her into a relationship she didn't want, and now she had learned a crazy man was stalking her every step.

If that wasn't enough, Wes Holden had complicated the situation by making her feel things she'd never felt before. The sad part of it all was that no matter what she did, she was going to come out the loser.

She stumbled into the bathroom, then into the shower, and washed until her skin was tingling. When she got out, she felt empty, both in heart and in spirit, but there were still things to be done. She put away the food that hadn't been eaten, cleaned dishes and cabinets and the floors she'd tracked up, and when there was nothing left to do, gave up and went to bed. But as hard as she tried, she couldn't get the sound of Wes Holden's voice out of her head.

You don't need to be here.

"God help me," she whispered, then pulled the covers up to her shoulders and closed her eyes.

Sometime later, Gideon came home. The thunderstorm had passed, leaving the roads muddy but the leaves and grass washed clean. He got out of the truck, took a deep, cleansing breath and stretched wearily. It felt good to be home.

Pete had pulled through surgery and, barring complications, would recover completely. Gideon was full of the news of the accident and wanted to talk, but then he remembered that Danny and Porter were in Charleston for the night. And even though the lights had been left on for him, he knew Ally would not have waited up. Ever since he'd introduced Freddie Joe into her life, she'd alternated between being angry and cold toward him. Still, Gideon was a man who rarely admitted he made mistakes, and so the fiasco continued. On Friday Freddie Joe and his three children would be here for a meal. Maybe the children would make a difference in Ally's eyes.

He locked the doors, checked the windows, then looked in on Ally as she slept. Despite the summer temperatures, she was curled up on her side with the covers pulled under her chin. He smiled. Even as a child, hot or cold, rain or shine, she had slept rolled up in her covers. Nothing had changed.

A short while later, the last light finally went out and the little house went dark. Buddy lay curled up by the door on the front porch, peacefully sleeping, while up on the mountain, peace was a long way from home.

The thunderstorm had passed and the sun was dropping at a lazy angle in the sky, but Wes hadn't gone directly home. He had decided on a reconnoiter and located Storm's truck. When he found it unlocked, he tried the keys he'd found. When they fit, it confirmed what he'd suspected. But had Storm been watching Wes—or Ally? He was inclined to believe it was a little bit of both, although he was still puzzled. In a twisted sort of way, he understood why Storm would be stalking Ally. She was a beautiful and single woman.

But why me?

The question kept looping through Wes's mind without coming back with an answer. Still, there had to be a reason why Wes's presence threatened Roland Storm enough to put him on the defensive. All he had to do was find it.

Wes looked up the road, then up at the sky. The storm had left enough clouds behind to bring on an early night, and he'd already had one experience coming down off this mountain in the dark. He wasn't in the mood to do it again.

He tossed the keys on the seat of the truck, locked and shut the doors, then started back down the road. Even though his strides were long, night caught him before he got home.

When he reached the little house, he unlocked the door, then locked it securely behind him after he entered. Then he turned on the lights, kicked off his shoes and dropped his wet clothes in the kitchen beside the washing machine. The thought of a slow, warm shower put speed in his step, and for once, he didn't care that the showerhead was too low and the room too small. The house was a haven of comfort at the end of a very bad day.

He showered quickly, pulled on a pair of shorts and then went back to the kitchen. The pan of soup was still on the stove where he'd left it. He set it on the burner and turned on the heat. While it was warming, he made himself a ham sandwich, got a bottle of beer from the refrigerator and set it all on the table. He gave the soup a quick stir, then went into the living room and began scanning the multitudes of books on the shelves for something to read.

After browsing through a shelf of fiction, he settled on a book he hadn't read in years. The cover was worn, the gilt-edged pages somewhat faded, but the author's name was still dark and vivid, as was the title.

John Steinbeck. *The Grapes Of Wrath.*

It wasn't the most uplifting book he'd ever read, but it fit the mood Wes was in. He carried it with him back into the kitchen, laid it beside his plate, then poured the soup into a bowl and took it to the table.

He sat down, taking a moment to savor the shelter of the odd little house and the simple fare he was about to eat. His belly growled, reminding him of how long it had been since he'd eaten, but he still took the time to feel the quiet.

Part of his training in Special Ops had been to ascertain as much of his surroundings as possible with senses other than sight. So he closed his eyes and took a slow, deep breath, letting the peace of this place settle deep in his heart.

The smell of tomato soup was right beneath his nose, as was the pungent scent of the mustard that he'd put on the ham. He could smell the fresh bread on the plate and the yeasty scent of the beer that he'd opened. But on a lesser level, he remembered the wet clothes he'd left in a pile by the washer when the scent of decaying leaves and wet cotton shifted through the air.

Somewhere behind him he heard a continuous drip of water and realized he hadn't turned the faucets all the way off at the sink. Outside, a slight breeze must have come up, because he could hear the intermittent sound of a tree branch scraping against a window and water dripping from the edges of the roof.

This was a safe place. A place of shelter and comfort. Slowly, a great pain shoved itself through his chest, pushing, then twisting at his lifeblood just to remind him that he still lived when his family did not.

He took another breath, this time shorter and infinitely more painful, but he took it just the same. Then he picked up the spoon, stirred it through the cooling soup and took his first swallow to satisfy the pangs of hunger.

It was good.

He took another and another, just to prove that he could—just to prove to himself that it was all right to satisfy one kind of pain while clinging to the other.

Then he opened the book and began to read. Every now and then he would take a bite of the sandwich or a drink from the beer until, little by little, he was done with his meal.

Regretfully, he marked his place in the book, washed his dishes and headed for bed, turning out the lights as he went. There was a clock by the bedside. He set it for 6:00 a.m. and started to go to bed when caution stopped him.

He got back up and walked through the dark house,

pausing to look outside from every window, then making sure the doors were locked and bolted. He had barred the cellar door from the inside, but he took the time to lock the door from the kitchen to the cellar, as well. There was safety within these walls, but there was treachery without.

Once he was satisfied that he'd done all he could to assure himself of a safe night's sleep, he took the switchblade from his pants pocket and carried it to the bed. He slid it beneath a pillow, then crawled into bed. Once his head hit the pillow, he was gone.

Just as he was falling asleep, a vague thought began to plague him that he'd forgotten something important. He rolled over on his side, pulled the switch out on the alarm so that he would be sure to wake up on time, and then pulled the covers back up over him.

The air from the window unit blew cool across his back and legs, and in his dreams, he stood at the end of a long road, watching his wife and son walking away without him. He kept calling to them, over and over, but each time he would call, they would simply turn and wave, then resume their journey. He began to cry, and then someone took him by the hand and told him he was no longer alone. When he looked to see, it was Ally.

He woke up with tears on his cheeks.

"Ah, God…if you're still there, make me understand why."

It's not your journey to understand.

Wes gasped. The voice was so loud it echoed in his head.

"I don't want to be here," he said softly.

It's not about what you want. It's about what you have to do.

The flesh crawled on the back of Wes's neck. Either he was having a moment with God, or he was losing his mind.

"I don't believe in You anymore," he muttered.

That's all right, son. I still believe in you.

At that point Wes lay back down and pulled the pillow over his head.

The next thing he knew, it was morning and the alarm was going off.

Twelve

Ally was up early, picking tomatoes from the garden before the day got too hot. Tomorrow was the inevitable supper with Freddie Joe. She could only imagine what Wes's appearance would do to the mix, but she couldn't make herself care. She knew she should feel guilty for putting him in such an awkward position, but she also knew he was more than capable of taking care of himself.

Buddy was trailing her up and down the rows, nosing beneath the staked plants and licking her fingers as she reached for the ripe produce. She patted him gently from time to time, but his presence was definitely a hindrance.

"Move, baby," she said, and gave him an easy push. "I'm not ever going to get finished if you keep getting in my way."

Buddy looked up at her and then licked her face before she could move back.

"Eew, Buddy…"

Grinning, she pulled up the hem of her T-shirt and wiped dog off her face. This behavior was out of the ordinary for him, and she wondered if he sensed how unsettled she felt. She patted him on the head and was still smiling when she turned around and saw Wes Holden walking down the road on his way to work.

She started to call out a hello when he saw her and waved.

"Don't forget tomorrow night!" she called.

He nodded and gave her a thumbs-up as he kept on walking.

The brief moment of seeing him gave her heart a lift and put a smile on her face that lasted through the morning.

The week had flown by with continuous rains. Wes's sleep had been restless. He'd had dreams that brought him to tears, which he hated. Before, he'd never cried. He'd been raised to be tough, and what his father hadn't taught him about a stiff upper lip, the army had. Most of the time he managed to subdue his emotions, but at night, when he was alone and at his weakest, the despair was there. The smallest things would make him think of Mikey, which in turn would remind him of the huge hole his son's passing had left behind.

He and Margie had talked more than once about what would happen if one or the other of them ever became a single parent. Usually it was Wes who was counseling Margie, because his life was so often on the line. He'd rarely thought of living on without her, let alone without his son, yet here he was, afoot on a mountain with a man who wanted him gone and a woman who made him remember just how much he had lost. It was in this mind-set that he started off to work.

He'd kissed her, and it had left him wanting more. Tomorrow night he would sit at a table with her and her family and suffer their scrutiny, as well as the antagonism her unwanted suitor would feel. It would be the most human contact he'd had in more than a year and it made him smile. One thing was for sure. He wouldn't be bored.

The road down to Blue Creek was still muddy and the ruts deep, but he stayed on the shoulder, walking in the grass instead. After yesterday and the hard, driving rain, the world smelled clean and fresh. Birds were everywhere, going from limb to ground to spear the earthworms that had been driven up to the surface, then back again, rejoicing in Mother Nature's smorgasbord. Wes felt obliged to share their happiness.

As he passed the Monroe property, he'd seen a flash of yellow out in the garden. When he'd realized it was Ally, his steps had slowed. She was down between the tomato rows and laughing at something the dog was doing. The faint sound of her laughter washed over him. Sunlight caught in the honey-colored hair she had tied at the nape of her neck. The ribbon was yellow, like her shirt. When she finally stood up, he saw that her jeans were old, almost white from repeated laundering, but so soft they molded to her long legs and trim figure.

An ache settled deep in his belly. He was supposed to be in mourning, even though it had been more than a year since they'd been gone. Then he'd heard himself call out a greeting. When she smiled and waved back, guilt disappeared. All he wanted was to sit in her presence and let the peace that surrounded her flow into his heart.

About a mile down the road, a pig farmer named Sylvester Smith recognized Wes from the feed store and offered him a ride. Wes took it gladly, which put him at Harold James's feed store thirty minutes early.

Harold was still across the street at the café drinking coffee when he noticed Wes sitting on the front steps of the feed store. He swallowed the last of his coffee in a gulp, tossed some money on the counter and hurried out the door. It wasn't good for the boss to be the last to work.

"Hey there," Harold said as he stepped up on the curb. "You're early."

Wes nodded. "Yeah, caught a ride with Mr. Smith."

"I suppose we might just as well open up. Who knows? Might start a trend," Harold said, and then grinned.

"I hope not, unless I'm lucky enough to catch a ride every morning."

Harold laughed, and so the morning began.

Danny and Porter were finally back from Charleston. They were full of themselves as they came into the house, dumping their dirty clothes by the door as they stole warm cookies from the tray Ally had just taken out of the oven.

Danny grinned and winked at her as he stuffed a whole one in his mouth.

Ally grinned back. It was impossible not to. His red hair and impish expression were infectious.

"These are good," he said, then added, "Did you miss us?"

"About as much as I missed those dirty clothes. Don't leave them at the door, mister. I didn't wear them."

Danny chuckled, but he picked up the bag.

"Don't get mad. We were going to wash the stuff all along."

"Uh-huh," Ally said, and slid the cookies onto a cooling rack.

Porter was Danny's opposite—tall where his brother was short, dark where Danny was red-headed and fair—and with a contrasting personality to boot. He was the polar opposite of Danny Monroe in every way possible. Danny was quick to anger—quick to fight—while Porter took a slower but more unforgiving approach to his enemies. But he, too, loved his sister's cookies. He took a couple from the cooling rack and eyed her as he took a bite. He ate until both were gone, then washed them down with a cold pop.

"Good stuff," he said as his eyes narrowed thoughtfully. "What's going on with you?"

Startled by his perceptiveness, she felt herself blushing even as she denied it.

"As always, nothing," she said, and began filling another cookie sheet with dough yet to be baked.

Porter kept watching her. He'd seen the color flood her face.

"You still mad at Dad about Freddie Joe?"

"Wouldn't you be?"

Porter shrugged.

"You don't have to do it," he said.

"I know that, and you know that. The only problem is Dad. He still treats us like children."

"Probably 'cause we're all still living under his roof," Porter offered.

Ally was surprised by his honesty.

"We all know why I'm still here," she said. "But why did you and Danny stay?"

"The path of least resistance?"

Ally shook her head.

Porter grinned wryly. "Yeah, I know…basically, you've made it easy for us all to stay, but if you hit it off with Freddie Joe, that could change."

"Don't count on that ever happening," Ally said. "He's lazy and mean."

Porter stared at her for a few moments, then grinned.

"Yeah, he is, isn't he?"

Ally made a face at him. "You and Danny are no help at all. The least you could do is back me up when Dad starts in on me again."

"'Fraid to," Porter said. "If he quits on you, he'll start in on me and Danny."

"Wretch," Ally muttered.

"I know." He took another cookie, bit into it with relish and then winked at her. "But you love us just the same."

"Not enough to do your laundry, though," she said.

He laughed, and Ally thought to herself how handsome he was—her eldest brother.

A few minutes later the washing machine was humming and Ally was taking the last tray of cookies from the oven when both brothers came back into the room.

"See you this evening after we get off work," Danny said.

Ally turned in surprise.

"Work?"

"Yeah, Porter and I start work for Roland Storm today."

She thought about telling them what Wes had said about Storm, then changed her mind. Nothing had really happened, and they needed the work.

"It's sort of late to be going to work," she said.

"We had to wait for good weather. He told us not to come until the rains had passed."

Ally had already given Danny her opinion of the job. Now there was nothing left for her to do but pray they wouldn't get into trouble.

"Does Dad know?" she asked.

"Porter told him."

Ally persisted. "Told him what?"

Danny's expression darkened. "Damn it, Ally. We've

already been through this. We're harvesting herbs. See you at supper."

"Don't forget, tomorrow is the night Freddie Joe and his children come to eat."

"Oh, yeah," Danny said.

"We wouldn't miss it for the world," Porter added.

"You both make me sick," Ally said.

They laughed. The screen door banged behind them, and she remembered Wes's warning and locked herself in.

There was nothing for Ally to do but watch them go. Once they were gone, the house seemed unusually quiet, even though she could hear the faint thump and hum of the washing machine in the shed outside.

She dropped the cookie sheets into the sink, then turned around. The house was empty again—just like her life. She tried not to feel sorry for herself, but it kept coming to the fore. People came and went in her life, while her life always stayed the same. She wondered what they thought of her—the cripple, the old maid, the woman nobody wanted—except, of course, Freddie Joe, and now Roland Storm.

She thought of the kiss she'd shared with Wes and suddenly felt as if she were going to explode. Even though she'd told her father she would have none of it, tomorrow Freddie Joe and his children would be sitting at this table, watching her every move and picturing her as the new woman in their lives. She couldn't stop them from coming, but they were all due for a big disappointment.

* * *

Roland Storm was up by daybreak to retrieve his stranded truck. By the time he started down the road with the second set of keys that he'd finally found, the sun was up and the sky was clear, but it didn't change his mood. He believed that everything he had going for him was in danger of being ruined. He needed to find out who was living in Dooley Brown's house and why he was there. He didn't think anyone had gotten wind of Triple H, but he couldn't be sure. If the need warranted, he would get rid of him just like he'd gotten rid of Dooley Brown.

Suddenly a twig snapped in the trees. Roland gasped and turned, certain he was about to come face-to-face with the knife-wielding stranger again. A moment later, a doe bolted from the forest, leapt across the road and disappeared into the trees on the other side.

"Shit," Roland muttered.

He was still shaking as he began to trot. The sooner he got his truck and drove home, the better he would feel. Being afoot made him feel vulnerable.

A short while later, he reached the truck and started to get in, then realized that the doors were locked. Almost certain that it hadn't been locked last night when he'd discovered his keys were missing, he frowned as he used the other key to unlock it.

The hinges on the door squeaked as it swung open. He started to slide into the seat when he suddenly stopped and leapt back. His eyes widened, then his heart skipped a beat. His keys—the keys he'd lost—were lying on the seat.

Roland's mind began to race. The keys hadn't been there before. He hadn't overlooked them in the dark, of that he was certain. That meant that someone had found them, followed him up the mountain without his knowledge, dropped them in the truck, then locked it as a taunt.

Roland's hand was shaking as he reached for the keys, then dropped them into his pocket. He slid into the seat and quickly locked the doors, then sat for a moment, gazing intently into the trees, then down the road, wondering if he was being watched at this very moment.

"You bastard," he muttered, then thrust the key into the ignition. "I will not be humiliated in this manner."

But his threat was empty, and he knew it. As soon as the engine fired, he put it in gear and stomped the accelerator. The tires spun on mud and leaves, then the truck suddenly shot out into the road and promptly slid sideways. There were a few nervous moments when he feared he would be in the ditch before he had the vehicle under control. He made himself calm down, the truck righted itself, and he drove home, keeping watch on the road ahead, as well as the road behind.

It wasn't until a couple of hours later that the Monroe brothers showed up. By that time, he'd worked himself into a state.

Danny and Porter were just getting out of their truck when Roland dashed out of the house.

"Who's the man who's living in that little toadstool house down the road? I won't be spied on! You hear me?"

In that moment, Danny felt the skin crawl on the back of his neck as his sister's warning echoed in his mind. Storm's eyes were bloodshot, and there was a speck of spittle at the corner of his lips.

Porter, however, took the greeting as an insult and pointed at Danny.

"Get back in the truck," Porter said. "We're going home."

Roland groaned. He needed these two men badly. They couldn't leave him in the lurch.

"Wait!" he cried.

Porter kept on walking, but Danny stopped.

Roland could tell he was going to have to do some fast talking to get himself out of this.

"I didn't mean to offend you, and I wasn't accusing you boys of anything. It's just that he's been giving me problems."

Danny frowned. "Who's been giving you problems?"

"The man who lives in that odd little house up the road from your place."

"No one lives in that house anymore," Porter said.

"Oh, yes they do," Roland said. "There's a man living there. I've seen him twice."

Porter stared at Danny. "You know anything about this?"

Danny shook his head. "No, but Ally might."

At the mention of their sister's name, Roland's anger scattered.

"Who's Ally?" he asked, although he knew very well who she was.

"Our sister," Porter said. "The house is hers now. It belonged to our mother's only brother. Ally inherited it when he died."

Roland felt his lips going numb. Uncle? He hadn't known they were related, but it didn't matter who Dooley Brown had been related to. Triple H was Roland's main concern.

"Regardless of who the house belongs to, there's a man living there who I believe is trying to steal my crop."

Danny frowned. "The herbs?"

"Yes, the herbs," Roland said.

Porter's eyes narrowed thoughtfully. He'd been doubtful of Storm's honesty from the moment Danny had mentioned what they were going to be paid.

"Are they worth all that?" Porter asked.

Roland turned on him in fury. It made Porter think of a rabid dog.

"They are to me," Roland said. "And they're ready for harvest."

Danny looked at Porter. Porter stared long and hard at Roland, then arched an eyebrow at Danny and gave his shoulders a shrug.

"What do we do first?" Danny asked.

"Follow me and I'll show you," Roland said.

They followed Storm to the barn, and began checking over the old tractor and equipment he intended them to use.

"Needs grease," Porter said as he kicked one of the tractor's front tires.

"In there," Roland said, pointing to a dusty cabinet. "Once the crop is down, you'll need to gather it by hand. You can use that flat-bed trailer to load the bundles. We'll be drying them in the old tobacco sheds."

Danny nodded and pulled a pair of gloves from his back pocket.

Roland watched their expressions, fearing that they would betray him, yet unable to do this without them. Maybe if he gave them the impression that the stuff was poison, they wouldn't be inclined to steal some of it for themselves.

"Look, in its raw form, the stuff could be toxic, but if you're wearing long-sleeved shirts and gloves, which you both are, you should be all right."

Porter held up his hands and started backing up.

"Whoa…now, wait a minute," he said. "No one said anything about toxicity."

Roland cursed himself. That had backfired nicely. The crop was ready to harvest, he couldn't do it by himself, and he didn't dare let these two men walk out of here and start spreading it around that he was growing something poisonous.

"Oh, for God's sake," Roland said. "I'm a specialist in these things. There are plenty of things we use that start out toxic, only we know how to process them to remove the dangers. These herbs are no exception."

"Name one thing," Porter stated.

Roland threw up his hands. "Hell, off the top of my head, the first thing I can think of is foxglove—it's the plant from which we derive digitalis, which is one of the medicines that keeps people with bad hearts from dying. But in its native state, it's a poison."

"Mama's aunt Phoebe used to gather foxglove and all kinds of herbs for treating sickness," Danny said.

"Yeah, I remember," Porter said.

Roland's hopes rose. Maybe this was going to work out after all.

"See? I'm not hiding anything illegal. I just believe in being careful."

"And the five thousand still holds?" Danny asked.

"Yes, yes. Five thousand," Roland echoed.

"Apiece?" Porter added.

"Yes! For God's sake, yes! Five thousand apiece. Now, are we going to begin the harvest today or not?"

The brothers looked at each other, then shrugged.

"I reckon so," Porter said.

"Just keep your skin covered and you'll be fine," Roland said.

Porter glared at Danny. "Yeah, we'll be just fine."

Danny wouldn't look at his brother. He'd gotten them into this, but it was obvious he hadn't asked enough questions before he'd committed them to the job. Still, five thousand dollars apiece for less than a couple of weeks' work was too good to pass up. Danny took the gloves out of his pocket and put them on.

"Okay, Storm. Show us where you want to start."

It was just before noon when Harold walked back into the storeroom and called out to Wes.

"Hey, Wes…I need a twenty-five pound sack of tuna-flavored cat food brought up front."

Wes nodded, then walked past the loaded pallets of feed and seed to the corner of the storeroom where the sacks of dog and cat food were stacked. He shouldered a sack and then headed for the front.

There was a tiny old woman standing at the counter as Wes entered the room.

"Which car?" Wes asked.

"The blue Ford truck," Harold said.

Wes walked through the store, then out the front door and put the sack in the rear of the truck. He was on his way back inside when the elderly woman came out of the store, guided by a younger woman who was very pregnant. It was then he realized the old woman was blind. Instead of speaking, he nodded cordially at the pregnant woman, then held the door for them as they passed by.

"Thank you kindly," the young woman said.

"You're welcome, ma'am," Wes answered.

The old woman stopped, tilted her head sideways like a little bird eyeing something new on the ground, and then spoke.

"I don't believe we've met," she said, and held out

her hand. "My name is Amelia Devon, but everyone just calls me Granny, and this is my niece, Charlotte."

When he took her hand, he was surprised by the strength in her grip, then even more surprised when she seemed to go off into a trance and began muttering some kind of rhyme.

"Man comes a cryin', runnin' for his life.
Lost his little boy. Lost his pretty wife.
Danger all around him. Danger up above.
Thinks his life is over. Gonna find new love."

Wes was so stunned by what she said that he forgot to turn loose of her hand. Then, by the time she was finished, it was too late. She started sliding toward the ground.

"Help me," Charlotte said as she grabbed at Granny's shoulders.

Wes caught her, lifted her up, then carried her to the truck.

"Here, let me get the door for you," Charlotte said.

"Don't we need to call an ambulance?"

"No…that's just Granny's way. Never know when the visions will hit her, but they always leave her weak as a kitten."

Wes figured this must have been how Alice felt when she fell down the rabbit hole. The only person who seemed to think this was all strange was him. He stared at the pregnant woman as if she'd just lost her mind.

"Visions?"

Charlotte nodded. "Yes. Granny was born blind, you know, but she sees more than any sighted person could."

"She has visions?"

Charlotte smiled sympathetically. "I know. It sounds strange, but it's true. You mind what she said to you. It always comes true."

"Yes, ma'am," Wes said, then shut the door to the truck, putting some much-needed distance between himself and the woman who called herself Granny Devon.

He stepped up on the curb and then strode into the store.

"Granny all right?" Harold asked.

"Seems so," Wes said shortly.

"Must have had herself a vision," Harold added.

Wes glared at Harold as he stomped through the shop to the storeroom.

This isn't the rabbit hole. It's the freakin' Twilight Zone.

He picked up a broom and started sweeping an already clean floor as Scooby the cat made a dive for calmer quarters. But the harder he swept, the more creepy he felt.

The first half of what she'd said had already happened, and he didn't want a goddamned thing to do with the last of it. Not the danger, and for certain not another love, even though there was no denying he was attracted to Ally Monroe. But it hurt too much to lose a love. He wasn't about to try anything that foolish again.

Still, when quitting time came and he started the walk back home, he caught himself thinking of seeing her tomorrow and began to walk faster. Even though the evening would probably wind up a disaster, he couldn't wait to see her again.

Thirteen

The midday heat was sweltering. What air was moving was unable to get past the trees surrounding the field where Danny and Porter were working. Their clothes were wet with sweat and stuck fast to their bodies. Adding to the misery were the tiny gnats that swarmed around their heads and up their noses. Danny tied a handkerchief across the lower half of his face, while Porter lit up a cigarette, using the smoke to keep the insects at bay. In their whole lives, they'd done just about every kind of job there was to do on a working farm, but this was, without doubt, the most miserable thing they'd ever encountered. And, as if the heat and bugs weren't enough, they kept finding small dead animals scattered throughout the field.

Porter finished cutting down a row and then stopped to help Danny load the trailer they were pulling behind the tractor. The cut ends oozed a clear, sticky sap that seemed to draw insects by the thousands. The stalks were crawling with ants and beetles, and when they loaded the trailer, the bugs crawled on them, too.

Porter flipped the cigarette he'd been smoking into the dirt, stomped it with the toe of his boot, then brushed a handful of ants from the front of his shirt.

"This is the most miserable, goddamned job I've ever had."

Danny took the handkerchief from his face and used it to blow his nose, blasting it with sweat, snot and bugs.

"I've never seen so many insects in a field in my life," Danny said.

"You're not telling me anything I didn't already know," Porter snapped, and swatted at a wasp buzzing near his ear. "I don't know what the hell kind of herb this is supposed to be, but I will lay odds it's illegal."

Danny sighed. "Yeah."

Porter's eyes narrowed. "We can walk away from this right now. Forfeit the money and leave Storm to stuff himself."

Danny sighed. "I know."

Porter stared at his brother. He knew him almost as well as he knew himself.

"But you're not going to, are you?" Porter said.

Danny hesitated, then shook his head.

"I can't. It wouldn't be right."

Porter smiled wryly. "Because you gave him your word, right?"

Danny shrugged. "Yeah."

Porter cursed beneath his breath, then laughed softly.

"Damn it, Danny. One of these days your sense of honor is gonna get us killed."

Danny frowned. "Don't say that!"

Porter laughed again. "Just teasing, brother. Just teasing."

"Well…it wasn't funny," Danny said, then bent down and picked up another armload of the cut stalks and laid them on the low flatbed trailer. "We've almost got another load," he said.

"I can get another half-dozen bunches on here, and then I think I'll take it in," Porter said.

Danny nodded. "I'll gather up some more bunches and leave them beside the rows while you're gone. Would you please bring me something cold to drink when you come back?"

"Will do," Porter said, and a few minutes later, he took off to the drying sheds, leaving Danny alone in the field.

Danny continued to gather the cut stalks, then pile them up for loading. As he bent down, the scent of something dead filled his nostrils. He moved some stalks and found another dead rabbit.

That in itself wasn't unusual, but that they kept finding them here in the field was weird. Another oddity was that they seemed to have died on their own. Normally, small animals like this fell prey to predators, such as foxes or big cats. And while this one had obviously been here for some time, Danny was still able to tell that it had died intact. Not only that, but no predators had fed from it, not even the buzzards, who never missed carrion. The first thing he thought of was rabies, so he sidestepped the small carcass.

A short while later, he heard Porter coming back and retraced his steps down the row, anxious for the cold drink and a chance to rest. In the process, he completely forgot to mention the newest carcass to Porter; then, when he thought of it again, Porter was already taking off with another load to the sheds. Danny hopped onto the back of the trailer and rode it down. When he jumped off and headed toward an outdoor water faucet, Storm came out of one of the sheds and yelled at him.

"Where are you going?" Roland yelled. "It's not quitting time."

Hot, tired and sick of sucking bugs up his nose, then spitting them out of his mouth, Danny turned on Roland with a vengeance.

"Look, mister! I'm only going over here to wash the fucking bugs off my face, then I'm going to help Porter unload the trailer. But if you open your pie hole and yell at me or Porter one more time, we're going home and we're not coming back. Do I make myself clear?"

Roland stopped. He wasn't accustomed to having his authority questioned, but from the looks on the Monroe brothers' faces, they meant what they said.

"You gave me your word," he muttered.

Danny sighed. "Yes, I know, and that's the only thing keeping us here." Then he pointed at the load on the trailer. "I don't know what kind of herb that is you're growing, but if those health-food nuts you're selling it to take to it as much as those bugs, you're gonna make a fortune."

Roland's expression stilled. "Bugs? What bugs?"

Porter snorted, then pointed to the load.

"Hellsfire, man, just look. The stalks are crawling with 'em."

The color disappeared from Roland's face. He hadn't taken any kind of infestation into consideration and hadn't noticed anything like this before. He stared at the insects crawling madly among the stalks. From there, his mind hopped to their predators—birds, wasps, spiders. Then to the rodents that ate insects. At that point, fear shot his calculations straight to the end of the chain, which was man. He was fine with killing off the scum of the world and those that pandered to it, but he hadn't counted on the destruction affecting himself, as well. Could this thing that he'd created become that deadly? He didn't know, but until he found out, he was going to have to make some changes.

"I'm going to start some smudge pots," he said. "We'll put them under the drying tables and hopefully smoke out the insects. If that works, I'll put some in the fields. That should take care of the problem."

"Sort of like smoking bees," Porter said.

"What?" Roland asked, thinking of at least three men he knew in the area who kept honeybees. "What about bees? There were bees in the field, too?"

"No...I mean, there could have been," Porter said.

"But I was referring to the smokers that beekeepers use so they can steal the honey from the hives."

"Oh, yes. Of course. Smoke the bees…smoke the insects… Yes, yes, I get it," Roland said, and then laughed.

Danny's gut knotted. The man not only acted crazy, he sounded crazy, too. That laugh was straight out of some Hollywood horror movie.

Porter got off the tractor and began unloading the bundles while Danny stripped the gloves from his hands, then turned on the faucet and ducked his head under the running water.

Porter grabbed an armload of the stalks and carried them into the shed, then strung them out across the drying tables that Roland had indicated. Later, they would have to tie them in bundles and hang them upside down for further drying, but for now, just getting them off the ground and into the sheds was the deal.

Sap was all over Porter's gloves, on the front of his shirt and the legs of his jeans. He hoped the stuff would wash off okay and thought of what a fit Ally would have when she saw their clothes. As he walked back for another load, something lit on the side of his face, then crawled toward his mouth. Before he thought, he swiped at it, stringing sap from his gloves all across the left side of his face.

"God Almighty," he muttered, and then took off his gloves and headed for the spigot that Danny had just vacated.

The sap was sticky on his cheek, and before he

thought about it, he'd licked his lips. Almost instantly, he panicked as he remembered Roland's warning about toxicity, then waited to see if he was going to drop dead. When he didn't, the relief was so great that he almost laughed.

God. What a scare! The sap wasn't poison, but it *was* sweet. Porter felt the end of his tongue tingle just the least little bit, but that was all. Happy to be alive, he grinned.

"What's so damned funny?" Danny asked.

Porter looked at his brother, then at the water running down his face and into the neck of his shirt, and laughed.

"I reckon it's you," he said, then bent over and stuck his own head under the flow of running water, washing away the sticky sap, as well as the sweat and bugs that were stuck to his skin.

As the day wore on, the excessive amount of bugs and the steamy heat began to wear on everyone's nerves. Roland had smudge fires going in the drying shed that weren't doing much good. The bugs on the plants were crawling on everything, even one another, in some kind of frenzy. Roland wondered if this was how von Braun must have felt when he realized he'd created the atomic bomb.

What bothered him most was that, not once in his research, had he seen signs of this. Yes, the need for more Triple H had been evident, and the more he'd given the rats, the more they'd needed for the next fix. But having something this addictive that could conceivably be transmitted between species was horrifying. He wasn't sure what he should do. He'd started this harvest with one goal in mind, but now all he wanted was to make it go away.

As he stared at the tables in growing panic, his cell phone began to ring. He checked the caller ID and frowned. It was his Chicago contact calling back, but now he didn't know what to say. It rang until voice mail picked up. He tossed the phone aside and then hurried outside.

From where he was standing, he could see the Monroe brothers bringing in another load. Then he looked past them to the field beyond. Less than a third of the crop had been cut.

What in hell was he going to do?

Porter and Danny were silent as they drove home that same day. Their faces were streaked with sweat and bugs, their clothes sticky from the sap. The muscles in Porter's jaw ached as if he'd been punched, and Danny had a headache that just wouldn't quit.

Porter pulled up in front of their home, parked the truck, then looked at Danny.

"Goin' back?"

Danny sighed.

"I guess."

"Shit."

Danny frowned. "You don't have to go."

Porter sat for a moment, letting the sound of the words settle the unease he kept feeling.

"That money isn't worth it," he said.

"It's not about the money," Danny said. "It's about being a quitter."

Then he got out of the truck and headed for the back of the house.

Porter followed.

Ally was taking loaves of fresh bread out of the oven when Danny came in the back door wearing nothing but a towel wrapped around his waist. She grinned and started to tease him, then saw the look on his face.

"Danny?"

He didn't answer but kept on walking.

Porter came in next, just as naked, but with an old shower curtain covering his nudity.

Ally's eyes widened.

"What on—"

"Don't touch those clothes that we put in the washing machine," he said shortly.

"But—"

He turned on her then, and she saw more than weariness on his face. His eyes were bloodshot, his nostrils flared, and there was a muscle twitching at the corner of his left eye.

"Don't argue with me, goddamn it! Whatever you do, don't touch those fucking clothes!"

Ally wadded the pot holders in her hands as she began to back up. It wasn't until she felt the cabinets against her legs that she stopped, and still she wasn't sure she was far enough away from Porter to be safe.

Porter heard himself talking and couldn't believe those words were coming out of his mouth. When he saw the look on his sister's face, he groaned, then dropped his head.

"I'm sorry. I'm sorry. Please forgive me. It's been one hell of a day."

"It's okay," Ally said. She started toward him, when Porter instinctively moved away.

"I'm filthy," he said, and headed for the bathroom behind Danny.

Ally had an overwhelming urge to cry and didn't know why. This behavior was so out of character for both her brothers. She knew where they'd been and what they had been doing. She trusted her brothers, but she didn't trust Roland Storm one bit.

She glanced toward the back door. From where she was standing, she could hear the sound of the washing machine filling with water. She couldn't imagine what they'd meant by not touching their clothes.

What had they done?

Even more to the point, what had they gotten themselves involved in?

With each passing day, Granny Devon's warning of danger and being her brothers' keeper wore on Ally's conscience. She was helpless to do anything to change the minds of two grown men who still treated her like their baby sister, but just maybe, if she knew what was happening, she would know who to go to for help. Still, that was something for another day. Tonight she had more on her plate than she could say grace over, and it was time to start frying chicken for the supper from hell.

Wes passed the Monroe house on his way home from getting groceries and noticed that Gideon Monroe was already home. But the brothers' truck was still missing, which meant they were still at work. A little surprised, he lengthened his stride, anxious to get home and clean up before coming back for supper. Instead of staying on the road, he decided to take the shortcut through the trees beyond the Monroes' yard.

He ran the last few yards to the house and hurried to unlock the door. Once inside, he put up his groceries, then began stripping off his clothes as he went and quickly jumped in the shower. A few minutes later, he was at the closet, sorting through his meager assortment of clothes for something to wear, then frowned at himself for being excited. It was just a meal with a woman who needed a favor. Granted, she was a pretty woman, and there was the fact that he was attracted, but that only meant he was still alive. A man would have to be dead not to be attracted to someone like Ally Monroe.

Choosing the least wrinkled of his clothes as the best bet, he dressed in jeans and a clean white T-shirt, grabbed a clean pair of socks and used his dirty ones to brush the dust off his boots.

Once he was dressed, he checked his appearance in the mirror—a holdover from his military days, when everything about him had to be spit-shined and in place.

Satisfied that he was presentable, he started for the door, then stopped. It was customary to take something to the hostess who was preparing the meal, and he wished he'd remembered that before he'd left Blue Creek. Then he thought of the wisteria blooming all over the roof. It would be perfect.

Quickly he went outside and cut an armful of the heavy, purple-hued blooms, then wrapped them in an empty brown paper sack from the supermarket and hit the road. It would take a little longer, but he wanted to arrive looking as neat as possible, and cutting through the forest was just asking for a torn shirt or leaves in his hair.

A short while later he was at the mailbox and starting up the Monroes' drive. The old hound was lying at the side of the driveway between the house and the road. When he saw Wes, he lifted his head and managed a soft bugle.

"Hey there, old fella," Wes said, and stopped to give the dog a pat.

Buddy took it in stride and then plopped back down, as if satisfied that he'd done his duty.

Wes shifted the flowers in his arms to a more comfortable position and looked up at the house. There were three vehicles in the driveway now, which probably meant he was the last guest to arrive.

"Well, Buddy, here goes nothing."

Fourteen

Ally was at her wits' end. Freddie Joe had arrived with his children, who were in sad need of care. The oldest, the only female of the trio, introduced herself as Loretta Lynn Detweiller. Freddie Joe filled in by mentioning her age. She was eleven and, in Ally's opinion, in serious need of a shampoo and a bra. The middle child was a boy who glared at her without speaking. Freddie Joe introduced him.

"His name is Freddie Joe Detweiller the third, but I call him Booger."

Ally considered it wise not to ask why he'd gotten that nickname and then bit the inside of her mouth to keep from laughing when he stuck a finger up one nostril and gave it a poke. He was eight.

The youngest child was four. And if Ally had been weak-minded and desperate, the little fellow would have been reason enough to marry his dad. Thankfully, she was neither weak-minded nor desperate, but she gave him a welcoming smile as he told her his name.

"My name is Toot. I four."

Again Ally refrained from asking about the nickname as Freddie Joe quickly filled in more blanks.

"That there is Johnny Cash Detweiller. I'm a big country music fan. How about you?" Freddie Joe asked.

"It's fine," Ally said. "But I'm partial to bluegrass."

Freddie Joe frowned. He couldn't abide a woman who argued, but he remembered that the last time he'd started to argue he'd been ushered out before he'd had time to eat his dessert. And since they had yet to sit down to supper and everything was smelling so good, he figured he would wait a bit to let her know who was boss.

"Food smells good."

"Thank you," Ally said, and ignored her father's beaming smile.

"Is it done yet?" Freddie Joe asked.

"Yes."

"Good. Kids are hungry. I reckon it's time to eat."

"Not yet," Ally said. "My brothers are still cleaning up, and we have one more guest who has yet to arrive."

Freddie Joe glared at Gideon.

"I didn't know this was gonna be a party," he said.

"It's not… I mean… Ally! What do you mean, someone else is coming? You knew I'd invited Freddie Joe and the kids."

She gave her father a sweet smile.

"Why yes, I knew you'd invited them. You've reminded me at least twice a day, so I thought since you were inviting your friends, the least I could do was add one of mine to the list. He should be here anytime."

Danny and Porter entered the living room just as Ally made her announcement.

Porter remembered Storm's complaint about the stranger in Uncle Doo's house, but before he could comment, there was a knock at the door.

"That must be him now," Ally said, and rushed to the door.

In truth, she was not only nervous but downright afraid that her family would do something to hurt Wes's feelings. Despite her request for Wes to act as a buffer, she was feeling guilty for having drawn him into the mess. Then she opened the door and saw him standing on the porch holding an armful of wisteria, and turned loose with a smile.

"Welcome," she said. "I'm so glad you're here."

Her smile rocked Wes where he stood, but he managed to maintain some good sense as she grabbed him by the arm and pulled him inside.

Immediately, Wes found himself facing the stares of four suspicious men and three curious children. He only glanced at the children, knowing that they could be the trigger to him coming undone.

The sweet, heady scent of wisteria beneath his nose suddenly reminded him of his manners. He handed Ally the bouquet.

"A small gift for the hostess," he said.

"They're wonderful," Ally said. "I'll put them in water just as soon as you're introduced." Then she blasted the men with a glare.

"Everyone…this is Wes Holden. He's renting Uncle Doo's house and working down in Blue Creek at the feed store."

If shock had been a physical emotion, Gideon Monroe would have been flat on the floor. Danny and Porter, having already been forewarned by Storm that he existed, were withholding their opinions, while Freddie Joe was in a panic, taking Wes's appearance as an immediate threat to his own plans for a wife.

Gideon was the first to recover.

"Ally Monroe! Why is this the first I've heard about this man's presence?"

"I don't know…. Maybe because not once in my entire life have I heard any of the three of you ever come into this house and ask me how my day went, or if I needed any help. If I thought you were interested in my business—and you do remember that house is my business—then I suppose I would have mentioned Wes earlier. However, he's here and the food is ready, and since Wes is my guest, I'll show him to the table and put the wisteria in water as we all sit down."

Wes stifled a smile. In her own house, Ally Monroe was a sight to behold. She'd taken the wind out of her father's anger and ignored the rest, leaving Freddie Joe to hustle his brood into the kitchen alone.

Ally laid the wisteria on the counter long enough to

get a large vase from the cabinet, then put them in water and set them in a prominent place on top of the sideboard, right next to three pies.

"Looks like you've been working at this meal all day," Wes said. "It smells wonderful."

Ally beamed.

Gideon frowned.

Freddie Joe fumed.

Danny and Porter thought the man was too slick and wondered if Storm had been right.

"Please, everyone, take a seat," Ally said. Then she turned to the children. "I know you'll want to sit beside your daddy. Freddie Joe, you sit here between Toot and Booger. Loretta Lynn can help me pour tea in the glasses." Then she looked at the young girl. "Is that okay, honey?"

Glad that someone else had cooked their meal tonight, Loretta Lynn was more than happy to assist.

"Yes, ma'am. I'd be proud to help."

Freddie Joe glared at Gideon, as if waiting for him to do something, but Gideon was too stunned by Ally's defiance to do anything but sit.

Wes followed Ally to the refrigerator, then took the bin of ice out of her hands and set it on the cabinet beside Freddie Joe's girl.

"Is there anything I can do to help?" he asked.

Ally was still reeling from turning around to find him nose-to-chest close. When he'd taken the ice as if it was too heavy for her to handle, she found she'd completely lost her train of thought.

"Uh…no, all I have to do is take the food out of the warming oven and—"

"I'll do that. Show me," he said.

Now Ally was staring at him, too.

"What?" Wes asked.

"Men don't do women's work," Freddie Joe snapped.

"Where I come from, men do whatever the hell they choose, and since Ally has done all the work of cooking this meal, I choose to help put it on the table."

Freddie Joe muttered beneath his breath.

Wes turned his back on them all, then wondered if that was wise. He'd seen enough "go to hell" looks to wind up with a table knife in his back.

He took two platters of fried chicken from the oven and carried them to the table, putting one at each end of the long table.

Freddie Joe frowned. "We had fried chicken last night," he said.

Ally's face reddened, but before she could answer, Porter decided he'd heard enough. He didn't know about this Wes Holden, but he did know about Freddie Joe, and he didn't like the little bastard.

"You don't plan to stay, then?" he asked.

Freddie Joe sputtered, then glared. "That's not what I said. I was just pointing out that—"

"Who wants iced tea and who wants lemonade?" Ally asked, purposefully interrupting before a real argument ensued.

The drinks were soon sorted out, with Loretta Lynn

proudly carrying the glasses to each place. By the time they were done, Wes had carried the last of the food from the oven. As if he hadn't done enough to antagonize the men, he stopped at Ally's chair and wouldn't sit down until he'd seated her.

Gideon wanted to comment, but every time he looked at Wes Holden, intuition told him to stay quiet. There was something in the way the man walked and the way he stood that said he was a force to be reckoned with. Seeing him beside Freddie Joe made Gideon horribly aware of how willing he'd been to cheat his daughter out of a true man. He was not only ashamed but embarrassed.

"The food looks fine, Ally honey...real fine."

"Why, thank you, Daddy," Ally said. "Would you give the blessing?"

"Please bow your heads," Gideon said.

And they did.

As Gideon began the ritual, Ally slipped her hand into Wes's and gave it a quick squeeze, as if to say thank-you for coming, for helping, for just being a friend.

Before he had time to think about reciprocating, she'd put both hands in her lap and bowed her head.

He had to be satisfied with the lingering warmth of her touch. Then the meal began, and Wes was forced to face the children, especially the little boy who called himself Toot.

"I like chicken legs," Toot announced.

Everyone smiled. Wes swallowed past the knot in his throat and picked up the platter of chicken. His hands were shaking, and there was a pain in his chest that hurt worse than dying, and still he made himself smile.

"My little boy liked them best, too," Wes said. "Which one looks best to you?"

Johnny Cash Detweiller pointed to the biggest, crustiest one, and then looked up at Wes with a smile that nearly ended him in front of them all.

"That would have been my pick, too," Wes said, then forked it from the platter onto Toot's plate, took a piece for himself and passed the chicken to Ally without looking up.

Freddie Joe had seen the writing on the wall. He didn't know where this man had come from, but with three kids and a receding hairline, he couldn't compete. The most he could hope to get out of this day was a home-cooked meal, and then he was back to square one.

But Toot, having decided that the chicken-man was friendly, did what all small children do—asked a question that was too hard to answer. As the food was being passed, he took a bite of the chicken leg, then looked up at Wes.

"Where's your little boy, mister? Would he like to play with me?"

Ally stifled a gasp, and all the color disappeared from Wes's face. But to his credit, he managed to answer.

"He's not here anymore, but if he was, I can promise he would have wanted to play with you."

Toot was satisfied with the answer and kept on eating, but like a cur dog sensing weakness in a foe, Freddie Joe figured the man was one of those deadbeat dads and wanted to put him in a bad light.

"So what did you do, walk out on him?" he asked.

"Freddie Joe! You don't know what you're saying!" Ally said, then turned to Wes. "I'm sorry. I should not have put you in this position, and I will understand perfectly if you want to leave."

"No, it's okay," Wes said, then made himself smile. "You don't think I'd walk out on all of this good food and company, do you?"

"What?" Freddie Joe asked. "What's the big deal? I still got my kids. What's so special about him walking out on his?"

"He didn't walk out on him," Ally said. "His son and his wife were killed in that bombing at Fort Benning last year, and you owe Wes an apology."

Freddie Joe wilted.

"Hell, man, I'm sorry. I know what it's like to lose a wife, and I'm real sorry about your little boy."

Toot wasn't sure what was going on, but he was sure his daddy was in trouble and felt obligated to put it right.

He leaned over and patted Wes on the arm.

"Hey, mister…I know a joke."

There was a moment of silence around the table; then everyone laughed.

"You do, do you?" Wes said.

Not one to be outdone, Booger offered his own skills to the assembly.

"Watch this," he said as he scooped a pea onto his

spoon, put it in his mouth, then snorted it out through his nose. It went flying across the table and landed on Danny's plate.

Freddie Joe froze.

Danny's face turned red; then he started to grin as Porter burst into laughter. Thankful that the tension was gone from his house, Gideon joined in the laughter. Loretta Lynn rolled her eyes, while Toot looked crestfallen. As always, his big brother had stolen his moment.

Ally looked wild-eyed at Wes, certain that he would think them all mad, but he didn't look upset. In fact, he was laughing. Breath caught in the back of Ally's throat. From the first, she'd thought Wes Holden handsome, but this was the first time she was seeing all of the man. His eyes were dancing, and his lips were turned up in pure joy.

Freddie Joe whopped his oldest boy on the side of his head.

"What?" Booger asked,

"What'd you go and do that for?" Freddie Joe said.

"'Cause Toot can't."

"I still know a joke," Toot offered.

The laughter rolled through the room again, filling Wes to overflowing. It took everything he had to get serious, although serious he had to be.

"So, Johnny Cash, tell me this good joke."

Toot beamed.

"Knock, knock." Then he patted Wes's arm. "You're 'apposed to say 'Come in.'"

Booger groaned. "See. Toot never can get 'em right. It's 'Who's there?' Toot. Not 'come in.'"

"Oh, yeah," Toot said, and looked to Wes, waiting for him to finish his part.

"Who's there?" Wes asked.

"Peanut butter," Toot said, then patted Wes again. "Now you say—"

"Oh, for Pete's sake, Toot! He knows how to do it," Booger muttered.

"Peanut butter who?" Wes said before Toot started to cry.

"Peanut butter and jelly samwich!" Toot cried, and then slapped his leg and laughed aloud.

Booger groaned as everyone laughed.

"That wasn't funny," Booger muttered.

Loretta Lynn punched him and frowned.

"That was a fine joke," Wes said, and forever became a hero in Johnny Cash Detweiller's eyes.

"I'll have another chicken leg," Toot announced.

Ally passed Wes the plate.

"I don't know if there's another leg left. Is there another piece of chicken that you like?"

"The butt," Toot announced, and pointed to a thigh.

The answer drew another round of chuckles, which Toot promptly ignored.

Later, after the meal had progressed to dessert, Freddie Joe hurried them through it and began to take his leave. He'd been humiliated enough for one day.

Ally was packing up some leftovers for the children

to take with them. Gideon and his sons had retired to the living room, leaving Wes alone in the kitchen with Ally and Loretta Lynn.

"Here you go, honey," Ally said. "It'll be enough for another meal."

"I thank you," the girl said. "I'm not much of a cook."

Ally's heart went out to her. "I wasn't, either, when my mother died, but I learned."

"I'm sorry you aren't gonna be our new ma," the girl said. "I think you would have worked out just fine."

Ally's heart went out to the young girl. "I'm sorry, too," she said. "But you can't pretend something you don't feel. Do you understand?"

"Oh, yes, ma'am. That's what Mommy always said. She also said to marry someone a sight smarter than Pa."

Ally bit her lip to keep from smiling as she handed the girl the sack of food.

Loretta Lynn Detweiller sighed, then eyed Wes, who was standing at the sink washing dishes.

"Hey, mister?"

Wes turned around.

"It was a pleasure to meet you," she said.

Wes smiled. "It was a pleasure to meet you, too," he said, and realized he meant it.

At that point Freddie Joe came in, looking for his last child.

"Hurry it up, girl. The boys are already in the car."

"Miss Monroe was just giving us some leftovers, Pa."

"Thank you," Freddie Joe said, then glanced at Wes one last time. "I'm real sorry for your loss."

Wes was touched by the simple fact that he realized the man meant it.

"Thank you, and I'm sorry for yours."

Freddie Joe felt shame all over again. "I didn't mean nothin' by what I said about your boy."

"I know," Wes said, and then added, "Would you do me a favor?"

Freddie Joe shrugged. "Like what?"

"Don't ever take your kids for granted."

Embarrassed that he felt real emotion, Freddie Joe nodded quickly. "Yeah. Yeah. See you around."

And then he was gone.

Ally took the dishcloth out of Wes's hand and pushed him toward the living room.

"Go sit with the men before they completely blow a fuse."

Wes grinned. "Is my helping you that bad?"

She rolled her eyes. "You have no idea. I can promise you that you're the first man they've ever seen who lifted a hand to help a woman in the kitchen."

"Then it was high time they did," Wes muttered.

Suddenly bashful, Ally ducked her head as she smiled.

"Thank you, though. More than you will ever know."

"I didn't do anything but eat your good food and laugh at the jokes."

"You did, and you know it," Ally said. "You're a special man, Wes Holden, and I wish you weren't so sad."

Wes sighed. "So do I, Ally, so do I. But thanks to you, I'm getting better every day. However, I think I'm going to leave before I outstay my welcome."

"Never," Ally said. "But I'll say goodbye to you here."

She stood on her tiptoes and gave him a quick kiss, then moved away before he could react.

"Don't stay away too long."

Wes touched her head, then ran his fingers down the length of her braid.

"Take care of yourself," he said, and the moment he said it, the mood shifted between them.

"You're talking about Roland Storm, aren't you?"

"Yes."

She nodded.

"Tell your father."

She frowned. "I'll think about it."

Wes had to accept that, for now, he had done all he could.

"I'll be seeing you," he said.

"Soon, I hope."

He nodded, then left the room.

Gideon looked up as Wes entered.

"Come sit down," he said.

"Thank you, sir, but I think I'd better be getting back. I have to get up pretty early."

"How do you get to work?" Porter asked.

"I walk."

Danny whistled softly between his teeth. "Dang, man, that's a long walk."

"It's not too bad," Wes said, then added, "It's been a pleasure meeting you…all of you."

Gideon stood and shook Wes's hand. "Same to you, son," he said.

Porter got up. "I'll give you a ride home."

"There's no need," Wes said. "It isn't far."

"No. I insist," Porter said.

Wes suspected there was more than a ride in the offer, but he didn't resist.

"Sure, why not?" he said, and followed Porter to his truck.

Porter didn't speak until they were out of the driveway and starting up the road.

"How did you come to be here?" he asked.

"What do you mean? West Virginia, or here in this place?"

"In this place…in my uncle Dooley's house…being friendly to my sister."

Wes sighed. This was no less than he would have done, had he been in Porter's place.

"In a manner of speaking, I guess I just ran away from home."

It was the last thing Porter expected, and because it sounded so honest, he relaxed his guard.

"You mean, because of what happened to your family?"

Wes shrugged. "That was part of it, but I was already pretty messed up before that. Basically, it was the last straw of what was left of my sanity."

Porter frowned. "Listen, mister. I'm the first one to

say you've had a hell of a deal handed to you, but I don't want my sister to get hurt."

"Your sister was kind to me when I needed it most. I would never hurt her...in any way."

"She's falling for you. I can see it on her face."

"I have feelings for her, too," Wes said. "But they're all mixed up with my grief. Bottom line is, I feel guilty for caring."

Porter frowned. "Nothing personal, but work it out— or get out."

Wes nodded. "Fair enough."

At that point, Porter pulled up in front of the little house.

"Heck of a house, isn't it?"

"My son would have loved it," Wes said, and got out. "Thanks for the ride."

Porter nodded, then put the truck in reverse, backed up and drove away.

Nightfall was just minutes away. Sunset had already come and gone, and the fireflies were out, flitting about from bush to tree doing whatever it was fireflies did. Too keyed up for sleep, Wes went into the house, got a can of pop from the refrigerator and went out the back door.

There was an old metal bench underneath a stand of hickory trees at the edge of the backyard. Wes brushed off the leaves, tossed aside a downed bird's nest that had blown out of the trees and eased himself down. He popped the top on the can and took his first drink. It was cold and sweet going down, with tiny shards of ice that melted instantly on his tongue. Margie always wanted her pop to be icy. She would have loved this one a lot. Wes stared at the can for a moment, then up at the darkening sky.

God. He'd just had a thought of his wife that hadn't made him want to scream. Oh, the pain was there, but not as heart-wrenching—not as hideously final—as it had been in the past.

He sat for a few minutes more, drinking from the swiftly warming can while the emptiness of his life shifted to a new place in his heart. He wasn't sure, but there was the possibility that he was learning how to remember the love without feeling the loss.

Finally, with one swallow left in the can and the sky awash in pink and purple hues, Wes stood. Acknowledging his weary body and aching muscles as having done a day's work, he lifted the can to the heavens, toasting the sunset, as well as the memory of his wife and his son.

"To you, my love, and to you, my little man," he said softly, and took the last drink.

Then he crumpled the can and went inside.

Back at the Monroe house, Gideon alternated between talking about Pete Randall's recovery and trying to pry information from his sons about their new job.

Danny and Porter were oddly noncommittal about their boss and what they were doing. All they would say was that it was the dirtiest job they'd ever had, and that Roland Storm was a half bubble off plumb.

Then Gideon made an out-of-character comment that

Storm looked like the cartoon version of Ichabod Crane. It was so unexpected that they all had to laugh. To Ally's relief, it lightened the mood and things shifted back to normal.

Later, as she was putting the last of the clean plates into the cabinet, Porter came inside carrying the freshly laundered clothes he and Danny had worn that day.

"I didn't know that dryer cycle had finished or I would have gotten those for you," Ally said.

Porter stopped. The nervous tic was back at the corner of his eye, as was the muscle jumping in his jaw.

"No. No. You don't touch what we wear to work." He started to walk away, then stopped again and looked her in the eye. "Ever."

Panic spread quickly, but she couldn't let him walk away without a better explanation.

"Damn it, Porter! You can't just say something like that and expect it to be all right."

"That's just it, honey. I don't know why, but I don't think anything is ever going to be all right again."

Ally pressed her fingers over her lips to keep from crying out. She wanted him to explain but was afraid she couldn't bear the truth.

"Please…Porter…whatever it is, just walk away."

He looked down at the clothes he was holding, then at his hands. They were shaking, and it was nothing to the shakes he had inside. He felt as if he was standing outside his body, watching himself coming apart. He didn't know what was happening, but he damn sure knew why. Whatever was in those "herbs" Roland Storm was growing, it was inside him now. He'd walked the earth that had given it life, breathed the air in which it had grown, and been symbolically washed in its blood from the constant flow of sap that had come out of the ends of the cut stems. He didn't know what it was, but he suspected it was deadly. The last thing he wanted was to go back up there again, but he'd already been exposed to whatever it was, and he and Danny had talked about it all the way home. They would finish harvesting the crop for Roland Storm. And when every last stalk was off the field and in the sheds, they were going to set fire to the whole thing and burn it to the ground. Then they were going to torch the fields and burn off the stubble. Whatever evil he'd created would be gone.

Saturday morning blew in with the wind. It whistled down the mountains and flew into Blue Creek without a by-your-leave, yanking freshly laundered clothes from the line and blowing trash cans about in the streets.

With the wind at Wes's back, he made good time going down the mountain to work, but he was hoping it would die down before noon, which was when the store closed on Saturdays, or it would be tough walking uphill against it.

After that, he would have a whole day and a half to himself. The yard needed to be mowed and the house to be cleaned, but nothing else was pressing. The thought of all that solitude made him nervous, although he thought he was ready to face it.

Scooby the cat wrapped himself around Wes's ankles as Wes slid a fifty-pound bag of sweet feed onto the dolly and wheeled it toward the loading dock where Melvin Peterson was waiting. The feed was for Melvin's son—or rather, his son's 4-H project, a little Hereford steer he called Doofus.

Wes had already seen pictures of both the son and the steer, which had done nothing but put him in a bad mood. Instead of accepting why he felt the need to lash out, he blamed his problems on the cat.

"Dang it, Scooby. You've already been fed. Go catch a mouse or something," he said shortly, then shrugged at the smile Melvin Peterson gave him. "He's a pest," Wes added.

"Good mouser, though," Melvin said.

Wes dumped the bag of sweet feed into the truck bed and then handed Melvin his paid ticket.

"Have a nice day," Wes said shortly.

Melvin eyed Wes thoughtfully, then nodded.

"Heard you saved them two men in the wreck the other day."

"I didn't save them," Wes said shortly. "I just put out a fire."

"Same thing," Melvin said, then settled his cap a little tighter on his head and drove away.

Wes picked up an empty bucket, but instead of hanging it on the wall, he drew back and flung it as far across the warehouse as it would go, just missing the side of Harold's head as he walked into the storeroom.

Had it been anyone else but Wes, Harold would have fired him on the spot. But he could tell by the look on Wes's face that he was already sorrier than a man had a right to be.

"I'm really sorry. I shouldn't have done that," Wes said.

"Was it something Melvin said?" Harold asked.

Wes shuddered visibly, then combed his fingers through his hair in mute frustration, but he didn't answer.

Harold frowned. "It's almost noon. Why don't you go on and clock yourself out, and get an early start on the weekend? I'll close up back here."

Wes didn't move. Instead, he stuffed his hands in his pockets. His shoulders hunched as if he was bracing for a blow; then he dropped his head.

For a while, neither man spoke, then it was Wes who broke the silence. He looked up, and Harold found himself staring into Wes Holden's eyes, unable to look away.

"Melvin showed me a picture of his kid and his steer," Wes said.

Harold grinned.

"Yeah, he's pretty proud of that boy. Only one him and Gretchen could have, but he does tend to run on a bit about the kid."

"I had a son," Wes said.

Harold heard the past tense and couldn't bring himself to ask more.

Wes turned away.

Harold could see him swallowing back tears. He felt like crying along with him.

Then Wes added. "The only thing he wanted in life was to be old enough to grow whiskers so he could shave. He didn't make it."

Harold cleared his throat, then yanked out his handkerchief and blew his nose.

"I'm real sorry, Wes."

Wes nodded. His footsteps were slow as he crossed the wooden floor, then moved into the front of the store. The bell jingled as the door swung shut, leaving Harold alone in the quiet. He stood there for a minute, then did something he hadn't done in years.

He closed the store early.

The way he figured, if someone's chickens had to go without scratch until Monday, then it was that someone's fault. Life was too short. He was going to go fishing.

Fifteen

Ally waved goodbye to her father as he left for work, watched her brothers walk out of the house as if they were going to a funeral, then sat down in the living room and cried. She was afraid—as afraid as she'd ever been. They'd been at this almost all weekend. She was even more afraid for them now than before. She needed to talk to someone, but there was no one she could trust. She didn't want to go to Granny Devon, mostly because she was afraid of what she might say, and she could no more betray her brothers by talking to her father than she could trust her father to understand.

But the longer she sat, the more convinced she became that she had to see for herself what was going on with Roland Storm. Convinced that she'd made a positive decision, she changed into a T-shirt and jeans, then traded her sandals for a pair of walking shoes. She could take Porter's ATV partway up the mountain, but she would have to park it at least a mile from Storm's house and walk the rest of the way so as not to be heard.

With purpose in every step, she hurried to the barn and threw the tarp off the ATV.

Ally was nervous as she started up the road. What she was going to do was as intrusive a thing as she'd ever done. She wasn't the kind of woman who butted into other people's business, nor was she a woman who ever passed gossip along. Yet here she was, going to snoop on her brothers and their employer. She hadn't even thought of what she would do if she found something wrong. All of her focus was on just getting there.

Roland was sitting in a corner of the third drying shed, staring at what the Monroe brothers had brought in today. Sap was oozing out of the ends of the stalks, spilling into puddles below the tables. Ants were every-where, crawling on the stalks and drowning themselves in the puddles. The brothers had told him about the dead animals they kept finding in the field, and Roland knew that unless he did something soon, this devasta-tion was only the beginning.

Last night, after he'd finally gone to bed, he'd had the satisfaction of realizing what he'd done wrong, but it gave him no peace of mind. During the years of his research, he'd only used the leaves, drying them the same way marijuana was cured. Each time he'd started a new phase of his research, he'd simply gone to the field and pulled leaves from the stalks. Not once had he cut the entire stalk and carried it into the lab. If he had, he wouldn't be facing this runaway disaster. Then again, if he had, he would probably already be dead.

Yesterday he'd learned that the stranger in the old house was an ex-soldier named Wes Holden. But that didn't explain his interest in Roland's business, and he was too bothered by his crop's mutation to delve further. After the Monroe brothers had gone home, he'd taken some of the stalks into the lab, then gone out to the barn and brought in the last of the lab rats he had on site. There was no time to run the proper tests, but if what he suspected was true, then time would be the least of his problems. He'd started by doing a quick-dry process on the leaves, then running his old set of tests on the first pair of rats. The rats had reacted as he expected—first highly agitated, then lethargic to the point of being rendered unconscious before starting the cycle all over again, so he knew that the property of the leaves was still the same.

Then he took another pair of rats and put them in the cage with oozing chunks of the stalks. The inside of the cage was soon coated with the stuff. The rats gnawed on the stalks, their behavior quickly changing to something approaching drunkenness. They staggered into each other, then into the walls of the cage as if they didn't know they were there, all the while snarling and snapping at each other.

But it was the third set of rats that proved his biggest fear was no longer a fear, but a fact. He taped their mouths shut so that they could neither lick nor eat any part of the stalks, then dipped them in the sap, rubbing it firmly into their skin. When they were thoroughly coated, he took the tape from their mouths and set them loose in a third cage. Within an hour, they had begun to gnaw on their own feet and on each other. Blood began to ooze from their eyes and ears, but it was their constant, high-pitched squeals of pain Roland couldn't forget.

They were both dead before midnight.

Roland wasn't certain if they were dead because they'd killed each other, or from blood loss due to the internal hemorrhages they'd both suffered. All he knew was that of the three sets he'd tested, they were the only ones that had died so quickly, proving it was the sap, not the leaves, that held the strongest concentration of Triple H. Roland hadn't created a new drug, he had created a monster. It was the ultimate high that kept on giving and giving until, ultimately, it took the only thing the user had left.

Life.

He thought about the sap that had been all over Danny's and Porter's skin and clothes, and felt sick. They were going to die. He didn't know when, but he knew it as surely as he knew his own name that they couldn't last long.

This wasn't supposed to happen, and he was scared as hell. He looked down at himself. Even though he'd taken extreme precautions, they might not have been enough. He'd worn two layers of clothing into the lab, plus his lab coat and surgical gloves and a mask.

Suddenly he couldn't get out of there fast enough. The sky was scattered with clouds as he ran outside, making it difficult for him to see, but he wasn't going to waste time going back inside to get a lantern. He could see enough to do what he had to do. He hurried to the shed, got a can of charcoal-starter fluid, then hurried over to the barrel he used to burn his garbage. He stripped where he stood, dropping everything into the barrel, including his shoes and socks. The gloves were the last things he removed.

The night was still, the air thick with humidity. He wondered if it would rain again before morning, then wondered why he cared. The harvest was a joke. There was nothing to harvest here but death.

He emptied the can of starter fluid into the barrel, then stepped back a couple of feet, struck a match and tossed it. As it passed over the barrel, the air ignited with a loud, roaring whoosh. Roland felt himself flying through the air backward, then landing on his back several feet away. When he could breathe without choking, he rolled over onto his hands and knees, and quickly crawled out of reach of the flames.

Finally, when he was far enough way to be safe, he stood up, then ran his fingers over his face and neck. The smell of singed hair was thick in his nostrils, and his skin felt as if he'd been out in the sun too long.

"Shit," he muttered, and then ran for the house.

That had been last night, and now here he was in the sheds, breathing air that was probably polluted with

Triple H and staring at the blackened grass around the barrel. There was a thin gray spiral of smoke still rising from the ashes.

It was the shoes.

Leather and rubber weren't easy to burn.

Out in the field, Danny and Porter Monroe worked like two madmen, slinging the cut stalks onto the wagon by the armfuls.

When they'd showed up for work this morning, he'd been surprised. Their attitudes the night before had not been good, yet they'd come back. Today, though, there had been a look in their eyes that left him nervous, and a purpose in their behavior he couldn't quite identify. A short while ago, he'd seen them accidentally run into each other out in the field, then throw down the stalks and trade punches.

He couldn't quit thinking about the last pair of rats— the ones that had started gnawing on each other's feet. When the Monroe brothers came back with this last load, he was sending them home. He didn't want to be anywhere in their vicinity when they began to come undone.

The last time Ally had been this far up the mountain, Clifton Nelson had still been alive. But after he'd passed and left his property to a distant nephew who turned out to be Roland Storm, she'd had no occasion to come back. Storm had taken up residence with the attitude that he wanted to be left alone, and the people in Blue Creek, as well as the ones on the mountain, had gladly abided by his wishes.

The ruts left from the recent rain were deep but beginning to dry. Still, the axles of regular vehicles were too far apart to match those of an ATV, so Ally was forced to make her own path along the side of the road, which made the going slow and rough.

Finally she began to recognize landmarks and knew she was close. Reluctantly, she drove the ATV off the road and hid it from sight, then started walking through the woods.

The going was harder than she had imagined. She stumbled often, nearly went down more than once, and before she'd gone a quarter of a mile, had taken a hard fall.

She caught her toe on a tree root that had been uncovered by the recent rains, and went flying. Winded from the impact, she struggled to catch a breath. Only when she was able to draw oxygen into her lungs did she begin to feel pain. Her chin was burning, as were the palms of her hands. Tears shot across her line of vision as she rolled over onto her back and willed herself not to cry.

"Damn stupid foot," she muttered, and slapped the ground with the flat of her hands.

Soon she was up, but the fall forced her to move slower, which only heightened her frustration. Frustration soon gave way to stress, and stress to strain, as she clambered over roots and rocks. She was making progress, but it was painfully slow.

Finally, when she saw the backside of the barn through the trees, she knew she'd arrived. As she paused, a case of nerves shot a dose of adrenaline racing through her system.

She'd done it.

She was here.

Now what?

She stood for a few moments, studying the lay of the land, then decided to move a little closer. If Danny and Porter were supposed to be helping Roland Storm harvest his herbs, then they should be in the field. In any other circumstances, she would have driven right up to Storm's property, then out to the fields and confronted them on the spot. But after the way Danny and Porter had behaved about their clothes, she was afraid.

She took care to stay concealed as she moved past the buildings, then to the fenced-in land beyond. She thought she could hear a tractor running, but the sound was muffled by distance, as well as the trees, and she wasn't sure.

Focused on nothing but seeing Danny and Porter, she all but fell over the dead buck in her path, then stifled a scream that was more disgust than fear. The scent of decaying flesh was strong as she circled it, and she couldn't help wondering why the hunter who'd shot it had left without taking either the rack or the meat. It wasn't until she got a closer look that she realized it hadn't been shot. The animal's face looked as if it had caved in. Over the years, she'd seen plenty of animals brought down for food, but never one quite like this. She vaguely noticed the blood head high on a tree near to the buck, but she had no idea what it meant and kept walking.

Less than fifty yards away, she came upon a dead possum, then, a bit farther on, a skunk. After that, she found a rabbit and three birds, then an owl, then an assortment of small rodents, and she realized that she could smell death in every direction. Also puzzling was the fact that no carnivores were among the dead, and that they had not fed off the carcasses. She couldn't help but wonder what they might know that humans didn't.

The hair on the back of her neck suddenly stood on end. Something was horribly wrong. She couldn't imagine what could be killing the wildlife with such abandon, but whatever it was, she had a bone-deep certainty that it involved her brothers. She began to hurry, desperate to find them. Then, when she finally did, she wished she hadn't.

She saw Danny first, Danny with the broad shoulders and round face and with skin as red as his hair. When he wasn't staggering, he was moving at a jerky, frenetic pace. Porter was on the other side of a wagon, tossing an armload of stalks into the air without aim. Somewhere he'd lost his hat, and he kept swiping at his face with his hands. She frowned as she watched him, thinking that she'd never seen Porter leave the house without shaving, but he must have, because she could see the dark stubble from here. The longer she stood, the more

she began to see she'd been wrong. That wasn't the beginnings of a beard on Porter's face; it was ants. Hundreds and hundreds of tiny black ants.

"Good Lord," Ally whispered, and suddenly looked
down at the ground, imagining that they were crawling
up her feet and legs, too.

Then, before she could panic, she heard what could
only be described as a scream. It was part rage and part
pain, and she looked up just as Porter began digging and
slapping at his face. When he began tearing off his
clothes, she started to shake.

He was screaming and shouting, cursing in obscen-
ities she'd never heard. Danny moved toward him and got
a punch in the face for his troubles. Blood spurted. When
she saw Danny bend over, then spit out what looked like
a tooth, she thought she was going to throw up.

"Oh, God…oh, God…please make them stop."

She didn't know she'd spoken aloud until a bird that
she'd startled lifted off from the branches over her head,
squawking as it flew.

Immediately, Danny and Porter stopped fighting and
looked into the trees. Even though she knew they
couldn't see her, she felt threatened.

While she was debating about what to do, Roland
Storm appeared in her line of vision. She watched her
brothers waving their arms and pointing, then saw
Storm pivot toward the trees where she was hiding and
realized they'd told him what they'd seen. Granted, it
was just a bird taking flight, but if something illicit was

going on out there, then they were likely to look into it, and she would be in danger.

To her horror, Storm waved his arms at her brothers, as if ordering them back to work, then began walking toward the woods.

Ally panicked. She wasn't sure what was going on, but she knew she couldn't let herself be found. She began running and within seconds was down again. This time her knees took the brunt of the fall. Ignoring the pain, she got up and ran, choosing the densest part of the forest to stay concealed.

She ran with limbs slapping her face and brush tearing at her clothes. The muscles in her ankle were burning from the fall, there was a stitch in her side that hurt when she drew breath, but she didn't stop, and she never looked back.

Just as she was reaching the end of her endurance, she saw the ATV. She didn't take time to push it out of the brush where she'd hidden it but instead leapt into the seat and started it up. Sobbing with relief as the motor revved, she put it in gear and took off.

The ATV flew out of the trees with Ally on it as if it had been shot from a gun. She went airborne over the ditch before landing hard in the road. It took all her skills to stay upright, and when she finally gained control, she rode off down the mountain as fast as the four-wheeler would take her.

One mile passed, then another and another, and just when she was convinced that she was going to make it, the engine began to sputter and the ATV began to slow, until finally it rolled to a stop.

"No, no, no," Ally muttered, and slapped the steering wheel with both hands.

She turned the key, trying to start it again, but all she got for her trouble was a sputter and a pop. That was when she noticed the fuel gauge. It was sitting on Empty.

She turned around, her heart hammering against her breast as she searched the road behind her. There was nothing there, but she thought she could hear the sound of a truck engine coming down the grade. Fear lent her new strength as she leapt off the ATV and once again rolled it off the road into the trees. This time, when she ran, she was running for her life.

It was almost one-thirty in the afternoon when Wes reached Dooley Brown's mailbox. He gave it a thump as he passed, then headed up the driveway, thinking of what he had in the refrigerator that he could eat without having to cook. He had the key in the lock and was turning the knob when he heard someone scream.

The skin crawled on the back of his neck as his mind slammed him back to the day of the bombing. Women had been crying and screaming then, but not Margie. She'd never had a chance to scream.

He turned abruptly, only to realize he wasn't at Fort Benning, after all. Instead, he was standing on the doorstep and watching Ally Monroe coming out of the trees. The braid had come undone, and her hair was flying out behind her like a sunlit veil. There was a tear in her shirt and blood on her face, but it was the terror in her scream that sent him toward her.

He caught her in midair, taking the full weight of her body as she clung to him in terror. Her arms were wrapped around his neck, her legs around his waist. Her breath was coming in short gasps and jerks, and she was trembling so hard that she couldn't speak.

"Ally! What happened? Talk to me! Did someone hurt you? Was it Storm?"

As soon as he mentioned the name, she moaned and hid her face against his neck. At first he thought she was just crying, but then he realized she was saying the same thing over and over again.

"Hide me," she begged. "Hide me…hide me…hide me."

Wes tightened his hold as he bolted for the house. The door was still ajar as he shoved his way in, then turned just as quickly to kick the door shut. He locked it behind him, then carried her to the sofa. Even as he was running his hands over her body to check for wounds, he could see that she was in shock. Her pupils were dilated, and she was bordering on unconscious.

There was blood on her shirt and scratches all over her face and arms, but he couldn't find a mortal wound anywhere.

"Ally…I need you to talk to me. Can you tell me what's wrong?"

"My brothers…dead birds…dead squirrels…dead

rabbits and skunks. Big deer…all dead…everything is dead." Then she pointed toward the door. "He's coming. Hide. We have to hide."

"Who's coming, Ally? Is it Storm?"

She moaned and then covered her face.

He took that as a yes and ran to the windows. When he was sure both the road and the yard were still clear, he made a quick sweep through his house, making sure everything was locked down, then ran back to the living room.

Ally was nowhere in sight.

His heart stopped.

The doors were still locked, so she couldn't be gone. A sudden flash of fear jabbed deep in his gut as he thought about her dead in his arms. Then he cursed, frustrated with the part of him that kept shifting from past to present. That was Margie, not Ally, who was dead. He shook off the fear and ran through the house, calling her name.

He found her down on her belly beside the bed and at first thought she trying to hide beneath it. He dropped down beside her.

"Ally…"

"The rifle. Uncle Doo's rifle."

Wes's eyes widened. He'd been sleeping on a gun?

"Under the bed?"

"Yes! Yes!" Then she sat up and grabbed Wes by both arms. "Something's wrong up there. Something terrible that he doesn't want anyone to know."

She covered her face with her hands and started to shake.

Wes dropped flat on his belly, then reached beneath the bed. Within seconds, he felt the barrel of a rifle, then the stock. It was tied to the frame! He yanked at the ropes. The rifle fell to the floor. He dragged it out, only to find it was unloaded.

"Ally?"

She heard him calling her name, but she couldn't make herself focus enough to look up.

Wes grabbed her by the shoulders.

"Ally! The gun isn't loaded. Where is the ammunition?"

She pointed beneath the bed again, this time toward the headboard.

Within seconds, Wes was back on his belly. He felt the first box almost instantly, and as he was dragging it out, found a second.

He spilled shells out onto the floor and loaded the gun where he sat.

"Stay here," he said shortly, and moments later he was gone.

Ally heard the front door open, then she heard it shut. By the time she got to her feet and into the front room, Wes was nowhere in sight. Scared out of her mind, she dragged herself into the kitchen, got a butcher knife from the drawer and then crawled into the pantry. With the door slightly ajar, she would be able to hear.

Then a new fear hit her. Exactly what was it that she

expected to hear? Wes coming back, of course, but what if he didn't? What if Roland Storm saw him first and ambushed him?

"Lord help us," Ally prayed. Besides being scared out of her mind that Storm might get to her, she couldn't bear to think of anything happening to Wes.

If only she had a phone to call the sheriff. Then she groaned. Exactly what would she tell him if she did call—that Roland Storm had hired her brothers to harvest a crop that had ants all over it? He hadn't threatened her. Truth was, he was the one who had a grievance. She had trespassed. She could mention the dead animals, but the sheriff would probably tell her to call the EPA in case there was bad water in the area. She had nothing concrete to tell him, even if she did have a phone. At that point, she started to cry.

"Please, God…keep my brothers safe—and let Wes Holden come back."

Wes ran out of his house with the rifle in his hand and ran straight into his past. Before he'd passed the mailbox, the trees and bushes had turned into sand dunes and the ditches had become bunkers.

He started up the road with the rifle held loosely at his side, running at a crouched lope. A small crop duster was buzzing the treetops as it made a wide loop to fly back to its target, but in Wes's mind, it was an Iraqi bomber. He looked up, watched the clouds turning into heat-seekers and went belly down in the ditch. The heat of the sun on the back of his neck turned into burns from a flash fire, and the screech of a hunting hawk turned into a dying man's screams. He buried his face in the crook of his arm, waiting for the barrage to pass.

His heart was still pounding as he raised himself up on his elbows, and as he did, a terrapin poked its head out of its shell only a few feet in front of him. For Wes, it was like turning off one switch and turning on another. All of a sudden, the bunker morphed back into a ditch, and the sand dunes into trees and hills.

"God in heaven," he muttered, and got up. He stared back at the house, trying to reconcile what was real with what was not.

Ally was real, and she was in trouble. There had been blood and scratches all over her face and clothes. She was hurt. Someone was after her.

Roland Storm.

He heard the sound of a truck engine coming over the hill, coming fast—too fast.

It had to be Storm.

"Please, God…if You're there, keep me sane."

He stepped out of the ditch and into the middle of the road, then took aim.

Storm was in a panic. Everything was going wrong. The brothers were out of control. He'd been about to send them home when they'd pointed out the bird in flight. Something had startled it from its roost, and while it could have been almost anything, at this point, he couldn't afford to take chances. He'd left Danny and Porter to themselves as he headed into the woods.

Once he'd broached the tree line, he'd been appalled by the number of dead animals. They were everywhere. All sizes and all species. From insects to birds to the warm-blooded mammals, they had all become infected.

"Oh, shit," Roland muttered. He'd been in the act of abandoning his search when he'd seen the first footprint. Then he'd seen another and another.

They were too small for a man, and there were no children on this side of the mountain. Then he noticed a distinct pattern in the steps. There was a step, then a drag mark—a mark that someone who walked with a limp might leave. A someone like Ally Monroe.

He didn't know where she was, but he would lay odds that she'd seen enough to ruin him. He thought about trying to catch her. She was lame, so he could easily outrun her, but she had that ATV. Last time he'd been right on top of her and she'd still eluded him. It wouldn't happen again.

He turned and started running for the house. He didn't notice that the Monroe brothers were no longer in the field, although his tractor and trailer were still there. He was too focused on getting to his truck and catching Ally. It was time for some damage control, and she was the first that had to go down.

Roland jumped in the truck and reached for the keys. They were missing. He slapped the steering wheel.

"Fuck! Fuck! Fuck!"

He jumped out of the truck and ran through the front door just as Danny and Porter went out the back. There was an odd scent inside the house, but Roland didn't take time to investigate. He had to stop Ally before she gave him away. He grabbed the keys from the dining room table and ran back outside. Anxiety made his long, jerky stride even clumsier than normal. Yards from his truck, he stumbled.

"Oh, n—"

Impact knocked the air from his lungs. For a few agonizing seconds he couldn't draw breath, then, when he did, it was a huge gulping gasp that ached all the way down. He rolled over on his back and stared up at the sky while his lungs reinflated in painful increments. As the pain began to ease, he absently noted a thin pillar of smoke drifting from south to north, then realized he'd lost the keys. He rolled to his hands and knees, and started a search.

One minute passed, then a second and a third, before he saw them hanging from the lower branches of a crepe myrtle bush.

He crawled over to the bush and grabbed the keys, then stumbled to the truck. When he jammed the key in the ignition, he smiled grimly as the engine fired.

Finally.

He put the truck in gear and spun out of the driveway, leaving a trail of flying debris and rocks as he went.

Above the trees behind his house, the thin pillar of smoke became thicker and darker, and at the base of the column, the fire that fed it began to spread. The first drying shed caught fire. Flying embers spread the fire to the second shed, then the third. As it burst into full flame, more embers drifted from the shed to the roof of the house. When the fire finally burned through the roof and dropped into the house below, the diesel fuel that Porter had tossed throughout the house ignited. Fed by the oxygen within, the fire rolled along the ceiling as if it was being sucked from room to room.

Beyond the house, the field was also aflame, the fire blessedly cremating everything in its path. When it reached the old tractor, the tires began to smolder as the rubber grew hotter and hotter. Suddenly the smoke turned to flame. Soon after, the fire reached the gas tank, and the old tractor blew, but Roland was too far away to realize what Danny and Porter had done.

He'd lost precious time in going back for the truck, then losing the keys, but now that he was speeding down the road, he began to regain mental control. There was no need to panic. One crippled woman would not be hard to find, and as much as he regretted the task, he would put her down just as he'd put down her uncle.

Roland tightened his grip on the steering wheel as he took a slow breath, making himself calm down while he concentrated on his driving. The drying ruts made it difficult to go fast, but he figured that Ally Monroe would have suffered a similar fate, so she couldn't be all that far ahead.

As he topped the hill just above the old Brown house

and started down the road, someone stepped out of the ditch and onto the road. He started to honk to wave him out of the way when he realized that the someone was Wes Holden and he was carrying a rifle—a rifle that was aimed directly at him.

At that point, every rational thought in his head went into meltdown. While he was trying to decide if he should hit the brakes or the accelerator, the first shot hit the passenger side of the windshield. It shattered like an icicle on a cold winter morning, leaving tiny chunks of glass all over the front seat and in his lap.

He hit the brakes as the second shot hit a headlight.

He started to scream.

"Stop! Stop, you crazy bastard! What are you doing? Do you know what you're doing?"

He watched Holden widen his stance as he braced for the next shot.

"I warned you!" Wes yelled. "I told you to leave her alone."

"I didn't touch her!" Roland screamed. "If she says different, she's lying."

Wes shot out the other headlight and took some satisfaction in the sudden hissing of steam that began to spew out from under the hood.

"Oh shit, oh hell, oh damn," Roland muttered. "The bastard is crazy. He's fucking crazy."

He slammed the truck in Reverse and stomped on the gas. The tires spun, seeking traction. Wes shouldered the rifle again.

Roland hit the brakes and put the truck in Park as he bailed out on the run. The way he figured it, his only chance was to get out of sight, and disappearing into the trees was his best bet.

Roland hit the woods and started running. Not once did he stop or take the time to look back. He ran until his chest hurt and his legs felt like rubber, and then, too weak to run anymore, he crawled into a natural indentation in the side of the hill and pulled some brush in over him.

He lay curled up in a fetal position with his hands over his head, while the blood hammered against his eardrums. And as he lay, listening for the sound of running feet, he thought he smelled smoke and remembered seeing that thin gray column rising up into the sky.

What if the mountain was on fire?

Sixteen

Wes watched Storm disappear into the trees and thought about going after him. But he was afraid that if he began a game of cat and mouse with the man on his own turf, Storm might be able to double back before Wes could catch up, and that would put Ally in harm's way. He'd already left her alone too long.

Reluctantly, he lowered the rifle to his side and headed back to the house, but this time, there was no confusion as to where he was. He kept remembering Ally as she'd come out of the trees, with her hair flying out behind her, remembering the way she'd felt in his arms, the tremble in her body, the warmth of her breath against his neck.

Damn it, he didn't want to feel this—but he did.

He ran all the way back to the house, then ran inside, calling her name as he went.

* * *

Ally had heard the shots, but it was the silence that had come afterward that frightened her most. If the shooting was over, then why didn't Wes come back? The longer she waited, the more terrified she became.

Finally she thought she heard someone at the front door, and when it opened abruptly, hitting the wall with a thump, she tightened her grip on the knife and got up. She was bracing herself for a fight when she heard Wes calling her name.

She dropped the knife and shoved the pantry door open.

"In here," she called, and stumbled out of the pantry into his arms.

He leaned the rifle against the wall, then pulled her close, wasting precious minutes of their getaway time just to assure himself she was okay, and Ally obviously felt the same. She began running her hands over his body and touching his face to reassure herself that he was whole.

"Are you all right? I heard shooting! Oh, Wes, I've never been so scared."

Wes looked down at her then, and for the first time allowed himself the pleasure of the woman in his arms. Her hair was heavy on his arms as he steadied her against his chest, and even with the scratches on her face and arms, and the blood on her shirt, she was soft and beautiful—so beautiful it made him ache. Then he shook off the thought and set her down.

"We've got to get out of here," he said.

"What's happening? Was that Storm?"

"Yes. I don't know what the hell you saw up there, but he's doing his best to make sure you don't tell."

"I don't know what he's growing, but I think it's very dangerous."

"How so?"

"There are dead animals everywhere, and something is wrong with Danny and Porter. They were acting as if they were drunk or crazy or a little of both. They were fighting, and Danny was bloody, and—"

"Damn it," Wes muttered. "I guess it could be anything from bio-terrorism to a new designer drug. At any rate, we've got to leave before he comes back."

Ally moaned, then threaded her fingers through her hair, combing it away from her face in frustration.

"This can't be happening," she said.

"But it is. Can you walk?"

She pointed down at her ankle. He saw the telltale bruising and swelling, and dropped to his knees. After a quick inspection of the muscles and tendons, he stood back up and grabbed his rifle.

"I'm sorry. I didn't know it was that bad."

"What are we going to do?" she asked. "I can't walk fast enough to keep up with you."

"You won't have to," Wes said, then turned around and squatted down. "Get on."

"You can't carry me," she argued. "I'm too heavy."

"I've carried heavier men who were dying a lot farther than the two miles to your house."

At that point it seemed futile to argue. She crawled up on his back, wrapping her arms around his neck and her legs around his waist. He grabbed her legs, holding them firmly as he stood, then tightened his grip on the rifle.

"Hold on to me, and don't let go."

"Okay," Ally said.

Wes hurried to the door, pausing only long enough to make sure Storm was nowhere in sight. Then he saw the smoke.

"Something's burning," he said. "Something big."

"Oh, my God," Ally said. "Despite that rain last week, this state is in the middle of a drought. The mountain will burn like paper."

Now there was a new danger behind them. Wes took off down the path that led to Ally's house, moving as fast as he could, aware that time was of the essence.

Ally buried her face against the back of his neck and hung on, knowing that their lives were teetering in the balance of a madman's plans. She wouldn't let herself think of what was happening to her brothers, or if they'd gotten caught in the fire. They knew the mountains like the backs of their hands. She had to trust that they would find a way to stay safe.

The mill where Gideon worked always closed at noon on Saturdays, but he'd had to stay late to help unload a load of logs. Afterward, he'd gone to Kathy's Café and gotten himself a burger and fries before heading home. His joints were aching, and he felt like he was getting a crick in his neck. It wasn't the first time lately that he'd thought about retiring. Lord knew he was past the age. He could apply for social security and take it easy for the rest of his life. But he wasn't sure how satisfied he would be by staying home alone, so he shelved the notion again.

He was almost home before he saw the smoke, and when he did, chills ran up his spine. It had been years since they'd had a fire on the mountain. This one looked huge, and Ally was all alone. Anxious to get to her, he stomped on the accelerator.

He was sliding to a stop in front of the house when he saw Wes Holden come running out of the trees, carrying Ally on his back. He jumped out of the truck and ran toward them. When he saw Ally's condition and her swollen ankle, he felt sick.

"Ally...honey...what happened?" he cried.

"Roland Storm is after her. Help me get her in the truck!" Wes ordered.

Gideon quickly ran back to the truck and opened the door. When Wes slid Ally into the seat, he accidentally bumped her ankle, causing her to cry out in pain.

"Oh, hell, oh, Ally...I'm so sorry," Wes said, and then he grabbed Gideon's arm. "I need to use your phone, then we've got to get out of here."

Gideon unlocked the front door for Wes. "By the chair," he said, pointing to the phone.

Wes quickly dialed the operator.

"This is an emergency," he said. "Get me the local office for the DEA in West Virginia, and hurry."

Gideon frowned. "Damn it, man, you need to be calling the fire department, not some government office."

"Go talk to Ally."

Gideon frowned, then ran back to the truck. Wes watched the expression on the old man's face as she began to explain; then his own attention shifted when his call was answered by a woman with a calm, businesslike voice.

"Drug Enforcement Agency, how may I direct your call?"

"I need to talk to the director, and hurry. This is an emergency."

"I'm sorry, sir, but—"

"Connect me now, damn it."

There was a long moment of silence; then Wes heard a buzz in his ear. At first he thought she'd disconnected him; then he heard a man answer.

"This is Mitch Collins. Start talking, and it better be good. I don't take kindly to people bullying my employees."

"Sir, I'm Colonel Wesley Holden, Army Special Ops. I'm on a mountain above a little town in West Virginia called Blue Creek. I need people from your office, as well as from the CDC, here as fast as you can get them, and probably the FBI, as well. There isn't time to explain everything now, but I believe we've got some kind of new drug being grown here, or some form of bio-terrorism being planned. We've got a whole bunch of dead animals in and around the place where the crop is growing. I don't know how they're connected, or even if they are, but I've got a bad feeling about this."

"Tell me your name again," the director said.

"Colonel Wesley Holden, Army Special Ops. Call the commander at Fort Benning, Georgia, for verification. Tell him I'm up and running, and that I'm serious as hell." Then he added, "And hurry."

"Do you have a number where I can reach you?" Collins asked.

"No. Due to a forest fire, we're evacuating this place as soon as I hang up. Call the local authorities in Blue Creek. They'll give you directions."

He hung up, then made a run for the truck.

Gideon was pale and shaking, and Ally looked as if she'd been crying. Wes shoved the old man into the seat between himself and Ally, then got behind the wheel.

"Hang on," he said. "This might be a rough ride going down."

"Did you call the fire department?" Gideon asked.

"No."

Ally stared. "Why ever not?"

He pointed. "Look at it," he said. Flames were licking above the treetops less than a mile away, and smoke was billowing up in the sky. "Remember what you saw up there?"

Ally frowned; then suddenly she understood.

"The fire…it will kill whatever is killing the animals, won't it?"

"We can hope," Wes said. "But we can't send men up there to fight that, knowing there could be something that would put them in far worse danger."

"Dear Lord," Gideon said, and then covered his face with his hands. "My sons."

Ally's chin quivered, but she wouldn't let herself cry. Instead, she looked at Wes.

"Get us out of here," she said.

Wes yanked the truck into gear and hit the gas.

Halfway down the mountain, they met the fire crews heading up. Wes braked to a halt and briefly explained enough to the fire chief and his crew that they turned around and headed back down to Blue Creek in a hurry.

Wes put the truck back in gear and followed them, driving as fast as he dared.

Ally was so scared she felt sick. Her father had aged years before her eyes. He seemed small and shrunken as he clung to her and cried.

"Wes?"

He answered without taking his eyes from the road. "What?"

"What's going to happen to us?"

"Nothing," he said. "I promise you that."

"What about my brothers? What about Storm?"

"God only knows," he muttered.

She leaned over her father, holding him closer and tighter as the miles sped by. Suddenly she saw the road leading to Granny Devon's house. They were past it before she could speak.

"Stop, Wes. Stop!"

He slammed on the brakes, sending the truck into a sideways skid. Smoke was bearing down on them in thick clouds, loaded with tiny flying embers.

"Granny Devon! Her house is just up that road. She'll die if we don't get her out!"

Wes wouldn't let himself look at how close the fire was behind them. Instead, he slammed the truck into Reverse and backed up to the driveway, then shifted into Drive and raced up the road.

The smoke was seeping into the cab of the truck now. Gideon started to cough. Ally grabbed the handkerchief from his back pocket and put it over his face.

"Here, Daddy, breathe through this," she said.

He clutched it against his face, and then slumped forward.

There was a muscle jumping at the corner of Wes's mouth as he struggled to speed on an unfamiliar road, and he kept feeling uncertain as to whether this was really happening or was part of his past.

"How much farther?" he asked.

"There!" Ally cried, and pointed through the smoke. "It's there!"

Wes barely missed the porch as he braked to a swift stop.

"Wait here!" he said, and jumped out on the run.

Within seconds he was gone, swallowed up by the

smoke. Ally couldn't see him, and the only thing she could hear was the roar and crackle as the fire jumped from treetop to treetop.

Just when she thought they were going to die, Wes appeared out of the smoke carrying the tiny woman in his arms.

Ally opened her door and held out her arms.

"Give her to me!" she cried. "She can sit in my lap."

Wes dropped Granny Devon inside and slammed the door on the run. The fire was so close that the skin on his face was starting to burn. His hair was singed, and the metal studs at the seams in his blue jeans were so hot they were burning his skin.

Granny Devon's voice was faint, and her body was trembling. She leaned against Ally for strength, as well as comfort.

"What's happening, Ally girl? I smell smoke."

"Forest fire, Granny. The mountain is on fire."

"Oh, Lord, poor Mr. Biddle. Thank you for comin' to get me, darlin'. I surely would have died."

"We're not out of danger yet," Ally said as Wes slid into the seat, turned the truck around and once again accelerated through the smoke. This time he was driving almost on instinct, because the road was barely visible. Once he ran into the ditch but quickly backed out, and twice he narrowly missed hitting a tree. Just when he thought they were done for, they emerged from Granny's drive, back onto the main road leading down to Blue Creek.

A wind was starting to blow, pushing the fire in a more easterly direction, which would bring it directly down their backs.

Granny shifted nervously in Ally's arms. Even though she couldn't see what was happening, she felt the power of the blaze, as well as Wes's erratic driving.

Ally tightened her grip on Granny's waist with one arm and held her father steady with the other as she looked at Wes. His shoulders were tensed, and he was holding on so tight to the steering wheel that his knuckles were white.

"Wes, are we going to get out of this?"

"I won't let you die. I swear." Then he suddenly swerved and cursed softly.

"What happened?" Ally cried.

"The wind's shifted. Hold on!"

He pounded the gas pedal all the way to the floor. Now they were going so fast that Ally thought they'd gone airborne. Sweat ran out of Wes's hair and into his eyes, momentarily blinding him. Blinking rapidly and ignoring the salty sting, he sped past a wild-eyed doe and her fawn. Their backs had been singed, and their tongues were foam-flecked and hanging out the sides of their mouths as they ran.

"Oh, God," Ally whispered, then looked away. Those poor animals were already dead and just didn't know it.

Up ahead, a tree at the side of the road began to crack, teetering from the pressure of fire and wind. Wes saw it swaying and knew it would be close if they made it past before it fell.

"The tree!" Ally screamed.

"It'll be all right," Granny said, and grabbed hold of Ally's hand.

She was right. They sailed past the tree mere seconds before it fell, blocking the road behind them. But they were safe, and yard by yard they drove out of the smoke, then, finally, away from the fire. When they finally reached the river for which Blue Creek was named, they knew they were safe.

Blue Creek Bridge had been built during the WPA days following the Great Depression. The iron spanning the wide, shallow river was rusty red and in need of painting. The creosote-treated lumber that had first made up the bridge bed had been replaced several times over the years, and stood up well to the wear and tear. But today, as Wes sped across it, the planks rattled long and loud. He'd been struggling to stay focused on reality ever since the smoke had caught up with them, but that sound was, in Wes's mind, so reminiscent of machine gun fire that he actually swerved and ducked.

Ally had been watching him, and when she saw his expression change from intent to distracted, she grabbed at his arm.

"Wes! Wes! We made it! We're across the bridge."

Her voice yanked his focus back in place, but it was her touch that settled the moment of confusion and panic. He shook his head slowly, as if shaking off a bad dream, then began to tap the brakes to slow down.

A dozen men were gathered just beyond the bridge. Wes recognized them as the firemen he'd turned back. When one of them hailed him, he braked to a stop. It was his boss, Harold, from the feed store. Harold leaned into the window and grabbed hold of Wes's arm.

"Wes…you don't know how glad we are to see you people, and thank God you got to Granny." Then he looked back up the mountain and frowned. "Where're Danny and Porter?"

Gideon moaned and covered his face.

"We don't know," Wes said, then added, "We need a doctor."

Harold turned to the man beside him.

"Is Doc Ferris still over at Kathy's Café?"

"Yeah."

"Go get him, will you? Gideon don't look too good." Then he noticed the blood on Ally's face and clothes. "Good grief, honey. Someone get Granny Devon out of Ally's lap. Looks like she's in need of a doctor, too."

Granny Devon patted Ally's hand.

"She's gonna be just fine, but I would appreciate it if someone would take me to my niece Charlotte's house. She's probably worried half to death."

Wes jumped out of the truck and raced around to open the door beside Ally. As he leaned in to lift Granny out of her lap, their gazes met.

For a moment, Ally felt as if time stopped. She could

see her reflection in the pupils of Wes's eyes and a streak of ash on the side of his cheek.

His expression softened as his gaze slid to her mouth, but when he saw her injuries up close, he frowned again. Then he remembered what he was supposed to be doing, and lifted Granny up and out.

"Easy does it, ma'am," Wes said. "Ally, watch her head for me, will you?"

"Yes, of course," Ally said, and helped ease the little woman out of the cab. "Take care, Granny," Ally called as they led her away.

Dr. Ferris appeared, took one look at the occupants inside the truck and frowned.

"I think we better get Gideon to the hospital, and we need to get those scratches on Ally's face cleaned up."

"Lead the way," Wes said, and got back into the truck and followed the doctor to the small country hospital.

As soon as they pulled up to the emergency room door, a nurse emerged with a wheelchair. Wes helped Gideon into the chair, then the nurse wheeled him into emergency, while Wes followed behind, carrying Ally. They put Gideon in a bed in one curtained area and Ally a short distance away in another.

Ally winced as she settled back against the pillow, then a nurse appeared.

"Hey, Marsha," Ally said.

Marsha had known the Monroe family all of her life and was obviously concerned by their condition.

"Hello, honey," she said. "What on earth happened to you and your daddy?"

"We got caught in the fire," Ally said.

Marsha gave Wes a curious look, but when he chose not to speak, she turned her attention to the job at hand. When she began to remove the shoe on Ally's injured foot, Ally bit her lip to keep from crying out in pain.

"That sore, honey?"

"Yes."

"Sorry. The doctor will be with you shortly."

"Yes, all right, but could you tell me how Daddy is doing?"

"We'll know something soon," Marsha said.

Wes watched the nurse as she poked and prodded at the bruising and swelling on Ally's foot and leg. Then, when she gave a slight twist to the foot and caused Ally even more pain, he grabbed her arm.

"That's enough," he said.

Marsha frowned. "Sir, I need to ask you to go sit in the waiting room."

"No."

Marsha was more than a bit taken aback. She'd had people argue with her before but never had one flatly refuse.

"I'm sorry, sir, but you can't—"

"You're hurting her unnecessarily," Wes said. "X-ray her foot or leave it alone."

Ally gave Wes's hand a quick squeeze.

"Marsha is just doing her job," she said softly.

The frown on Wes's face just got deeper.

"I didn't say she wasn't," he muttered. "I just told her to do it better."

Marsha laughed in spite of herself. "It's all right, honey. He's sort of right, you know. We poke and prod on so many people, we often forget there's pain behind the reason they're here. Just rest easy. Someone will be down in a bit to take you to X ray."

Wes watched until she was gone, then turned back to Ally. She looked so small and hurt, lying there on the bed. And he kept remembering the fear on her face when she'd come running out of the trees. He laid the back of his hand against her cheek, taking care not to touch the scratches.

"What did he do to you?" Wes asked.

Ally shuddered. The look in Wes's eyes was deadly.

"He never touched me," she said. "But not for lack of trying. He was chasing me. The ATV ran out of fuel. I pushed it off the road and started running." Then she grabbed Wes's hand. "Thank God you were home."

"What the hell were you doing up there? I told you he was stalking you. You had to know it was dangerous."

His anger fueled her own. She rose up on her elbows.

"Family matters to me," she said. "You didn't see how Porter and Danny had been behaving. They were scared of what was up there, and yet they went back. I had to know why."

Wes frowned. "Scared…how do you mean?"

Ally shuddered. "I don't quite know how to explain,

but you didn't see them. The first day they worked for him, they came home in a terrible mood. It was like they were mad at each other and everyone else, which is just not normal for them. And their clothes... Porter wouldn't let me touch their clothes. They stripped off outside and put them in the washer, and then he told me not to touch them—ever. Every day they were there was worse than the last. Then today, when I got to Storm's property, they were like crazy men, slapping at themselves, and digging at their eyes as if they were trying to rip them out of their sockets. There were insects crawling over them like some God-driven plague, and then they were fighting. It was awful. They never fight. Not physically—ever. And there were the animals."

"The dead ones?" Wes asked.

"Yes. They were everywhere. Skunks, raccoons, squirrels, deer, birds, everything. But nothing was eating them. They were just there...rotting."

She covered her face. "I can't explain it, but I think the Devil is on the mountain."

Wes's gut knotted. He'd felt the same thing the night he'd snuck onto Storm's property, but he hadn't been able to put it in words. Ally had.

Ally clung to him again. "I'm afraid...for my brothers...for us...for everyone." Then her face suddenly crumpled as tears spilled down her face.

"What?" Wes asked.

"Buddy. I just remembered him. He was such a good dog. He didn't deserve such a terrible end."

"Yeah, death hardly ever announces its arrival."

Immediately, Ally realized what she'd said.

"Oh, Wes, I'm so sorry. Here I am moaning over a dog, when you lost your whole family. Forgive me for being so insensitive."

"No. Don't do that," he said.

"Do what?"

"You can't measure regret and sadness against whose loss is the greater. Grief is part of healing, or so I've been told. I do know this. You have to grieve for what you loved, so it seems okay to me to be sad about Buddy. He was a really good dog."

Ally leaned toward him and closed her eyes. "I'm so scared."

She spoke so softly, he almost didn't hear. He scooted onto the side of the bed and put his arms around her.

"I won't let anything happen to you," Wes said.

Ally slid her arms around his waist. "I'm sorry, Wes Holden."

"For what?"

"For delaying your journey. If I hadn't offered you my house, you would have been long gone and free of this awful mess."

"My life was already a mess before I got here," he said. "Knowing you has made it better."

Ally shivered. She'd come close to dying today, and she knew if she didn't say what was in her heart, she would regret it for the rest of her life.

"It wasn't just kindness that made me offer you a place to stay."

"What do you mean?"

"This is going to sound crazy, but after what we've been through, leaving it unsaid is even crazier. All my life, I've had the same dream. I used to imagine that a stranger would come walking out of the trees behind the house and into my life. Just like you did. When I saw you, I thought you were nothing but a manifestation of those dreams. You asked for a drink of water, just like in my dream, so you see, I had no choice but to offer you shelter, because I have been waiting for you to come."

Wes was touched, and yet so torn. She deserved so much, and what was left of him was hardly worth having. He felt as if he would be cheating her if he took advantage of her affection.

"Oh, Ally, I am so messed up."

"And I am falling in love with you," she said.

Wes took her in his arms. "What if I hurt you?"

"What if I die without ever having known what it's like to love a man?"

He stilled, his voice barely above a whisper as he laid a hand at her waist. "You've never been with a man?"

"No."

He willed his heartbeat to a slower rhythm and then leaned down. And while Ally was waiting for the rest of her life to begin, Wes kissed her.

Her lips were soft, but her will was strong. The salty taste of her blood was on his lips, and still he couldn't bring himself to pull away. It wasn't until he felt her hand at the back of his neck that he remembered where they were.

He tore himself away from the kiss, then held her face, staring long and hard into her eyes.

"Look at me," he said, and when she would have looked away in embarrassment, he said it again, only louder. "No. Don't turn away. Look at me. I'm all messed up in the head. Odd things trigger flashbacks that make me think I'm still at war. What if I hurt you?"

"Just think of what my life would have been like if you hadn't come. Roland Storm was already here, creating God knows what. My brothers would still have been working for him, and I would have done nothing different than what I've already done. But if you hadn't been here, I wouldn't have been able to outrun Storm or the fire. That's what would have hurt me. Not you."

Wes felt as if he'd just been kicked in the gut. She was right.

"Okay, but nothing matters right now but getting you and your father well, and finding a place to keep you safe."

"And finding out what happened to Danny and Porter."

Wes nodded, but it would have been very difficult, if not impossible, to get past the power of that fire. If they'd been caught in its path, there was no way they could have survived.

As Wes and Ally made their escape down the mountain to Ally's home, Roland was crawling out of the little indentation in which he'd been hiding. He'd smelled the smoke at the same time he'd taken cover, and after thinking about the smoke he'd seen earlier at his home, it made him nervous to be on the mountain without knowing what was going on. He knew the drought that West Virginia had been suffering would make putting out a forest fire extremely difficult, but he still couldn't see much except a little smoke over the treetops. The only thing that caused him much worry was that the smoke was moving in his direction. Anxious to see exactly what he was facing, he ran to the road for a clearer view.

To his horror, about a mile away was a rapidly approaching wall of smoke. As he stood, he thought he could hear the pop and crackle of the fire as it ate its way through the trees. At that point, he knew he was facing the tenuousness of his mortality. Without a moment of hesitation, he turned around and began to run.

His long legs covered the distance quickly, but he was sadly out of shape. The years he'd spent in labs had left his muscles soft and flaccid. Fear lent speed to his stride as he plunged headlong down the road, but before long he was winded and in serious pain. The muscles in his legs were racked by spasms, and there was a pain in his side that went all the way to his toes. He needed to stop—at the least to catch his breath—but rest was for the living, and unless he kept running, that wouldn't be him.

Within a few minutes the smoke was so thick he could barely see the road. The roar of the fire behind him was now a certain and constant presence. Tears ran freely down his face from the smoke and the heat, until finally, in fear, he began to cry in earnest. It wasn't fair. He didn't deserve to die like this.

Eventually he began to stumble, then his legs gave way completely. He dropped to the ground, choking and coughing, painfully aware that he was going to die. Down on his hands and knees, and with his back arched in protest, he began to hack. The sinuous strands of smoke slid easily down his throat, soaking up oxygen like a sponge and scalding the inside of his mouth. Then a gust of wind came, and for a brief moment Roland could see clearly in front of him. When he realized he was staring at the backside of salvation, he crawled to his feet.

It was his truck.

"Thank you, God," Roland muttered, and staggered the rest of the way to the truck.

The keys were still in the ignition, but after the way Wes Holden had shot it up, he wasn't sure it would start. His hands were trembling as he reached for the key. The engine sputtered once, then caught. The pistons began to pump, the engine revved, and except for the fact that one of Wes's bullets had hit the radiator earlier and it was without fluid, Roland had wheels. The truck was mobile, and that was all that mattered. He jerked it into gear and stepped hard on the accelerator. To his overwhelming relief, it began to roll, gaining speed with every foot. As he sped past the house where

Wes Holden had been staying, he smirked. Stupid man—he could have used this truck to get away. He hoped both he and Ally Monroe fried.

But his elation soon faded. The wind was pushing the fire closer and closer—the smoke was catching up. He tried going faster but the truck, minus a radiator and apparently empty of oil, he noticed, staring at the gauges, was beginning to seize. No matter how hard he pressed the accelerator, the truck wasn't responding.

When the smoke began to fill the cab, he started to wail, this time cursing the same God he'd thanked only minutes earlier. At that point the engine started knocking, as if reminding Roland of who was really in charge. That lasted exactly fifteen seconds and was followed by a sudden explosion.

The hood blew up, blocking what was left of Roland's vision. He tried to steer to a stop, but the wheels wouldn't respond. At fifteen miles an hour, it bounced through a ditch, tossing Roland up so high that his head crashed against the ceiling of the cab. When he came down, he hit the steering wheel with his chin. A few seconds later, the truck slammed into some trees, throwing Roland headfirst against the dash.

For a few moments the only thing he could hear was the ringing of his ears, and then something cracked and fell across the bed of the truck. Groggy from the impact and bleeding from his nose and chin, he saw nothing but fire. At that point he reached for the door. But the door wouldn't open.

In desperation, he crawled across the seat and tried to get out on the passenger side, but that door, too, was stuck—bent inward from the impact of hitting a tree.

"No, no, no!" he screamed, and began beating on the doors, trying to get out. "Help! Somebody help me!"

Again, fate intervened. A large limb suddenly swung loose and fell, moving with such force that it sheared off the hood, leaving him free to exit via the hole where the windshield had been.

Roland crawled through the opening and then fell off the fender onto the ground. He scrambled to his feet and began running, saved from the pain in his body by the adrenaline rush of being free. With visibility often less than a foot in front of him, he ran headlong through the forest, often running into trees. But each time he crashed into one, he somehow managed to get back up and keep running.

Now he could feel the heat on his back. When he smelled his hair starting to fry, he began to scream. His shoes were burning his feet, and the air was so hot it was scorching his lungs. The hideous roar of the fire was on him—the maw of the great blaze open and ready to swallow him.

It was over.

Still running in an all-out stretch, he lifted his arms to the heavens, expecting to be engulfed.

One second he was running, and the next thing he knew the ground had gone out from under him. He fell down, down through the air, windmilling his arms and legs as he fell, then landed abruptly with a splash. The blessed relief of water on his body was unbelievable.

He'd fallen into Blue Creek.

The river had saved him.

Still aware of the roar and the heat, he began to swim forward as fast as he could and didn't stop until he was as far from the bank as possible. He chanced one last look over his shoulder, saw the flames in the treetops reaching out to grab him, then held his breath and went under.

Danny and Porter were at the backside of the field they'd been harvesting, watching the fire as it began to gain ground. It didn't make sense that the green stalks would burn, but burn they did, finally bursting and overflowing, as if the sap inside had boiled over and spilled out.

Danny's head was hurting, and he felt as if his chest was about to explode. He kept grabbing at his ears, as if causing himself pain would alleviate the pressure, but it was to no avail. His sobs turned to gasps, and then to guttural growls. He could see the flames as the fire ate through the field, dancing, teasing, taunting him to follow.

"Fire," he mumbled, and pointed to its path. "Fire, fire, *fire!*" he screamed, as his eyes rolled back in his head and he fell to the ground in a fit.

Porter was on his knees behind Danny. He'd been vomiting for what felt like forever. The scent of the stalks had become a part of him—on his skin, on his clothes, up his nose. Between bouts of nausea, he would slap at himself, still fighting the ants that were all over him, crawling in and out of his ears and his mouth. He'd tasted them, even spat them out, and had torn off all of his clothing but his pants and shoes in an effort to get rid of the crawling little devils, leaving him bared to the hot summer sun.

Swept by another wave of nausea, his back bowed as his head dropped. Gagging and spitting until nothing more could come up, Porter passed out. When he came to, he was staring up at the sky. The sun was coming at him like a freight train, bearing down on the spot where he lay. He held up his hands to ward off the impact, then arched up off the ground in agonizing pain as it hit. The blood boiled in his brain, and the tree limbs above him were turning into snakes, rolling, coiling, then striking. He screamed in horror as one struck him, then he managed to crawl out of reach. Finally he sat up, and with no thought in his mind, began playing with the blood dripping from his nose.

Danny was spread-eagled among the smoldering stalks, mumbling Bible verses that he'd learned as a child as his clothes began to smoke. When his shirt suddenly burst into flames, he would have cremated himself where he lay if Porter hadn't grabbed him by the ankles and pulled him forward.

"Ants," he muttered, as he began pounding at Danny's shirt, slapping and yanking until he'd ripped it straight off his body. "Goddamn ants all over…stop the ants…no more ants."

The blood from Porter's nose dripped onto Danny's belly and face, but Danny was blind to the gore and numb to the pain. Blisters began coming up on his skin as he staggered to his feet and started walking in the opposite direction from the fire.

Porter stared at his hands, believing that the blood on his body had, like the ants, begun to crawl across his skin. In a panic, he began wiping them in the grass and all over his pants.

"Ants…got to kill all the ants."

Suddenly a crazed deer, burned and nearly blind from the fire it had barely escaped, came running across the smoldering field and followed Danny into the trees.

Porter's eyes widened as he stared after the animal, which appeared to be glowing.

"Going hunting…time to hunt."

For no reason, he pulled off his shoes, felt at his waist for the hunting knife he'd been using to trim the harvested stalks and moved into the trees at a lope.

Seventeen

The fire burned out when it reached the river. Because of Wes's warning, the local authorities had shut off access to the bridge. No one was allowed back up this side of the mountain until further notice. Trees were still smoldering at nightfall, and when true darkness came, the tiny fires up on the mountain looked like flickering red lights on a Christmas tree.

Dr. Ferris kept Ally in the hospital overnight for observation and, because Gideon's blood pressure was so high, admitted him into Intensive Care, convinced he was bordering on a stroke.

Wes took a room at the only motel in town, which was a good thing, because by sunrise, there were no parking spaces or rooms to be had. The government had arrived.

The FBI were on site, in case Wes's claims of bioterrorism proved to be true. The DEA had come in force, ready to stop the illegal growing and selling of drugs, and, as requested by Wes, two vans from the Centers for Disease Control were there, as well.

Wes woke up to a knock on the door. He rolled out of bed with a groan and pulled on his jeans, his nose rebelling at the smoke-scented odor.

He opened the door, then was forced to deal with a barrage of men in uniforms and suits. An army major chose to introduce himself first.

"Colonel Wesley Holden?"

"Yes, but now retired."

"Major Arnold Poteet at your service." He saluted Wes sharply, then nodded as Wes saluted back.

"Come in, all of you," Wes said, "but you'll have to excuse the state of my attire. It's been somewhat compromised."

"Spoken like a true military man," Poteet said. "I represent the commanding chief at Fort Benning. He sends his regards and asks that you call him at your earliest convenience."

"Thank you," Wes said, then eyed the other men as they stepped forward.

"DEA Agent Hurley."

Wes nodded.

"Agent Black, with the Federal Bureau of Investigation."

"Agent Black," Wes echoed.

"Dr. Christopher Shero, CDC."

"Dr. Shero," Wes said, then pointed toward the bed

and chairs. "Have a seat, all of you. I'll be back in a minute."

He grabbed his shirt on the way into the bathroom, washed his face and combed his hair with his fingers, pulled the smoky shirt over his head, then frowned at his appearance.

When he came back out, one more officer had been added to the group—a young lieutenant who was waiting with a cup of hot coffee.

"Lieutenant Williams at your service, sir. Major Poteet thought you might like some coffee."

Wes smiled. "Major Poteet was right. Thank you for the courtesy, Lieutenant. At ease, and find yourself a seat."

The young lieutenant took a seat near the door as the questioning began. DEA Agent Hurley was the first to begin.

"Colonel Holden, can you—"

"Please," Wes said. "For the sake of expediency, call me Wes."

Hurley nodded, then continued. "Without intending any insult, we're here mostly because of the credibility given to your concern from your commanding officer. We don't normally swarm like this without good reason, so what can you tell me?"

Wes sighed. "I understand, and trust me, the good faith is appreciated. What I'll tell you is what I know, then I suggest that you speak next to a Miss Ally Monroe. At present she's in the local hospital under observation. She has information pertaining to the investigation, but separate from mine."

"Noted," Hurley said. "So who is it you suspect is involved with illegal drugs?"

"A man named Roland Storm has a place at the top of the mountain, up the same road as where the fire began. For reasons I don't understand, he was instantly suspicious of my presence on the mountain. He tried intimidation, then stalking. I decided to reconnoiter on my own, and searched his home and property."

"Where was Storm during this search?" Agent Black asked.

"Asleep in the bed down the hall."

Black nodded as he made notes.

Hurley blinked, eyeing Wes with new respect as he turned to one of his subordinates.

"Vernon, run that name through the database, see if we come up with any hits."

Agent Vernon left the room as Hurley continued.

"What did you find in the house that made you suspicious of his activities?"

"Not much—until I went down into the basement. He had turned it into a lab, and from the looks of the setup, a pretty high-tech one, at that. It appeared innocent enough, until I found a large waste bin full of dissected rodents. However, my only motive at that time was just to find out a little about the man who was targeting me."

Hurley nodded. "Go on."

"What I did learn was that he was growing some

kind of crop in a field near the house. We later learned he referred to it as Chinese herbs he was growing for market. Right after I left the house, he woke up. Instinct, I guess. Ever since my arrival here in Blue Creek, he's taken offense and has basically been stalking me. So when I started walking back home that night, I heard a truck coming down the road behind me and knew it was him. I had to get back to my house before he got there and found me gone. It would have confirmed his suspicions that I was the one who had been in his house."

"So what did he do when he got there and found you gone?" Hurley asked.

"I made it back in time to answer the door."

Hurley shook his head, but his respect for Wes Holden's abilities continued to grow.

Then Wes added, "And then there were the dead animals."

At that point, Dr. Shero from the CDC interrupted.

"Are you referring to the dissected rats you had found?"

"No," Wes said. "Wild animals…indigenous to the area. Deer, birds, skunks, squirrels and the like. Miss Monroe will confirm this. She saw a lot more than I did, along with some distinct behavior and personality changes in two of her family members who'd gone to work for Roland Storm, harvesting his crop."

Shero frowned. "But what led you to believe that this was anything more than, oh, I don't know…illegal weed, for God's sake, and maybe some people using animals for target practice?"

"The animals weren't shot…nor had they been devoured in any way by their normal predators. As Ally described, they were just there…rotting, which is definitely not the way the food chain operates, and you know it."

"And were these animals found throughout the forest?"

"I couldn't say," Wes said. "The ones Miss Monroe saw were confined to the perimeter around Roland Storm's property."

Hurley pointed at Wes with his pen. "Why did you think this was more than weed?"

"Danny and Porter Monroe, who are Ally Monroe's brothers—and by the way, still missing—were offered five thousand dollars apiece from Roland Storm to harvest the crop and keep quiet."

"Okay, you've got my attention," the DEA agent said.

"I still have questions," Dr. Shero countered. "I don't see any correlation between illegal drugs and an out-of-control disease."

"Something killed all the animals. Something turned two loving brothers into madmen. Something incited the insect world to the point of mass hysteria."

Shero leaned forward. "The insect world?"

"Ask Ally."

"We'll do just that."

"And for the record," Wes said, "I've been in a lot of places and dealt with chemical warfare, but I wouldn't set foot up there without a full protection suit and a tank of air on my back. I don't know for sure what's there, but I don't want any part of it."

Shero nodded, then eyed the other men. "Gentlemen, if you're through here, then I suggest we adjourn to the hospital to question Miss Monroe before we make any decisions as to what we should do."

Agent Black stood. "For sure we want to talk to Miss Monroe, but your business and mine don't necessarily coincide."

Hurley nodded. "I already have enough suspicion to investigate drug activity…with protective gear, of course," he added to satisfy Wes.

Wes began pocketing his things and looking for his room key.

"I'll be going with you," he said.

"We would prefer to talk to Miss Monroe alone," Hurley said.

"Yeah, well, we don't always get what we want," Wes said. "I'm not going to interfere in any way, but I'm not having her be questioned as if she was the one who'd committed some guilty act, and before you get all pissy, you know that's how your mind works. If her brothers were involved, then in your mind, that makes her a guilty party, too."

Hurley's face turned a dark, angry red.

"Listen, mister, you can't tell me how to run my business."

"I don't give a shit about your business," Wes said.

"But I care about these people, and something bad was going on up there. I don't know what started the fire, or how high up it was when it started, but if there's anything left of Storm's property, I wouldn't touch it with a ten-foot-pole."

Major Poteet moved to Wes's side.

"Colonel, you've made your point, and I'm sure these gentlemen will agree that there's nothing wrong with you being witness to Miss Monroe's statement. We have no reason to assign blame."

"And we have no reason to feel guilty," Wes said. "Think about it, for God's sake. If we did, do you think we would have called the government in?"

"You've made your point," Dr. Shero said. "Just don't interrupt our interrogation."

Wes pointed at him. "That's exactly what I was talking about. There's not going to be an interrogation. She's going to give you a statement regarding her serious concerns about her brothers and what she witnessed. It nearly cost her her life."

"How so?" Hurley asked.

"Ask her for the details," Wes said. "But Roland Storm chased her down the mountain with evil on his mind, and if I hadn't arrived home when I did, she would have become a victim instead of a witness."

"So let's go see the woman," Agent Black said.

At that point they all filed out the door. Wes got in Gideon's truck and drove himself to the hospital with the others falling in behind.

Ally was sitting up in bed, braiding her hair, when he walked into the room. He didn't intend to do any more than say hello, but when her face lit up at the sight of him, he walked straight over to the bed and took her into his arms.

"Did you sleep well?" he asked.

Her expression fell. "No. I'm worried sick about Danny and Porter."

"I know, honey, I know." Then he took the braid out of her hands and began to undo everything that she'd done.

"Wes…what are you—"

"It's so beautiful down," he said softly. "How's your dad?"

His nimble fingers quickly undid the braid, and when he combed his fingers through the tresses to remove the separations, she shivered with longing.

"He's stable and improving."

Before Wes could comment, the government arrived. When Ally saw all the strangers, she frowned.

"Wes…who are these men?"

"Remember the calls I made at your father's house?" She nodded.

"They responded." Then he pointed them out in succession. "Agent Hurley, DEA. Agent Black, FBI. Dr. Christopher Shero, CDC. Major Poteet and Lieutenant Williams from Fort Benning. They want to ask you some questions about Roland Storm and your brothers. Okay?"

"Oh. Yes, gladly," Ally said, then scooted over so that Wes could sit on the bed beside her

"I'll just stand over here out of the way," Wes said.

She frowned but didn't insist, and the questioning began. She answered as best as she could but felt they were missing the point. Frowning, she finally interrupted Dr. Shero with a wave of her hand.

"Please…all of you…I don't think you're getting what I'm trying to say. May I just tell you what I know, and then you can ask specific questions later?"

Then, without waiting for them to give their consent, she began to talk.

"It began with my brothers looking for work. There's not much work around these parts, and Danny had just been laid off. He came home one day all happy because he'd gotten both himself and Porter a job. They were to harvest a crop of Chinese herbs for Roland Storm, and he was going to pay them five thousand dollars apiece. I didn't like it and said so, accusing my brothers of knowingly hiring on to harvest some kind of illegal drug. They denied it, but I think they both had their suspicions. It was at the end of their first day of work that everything changed."

She took a deep breath, then her voice started to shake. "Right now, we don't know if they're alive or dead."

"It's all right, Ally," Wes said. "They've seen tears before. If it makes you feel better, honey, then cry."

Dr. Shero scooted a box of tissues toward her, and Hurley pretended to check a spot on his shoe as they waited for her to regain her composure. Finally she was able to continue.

"As I was saying, the first night, when they came home, they were filthy. I've never seen anything like it in my life. And they'd stripped out of their clothes outside. You see, our laundry room is in a shed attached to the side of the house, so they had put their own clothing in to wash before coming into the house. I can't stress enough how unusual that was. Anyway, Danny wouldn't even speak, which is completely opposite to his personality, and Porter, my oldest brother, was angry, almost mean. He scared me."

She looked into each man's face as she continued.

"I've never been afraid of a member of my family…until that day. When I offered to wash their clothing, Porter turned on me. He was like a rabid dog. There was spittle at the corner of his mouth, his eyes were bloodshot, and the muscles in his face were twitching, as if he had some kind of facial tic. He yelled at me and told me never to touch anything they wore while working for Roland Storm. Then later, he said it again when I offered to get the clean clothes from the dryer. When I questioned him, he all but admitted he knew something was wrong, but he said that Danny wouldn't quit, and he wouldn't let his younger brother go back without him."

Hurley sighed. "Look, Miss Monroe, this is all interesting, but so far you haven't given me any concrete evidence to make me believe it was anything but some dealer growing weed. Your brothers' behaviors could have been nothing more than them coming down off a high."

His arrogance infuriated Ally. She swung her legs out from under the covers, giving them a perfect view of her injuries, as well as her crippled foot.

"My brothers do not do drugs. Besides that, after several days, their behavior changed to what I can only refer to as crazy. Before, they rarely ever disagreed with each other, but it got to the point where all they did was fight and snarl at each other. I was so upset and concerned for what they were doing that I snuck up to the property to see for myself. As you can see, I'm not exactly built for uphill hikes, so I rode an ATV partway, then managed about a mile walk to see for myself what was going on. A short distance from the field where my brothers were working, I began to find dead animals. Deer, squirrels, skunks, birds, you name it. It was as if they'd just dropped where they lay, only no carnivores had fed on the carcasses, and I can tell you, there are plenty of carnivores up in the hills. It was eerie. When I got to the field, my brothers were…frenzied. They were just walking around and tossing these long green stalks toward a flatbed trailer without paying attention to whether they landed on it or not. Danny was digging at his face and pulling at his hair and ears, and then he walked too close to Porter. Porter just turned around and punched him in the mouth and knocked out one of Danny's teeth. I saw him spit it out from where I was standing."

"Did they see you?" Hurley asked.

"Not then. It wasn't until I realized that Porter was

covered in ants that I cried out. There were thousands of them, crawling on Porter's face and arms and all over his clothes. He was slapping himself in the face and on the head. I was so horrified, I guess I cried out."

Then she sighed and looked at Wes. She could tell he was just as appalled as the other men appeared to be.

Dr. Shero stepped forward. "Your brothers…what did they do next?" he asked.

"My cry startled a bird in a tree above me. It flew out, and they saw it. I guess they figured something or someone had spooked it, and at that moment Roland Storm appeared. They pointed to the forest where I was hiding. I think he gave them some kind of orders, and then he started toward where I was hiding. I tried to run…but as you can see, that's not as easy for me as for some. I fell more times than I could count, but I made it to where I'd hidden my ATV. I would have gotten away, only it ran out of gas. Then I ran for my life, with Roland Storm in his truck right behind me. I made it to Wes's house and told him what was happening. Only he doesn't have a phone, so he carried me the two miles down the mountain to my house, and after I told him what I've just told you, he started making calls."

"What happened to Storm?" Hurley asked.

"I stopped him," Wes said.

Hurley frowned. "How?"

"I took a rifle and waited in the road for him. I could hear his truck coming over the hill. When he appeared,

I aimed at him. He didn't stop soon enough, so I stopped him."

"Did you hit him? Is he dead?"

"No…all I shot was the truck. He bailed out, and I sent him back up the mountain on foot."

Hurley's smile widened. "Okay…so you dispatched Mr. Storm for the moment, then went to Miss Monroe's home. What happened next?"

Ally resumed her story.

"My father arrived about the same time we realized there was a fire on the mountain. We started for town and almost didn't make it. Wes saved our lives, and here we are."

"Well, that's enough info for me to warrant an investigation," Hurley said.

"You'd better let my crew go in first and sweep the area to make sure it's safe," Dr. Shero added. "If there's some kind of contaminant up there, we don't want to spread it."

"What if it burned?" Wes asked. "Then wouldn't everything be safe?"

"Not necessarily," Dr. Shero said. "I'm uneasy about the dead animals, but I'm most concerned about the insects being involved. What Miss Monroe described is most definitely abnormal."

"What about fire ants?" Wes said. "They swarm on people."

"Yes, but they also sting. The way she described it, the ants were simply crawling all over the men in some kind of frenzy. If the men were being stung, they wouldn't have lived five minutes."

"Oh, Lord," Ally said, and pressed her hands to her lips to keep from screaming.

Wes moved to her side as Black added his two cents into the conversation.

"You were right to be concerned, but I'm going to have to ask you two to sit back now and let us work our investigations. If we have further questions, we'll be in touch."

Before they could leave, Agent Vernon came back and handed Hurley a computer printout.

At first Hurley only glanced at it, then suddenly he was muttering under his breath.

"What is it?" Wes asked.

Hurley looked up. "There may be something more to this after all. Among other things, Roland Storm is a geneticist. He has a background in chemistry and science, and was let go from Lackey Laboratories after some research project ended. He was picked up once for suspicion of making designer drugs for some dealer in Chicago but later released."

"May I see that?" Shero asked.

Hurley handed him the printout.

"I need to make some calls," Shero said, then glanced back at Ally and Wes. "We'll be in touch."

Everyone filed out, leaving Wes and Ally alone.

She started to shiver, then held out her arms.

"Get me out of here," she begged. "I don't want to be here anymore."

Eighteen

Wes drove up to the motel, then carried Ally inside. Her clothing reeked of smoke, and the scent made her sick. She'd seen the smoking black scar on the mountain as they'd turned toward the motel, and it had been all she could do not to tear her hair and wail.

She didn't have to ask to know that everything that had meant home to her was gone. Not only had she lost the house and the old family pet, but her father's recovery was shaky and her brothers' whereabouts unknown. The only constant in her life was Wes Holden, and although they'd known each other little more than a couple of weeks, it seemed like forever. They'd shared laughter and tears, as well as the depths of despair, and all she could think was, thank God he was here.

Wes touched the side of her face with a finger. "You got burned."

She lay back against the pillows, watching the expression on his face as he smoothed the hair away from her forehead, then fingered the strands spilling across the pillows.

"I'm filthy," Ally said. "So are my clothes."

"Hair will wash, clothes can be replaced," he said softly.

"When this is over, are you going to leave?" she asked.

A frown furrowed his forehead. "No, I'm not going to leave you."

Ally's heart skipped a beat. She had asked one thing. He had answered another.

"Wes…"

"I don't want to lose another woman I care for."

She closed her eyes briefly, letting his vow settle deep in her heart. It had been so long in coming, this loving of a man, that she didn't want to forget a moment of how she felt.

Then she felt his mouth on her lips and his hands on her waist. That was when she opened her eyes. She'd waited even longer for this day to come, and she wasn't going to blind herself to a second of it.

"Are we going to make love now?" she asked.

Her question hit him like a fist to the gut, bringing him to an instant aching need, and at the same time, scaring him half to death.

"I damn sure want to," Wes whispered.

"Why do I sense there's a 'but' in that answer?"

"Because my feelings for you are all mixed up with sadness and guilt."

Ally sat up, then began unbuttoning her blouse.

"What are you doing?" Wes said.

"Taking the problem out of your hands. Later, if you have to, you can tell yourself I made you do it."

Wes grabbed her hands.

"Wait."

Her expression fell.

"Let me," Wes said, and began to take off her clothes.

After that, it seemed time stood still.

Between slow caresses and hot kisses, he removed every piece of her clothing, leaving her trembling with need. Then when she was bare for the taking, he stripped, too, removing the last of the barriers from between them.

"I have no protection," he said.

"Nor do I," Ally said.

He sat for a moment, thinking of the consequences and weighing them against her virginity.

"We can stop this right now," he said.

She held his face between the palms of her hands.

"Never. From this moment on, whatever happens between us is God-given. There is nothing about you that I would refuse or regret, and that includes bearing your child."

Wes shuddered. The thought was breathtaking, but, at the same time, agonizingly painful. He would never see a child without thinking of Mikey.

Ally saw through his silence and gave ease to his pain.

"Wes."

He looked down into her eyes and saw salvation.

"What you had before was precious. Nothing will ever change that or the memories that you keep. I wouldn't want it any other way. I have no wish or intention of trying to make you forget any part of your past. I just want to be a part of your future."

"You already are," he said. "And I wish that what we're about to do wasn't going to hurt you."

"Mama used to say that the pain of first taking a man into your body was not unlike the pain of giving him your heart. She said it's all about trusting that he won't damage either one. I never knew what she meant until now."

"Do you trust me, Ally?"

"Forever."

"I wish to God I trusted myself."

"You won't hurt me, Wes. It isn't in you."

He covered her lips with his own, then sighed when her hands slid from his face to his back. It had been a long time since he'd been with a woman. In a way, it was a first time for both of them.

With exquisite torture, Wes kissed every morsel of skin on her body, even tracing the faint but healing scratches with the tip of his tongue. Her skin was satin to the touch and warm beneath his lips. Her breasts were heavy in his hands, the nipples peaked and swollen from the laving of his tongue. More than once, he slipped his hand between her legs and stroked her to a fever pitch, but each time he withdrew before it was too late. She'd waited a very long time for this day to come; he didn't want it to be over before it had begun.

They lost track of time. When she began moaning and clutching at his body, begging for something she had yet to know, he increased the pressure of his touch. Her breath began coming in shorter and shorter gasps, and she was beginning to buck against his strokes. He could feel the beginnings of her climax as her muscles trembled beneath his touch. Then, at the moment it took her, he rose up and slid between her parted legs. In one targeted stroke, he drove himself into the spiraling heat. Her body resisted, but only fleetingly as the barrier tore.

Ally cried out once as he claimed her, but then he began to move, and the climax crashed through her, emptying her to everything but the man. Blood pounded against her eardrums as her heart hammered within her chest. She had lost all sensation except in the valley between her thighs. Where she had been empty, now she was filled. She felt weightless and, at the same time, too heavy to move. When the spasms began to subside and she thought it was over, Wes rose up, braced himself with a hand on either side of her shoulders, slid a little deeper into her heat and began to rock.

When she realized he was still inside her—and he was hard and hurting in the same way that she'd been only moments earlier—she gave herself up to his need. She could see the tension in his muscles and the agony on his face as he chased that elusive mistress called lust.

Instinct led her to wrap her legs around his back, changing the angle of his thrust. Almost instantly, she felt a renewal in herself and began to rock her body against him, man to woman—heart to heart.

For Wes, it had been too long since he'd been with a woman for him to maintain any semblance of control. One moment he'd been riding the slowly building feeling, and the next thing he knew, she'd pulled him under. The sudden rush of blood from his head to his groin was instantaneous. He began to groan, spilling himself into her over and over until he was spent. Every muscle in his body was quivering as the echoes of their passion still held him where he lay.

It seemed like forever before he could move, and when he did, he took her with him until she was the one on top. He wrapped his arms around her, and began stroking her body and smoothing the long tangles of her hair away from her face. He could feel her trembling, then heard what sounded like a muffled sob. At that point, he panicked. He must have hurt her, and it was the last thing he had intended to do.

"Ally…sweetheart…I'm so sorry. I didn't mean to hurt you."

She shook her head, then raised her eyes to meet his.

"Wes, you didn't hurt me. I just… I never knew." Then she buried her face against his chest, a little embarrassed. "I'm so glad it was you."

He sighed with relief and held her a little bit tighter as he struggled to control his own emotions. With her trust and her love, she'd given him something precious, too—a new reason to live.

"Yes, honey, me, too," he said softly, then scooted out from under her and slipped into the bathroom.

Moments later, Ally heard the sound of running water. She rolled over onto her side, wincing from the pain in her ankle and the unfamiliar pain between her thighs.

The bathroom door opened. Wes came out, picked her up, kissed her soundly again, then carried her into the bathroom, where he was running her a bath.

"This will help take the soreness out of your body," he said.

She blushed but was grateful.

"Thank you," she said.

He stroked a finger against the side of her face, then handed her a clean washcloth and the motel's only bar of soap.

"No…thank you," he said gently. "Take your time. We've got all day to get some more clothes, and the rest of our lives to worry about everything else."

"Oh, Wes…the rest of our lives?"

A dark expression came and went on his face, then he managed a small smile.

"I am so falling in love with you, girl."

She wanted to cry from the joy of this moment, but instead she settled for the brief kiss he gave her as he left her to her bath.

Later, they had managed to get dressed and were

about to go in search of new clothing, when there was a knock at the door.

Ally's face went pale. She clutched her hands against her middle as if she was about to be ill, then looked to Wes for strength.

"What if it's news about my brothers?"

"There's only one way to find out."

Charlie Frame had been back at Fort Benning for almost a month and was still worrying about Wes. After he'd been sent Stateside from Iraq, he'd gone home to Tulsa to visit his family, making all the usual stops in his hometown to catch up on the news of the people who had formed the center of the universe when he was growing up. But once he'd returned to base, his thoughts had immediately gone to his friend.

As soon as he'd reported back for duty, he'd expected to find Wes out of the hospital, at the least, and hopefully moving on with his life. When he'd discovered that Wes's recovery had been nil, and that a stepbrother had arrived with power of attorney and checked him out of the hospital, he'd been stunned.

He'd tried to let it go, telling himself that it was just part of life, and that he and Wes had moved in separate directions, but he couldn't. Finally he requested a short leave of absence so he could head for Miami. He needed to see Wes one more time—just to satisfy himself that everything possible had been done for his best friend.

Now Charlie left his uniform behind and, with Aaron

Clancy's address in hand, arrived in Miami before noon, checked into a hotel and caught a cab. The first sign that all was not as it should be was when he arrived at the address.

The apartment building was in a less-than-desirable part of the city. The concrete around the area was covered in graffiti. The turquoise paint on the building was peeling off the outer walls, and there were bars on the windows.

"Wait here," he told the cabbie.

"Yes, sir… I will wait," the driver said, but he took care to lock himself in as Charlie exited the cab.

Charlie couldn't bear to think of Wes in a place like this and hoped that looks were deceiving. But when he got inside, the size of the cockroaches running up the walls was not encouraging. He checked the address one more time, then started up to the fourth floor, looking for 413.

Somewhere on the second floor, a baby was crying and a woman was screaming to someone else in Spanish. He sidestepped a yellow tomcat sitting on the stairs and got hissed at for his trouble before making it up to the fourth floor. Since it was still before noon on a Saturday, he was counting on Aaron having slept in and not being at work.

Once at the landing, he took a right turn and went four doors down before coming to 413. The scent of urine and cooking odors was stronger up here, and he'd already decided to beat the hell out of Aaron Clancy on general principles, and if Wes wasn't okay… Already pissed, he made a fist and hammered on the door.

At first, there was no answer.

He hammered on the door again, and as he did, some-one down the hall opened a door and yelled at him to be quiet. His response to the request was to beat on the door again, this time adding his voice to the noise.

"Aaron! Aaron Clancy!"

Finally he heard life behind the door as someone began cursing. Seconds later the door swung inward.

Charlie glowered at the whisker-faced, shaggy-haired man.

"Are you Aaron Clancy?"

"Who the fuck wants to know?"

"Wes Holden's best friend, that's who."

He pushed his way past Aaron and strode into the apartment. Immediately, his nostrils flared. The stench in here was worse than out in the hall, but he wasn't as concerned with Clancy's housekeeping skills as he was by the fact that there was no sign of Wes in this place. He turned around, fixing Clancy with a look that made the man's gut tighten.

"Where is he?" Charlie asked.

"Who? Where's who?" Aaron asked.

Charlie jabbed a finger hard against Aaron's chest. "You know who I mean. Where's Wes?"

Aaron shuddered. He'd gotten fired less than a week after Wes's disappearance and had been living high on Wes's money ever since. He'd made no attempt to find another job, but it looked like that was about to change.

"He's, uh… I had him put in a…a…hospital."

"Where? What's the phone number? I want to talk to his doctor. Now."

Aaron's mind was reeling. If he could just get this man out of his apartment, he would have time to make a getaway before he figured out he'd been duped.

"I don't have a phone number…just the name and address of the place."

"Tell me," Charlie said.

Aaron took a deep breath, and, as his daddy used to say, pulled a name out of his ass.

"Ten Palms Sanitarium on Sepulveda. Here, I'll write it down for you."

"Don't bother," Charlie said. "I'll call Information and get directions."

To Clancy's horror, Charlie strolled over to his phone and dialed Information.

"Operator…how may I help you?"

"I need a listing in Miami, Florida, for Ten Palms Sanitarium. I believe it's on Sepulveda."

Aaron began pulling on his jeans and looking for his shirt. He found one he'd worn a few days earlier and pulled it over his head, then put on his socks and shoes. When he reached for the doorknob, Charlie turned and pointed.

It was only his finger that Charlie pointed with, but it might as well have been a gun. Aaron knew he couldn't outrun him, and he couldn't beat him in a fair fight. What he needed was a weapon, but the only thing within reach was a throw pillow.

As Charlie waited, the operator came back on the line.

"I'm sorry, sir, but I don't have a listing for Ten Palms on Sepulveda or anywhere else in Miami."

"Thank you, operator," Charlie said, and carefully replaced the receiver. Then he smiled at Aaron.

Aaron began to relax. If the man was smiling, that must mean he was happy.

"You lying, sorry-ass son of a bitch, what have you done with my friend?"

Aaron groaned. People shouldn't be allowed to smile unless they meant it. He backed up, but not far enough. Suddenly the man had him around the throat, then slammed him against the door.

"Talk. And you better not lie to me again, you little bastard, or I will cut you in to tiny little pieces and flush your sorry ass down the toilet."

"I don't know where he is," Aaron said.

Charlie tightened his grip on Aaron's throat.

"It's true!" Aaron squealed, and began trying to pull free. "I swear. I went to work one day, and when I came home, he was gone."

"Are you telling me the truth?"

"Yes! Yes! I swear!" Aaron cried.

"What did the police say? Do they have any leads?"

Aaron began to whimper.

"Please…please let me go."

"The police!" Charlie shouted. "What did they say?"

"I didn't report it," Aaron said, and then burst into tears.

Charlie froze. "Why not?"

"Because the stupid bastard had been playing me, that's why! I thought he was out of it. You know. Wouldn't talk. Wouldn't feed himself. I sat him in a chair in the morning, and he was there when I came home. That went on for a almost week, and then one day I came home and he was gone. He'd taken all his clothes and the money out of my stash here at the house and disappeared. Hell…he was making everyone nervous here in the building. He did me a favor by running out."

Charlie was so angry he was shaking.

"Let me see if I understand this correctly. You checked your brother out of the hospital, got his power of attorney, dumped him in this shit-hole and banked his money without using it for his care. Have I missed anything?"

"It's not my fault he checked out of here," Aaron said.

"You're not following me," Charlie said. "If you are no longer caring for your brother, then why are you still cashing his checks?"

Aaron's face paled.

"I…uh…was just waiting for him to come back to—"

Charlie drew back and punched him in the nose. Blood spurted.

Aaron grabbed his face as he dropped to the floor.

"You broke my nose."

"Be glad it wasn't your neck," Charlie said, and dragged Aaron back to the phone.

When Charlie picked up the receiver, Aaron began to struggle, trying to get free.

Charlie yanked him off his feet with one hand, then tossed him into the corner of the room.

"Stay there," he ordered. "Don't talk to me, and don't move."

Aaron did as he was told.

Charlie dialed the operator; when the call was answered, his request was brief.

"Give me the police."

Aaron covered his face and groaned. He'd known it wouldn't last forever, but this wasn't exactly the ending he'd planned for.

A short while later, two officers arrived, took Charlie's statement and then dragged Aaron to his feet.

"What did I do that was so awful?" Aaron yelled as the officer handcuffed him. "Tell me. I didn't hurt anybody. This ain't right."

"Well, for starters, you've been defrauding the federal government for the better part of a year," Charlie said.

"I what?"

"You've been cashing retirement checks belonging to a military veteran. They frown on stuff like that."

Aaron groaned. "But it was all legal. I had his power of attorney."

"And you were also responsible for his care. You made your first mistake when you didn't report him missing, and I can tell you now, if anything has happened to that man, I will see you in hell."

Aaron shrank back against the Miami policeman and started to whine.

"You heard that. You're my witness. He threatened me with bodily harm."

The officer glanced at Charlie and then frowned.

"No. I didn't hear anything like that at all. All he said was that he would see you in hell. Now, I don't know what Mr. Frame's position on religion is, but I can swear to the fact that unless you change your tune, hell is right where you're headed."

Charlie had the satisfaction of seeing Aaron taken into custody, but he was even more concerned about Wes now than when he'd arrived. Then he remembered the cab driver he'd told to wait. He looked out the window. The good news was that he was still there. The bad news was that the meter was still running.

With a heavy heart, he took the next plane back to Fort Benning and reported his findings to the commandant, then went to the Officers' Club to drown his sorrows.

Two days later he was called back to headquarters, only this time with news he hadn't expected. Wesley Holden was not only alive and well, but ass-deep in big trouble in a place called Blue Creek, West Virginia.

"Sir…with your permission, I would like to go to—"

"I've already sent representatives on our behalf. Major Poteet and his assistant, Lieutenant Williams, are already on their way. However, considering your and Holden's history, I'm giving you three days to go satisfy yourself that he's okay."

Charlie grinned, then saluted smartly.

"Yes, sir! Thank you, sir."

"Dismissed," the commandant said.

Charlie called the airport from his cell phone as he hurried back to his house. Two hours later, he was on a plane. He needed to look into Wes's face and know that the man he called friend was okay.

Nineteen

Wes glanced back at Ally, making sure she was through dressing before he opened the door. Her foot was too swollen for her to wear a shoe, and her hair was still damp from her bath. She was a sad sight in her crumpled, soot-streaked clothes, yet beautiful in his eyes.

"You ready for company?" he asked.

She nodded.

Still, Wes hesitated, and Ally began to worry if he was regretting what they'd done.

"Wes?"

Emotion welled in Wes's heart. He'd just made love to her. They had not just "had sex." They'd made love. There had been a time not so long ago when he would have sworn that would never happen again. But then he'd met Ally, and she'd given him back his life.

"I love you, honey."

Her face crumpled. "Oh, Wes…I love you, too."

Another knock sounded.

"Hold that thought," he said softly, then opened the door.

There was a moment of stunned silence, and then a loud shout of laughter.

"It *is* you! By God, I've never been so glad to see anyone in my life!" Charlie Frame shouted, then gave Wes a bear hug of a greeting before looking intently into his eyes.

"It's you in there, isn't it, buddy?"

Wes grinned somewhat shamefacedly as he returned Charlie's hug. "Yeah, Charlie, it's me."

Charlie hugged him again, this time thumping him soundly on the back.

"I knew it! I knew you could do it. I knew you'd find your way back to us."

Wes finally managed to extricate himself from Charlie's grip, and as he did, Charlie saw the woman on the bed.

"Man, I'm sorry, I hope I wasn't intruding on—"

"No intrusion... Ally, this crazy man is my best friend, Colonel Charles Frame."

"Call me Charlie," he said, and walked over to the bed to shake hands. That was when he realized she was injured. He pointed to her foot. "That looks bad. Did you have an accident?"

"In a manner of speaking," Ally said, and calmly shook Charlie's hand. "I'm very glad to meet you, Charlie Frame."

Charlie was immediately taken with her gentle manner and sweet voice, but he couldn't help thinking of Margie.

When he turned around, Wes saw it on his face.

"Ally settled the pain," he said.

Charlie nodded, remembering Wes's condition when he'd left him. Looking at him now, he'd find it difficult to imagine him as anything but a man in control. He eyed Ally with new respect.

"You must be something special."

"What I am right now is a mess," Ally said.

"We got caught in the fire on the mountain," Wes explained. "Came too damned close to not making it out. Her father is in the hospital. Her brothers' whereabouts are as yet unknown."

Charlie's expression changed. He'd had no idea that the situation in Blue Creek had been so serious.

"Forgive me," he said. "I had no idea. I was just so focused on finding Wes that…"

"It's not your fault," Ally said. "You were justifiably happy to see Wes. I know the feeling. Seeing him strikes me the same way."

Charlie grinned. "Whoa, honey, you've got it bad, don't you?"

Ally looked up at Wes, then sighed. "Actually, it's just the opposite. I've got it good."

"You win," Charlie said. "Now tell me, Wes, what's the deal with the CDC and the DEA all over the place out there?"

"In a nutshell…there's a chance that a local 'mad scientist' has created some new form of bioterrorism, or just some drug that makes things go crazy."

Charlie's mouth dropped. "Here?"

"Up on the mountain," Wes said.

Before Charlie could question them further, the telephone rang. Ally was sitting right beside it. She answered on the second ring.

"Hello."

"Miss Monroe…this is Agent Hurley. Is Wes Holden there?"

"Yes. Just a minute please." She held up the phone. "Wes, it's Agent Hurley for you."

"Who's Hurley?" Charlie whispered as Wes took the phone.

"DEA," Ally said.

"This is Holden," Wes said. "What's up?"

"I'm asking you not to react visibly as I speak. I think it would be better if you didn't indicate to Miss Monroe in any way that we have some serious news regarding her brothers."

Wes felt as if he'd been sideswiped. He'd hoped against hope that they would have good news, but this didn't sound like it. Still, like Hurley, he didn't want Ally to suffer needlessly.

"Oh. I see. So what do you think?" Wes asked.

"I don't think. I know. We have a situation, and the sooner you get here, the better."

Wes nodded and smiled, then turned to Ally and winked, as if nothing was amiss.

"Sure. I can do that. Are you sending a car?"

"There's one already waiting. Oh…and don't worry about contaminants. We'll take care of that when you get here."

"Okay. See you shortly."

Then he hung up the phone and turned to Ally.

"Honey, I'm afraid shopping for new clothes is going to have to wait."

"Is it something about my brothers?" she asked.

He frowned, as if considering the conversation he'd just had, and felt horrible for lying.

"No. At least, I don't think so. Hurley didn't mention them by name. He wants to go over some of the details of my run-in with Storm again. I hate to leave you, but I shouldn't be long."

"I want to go with you," she said.

He looked at her foot and then frowned.

"You're in no shape for that, and you know it. You can't even wear a shoe, and with all those unhealed cuts and scratches, I don't think you should be anywhere around all that soot and debris. But if you don't want to stay here in the motel by yourself, I could take you to Granny Devon's niece."

Ally frowned. She didn't like the idea of being left behind, but she also didn't want to visit and chitchat when her world was coming apart.

"If you'll bring me a bucket of ice and a cold pop from the machine outside, I think I'd rather just stay here," she said. "I can watch TV and maybe catch up on the sleep I didn't get in the hospital last night."

"Good girl," Wes said. "I shouldn't be gone too long, and if I'm delayed, I'll call."

"I'll get the ice and pop," Charlie offered. "What's your poison?"

Ally grinned. "Anything brown. I'm not a big fan of the lemony-lime tastes."

Charlie hurried to run the errand as Wes kissed her goodbye, then, when he would have walked away, turned and kissed her again. Ally sighed with contentment. Despite having lost her home, if there could be good news about her brothers, she would consider her life about perfect.

"Wes?"

"What, honey?"

"You promise to let me know immediately if there's news?"

"Yes."

"Good or bad…I still want to know."

"It's a promise."

Charlie returned with two Cokes, a bucket of ice and three candy bars.

"Three?" Ally asked, as he dumped a Snickers bar, a Milky Way bar and a Butterfinger in her lap.

"Better too many than not enough," he said.

Ally grinned. "Bringing a woman chocolate in bed is dangerous stuff."

Wes grabbed Charlie by the arm. "Let's go before I have to fight you for my woman."

Laughter followed the two men out of the room. Ally settled back against the pillows with a cold can of pop and reached for the remote. After she'd chosen a station, she laid the remote aside and picked up the Milky Way.

"He called me his woman," she said, and then stifled a giggle. "I think this calls for a celebration." She tore the wrapper from the candy bar and took a big bite as *The Price Is Right* came back on air after a commercial and Bob Barker called for another contestant to "Come on down."

Once outside, Wes's demeanor changed. Charlie frowned.

"Something's wrong, isn't it?" he asked.

"Maybe," Wes said.

"I'm going with you."

"Then get in," Wes said, pointing to the van that was waiting near the office.

As they drove through Blue Creek, Charlie talked, and Wes mostly just listened. Everything Charlie was talking about was no longer as pertinent to Wes's world as it had once been. The politics of the military and war were understood best by those who'd lived it, and while he understood that life, he wanted no more of it. But there were things Charlie could tell him that he desperately wanted to know. He knew nothing of the days after the bombing, things that he needed to know.

As the driver crossed the bridge over Blue Creek, the planks rattled beneath the tires, and once again the sound reminded Wes of machine-gun fire. Unconsciously, his fingers curled around the edges of the seat as sweat broke out across his forehead. He made himself focus on the black burn scar on the mountain.

Charlie didn't know what had just happened, but he saw the change in Wes's expression and knew he was in trouble.

"Wes?"

Wes's gaze was fixed, his senses tuning out everything as images of the past threatened his hold on the present.

Charlie frowned, grabbing Wes's arm.

"Wes! Hey! Where did you go?"

Wes flinched, then shuddered as Charlie's insistence finally soaked through. He blinked, then took a slow, deep breath as he turned his gaze to his friend.

"What did you say?"

Charlie groaned. "Man, you're still battling it, aren't you?"

Wes had to think about what Charlie meant before he could answer.

"You mean the flashbacks? Hell, yes."

Suddenly all the crap Charlie had been rattling on about seemed trivial.

"I'm sorry, buddy. It's just that you looked so good standing there in that motel room that I forgot looks can be deceiving."

Wes shrugged. "It's all right. Mostly I do okay, but once in a while, something will trigger a memory and I lose it."

"Do you remember much about being taken prisoner?"

Wes's lips thinned as he looked away. "Enough."

"Sorry. End of questions, okay?"

"I've got some for you," Wes said.

"Shoot," Charlie said, and then grinned. "Sorry, poor choice of words."

"Where did they bury Margie and Michael?"

Again Charlie felt like a heel. He kept making jokes, and Wes kept breaking his heart.

"Margie's parents claimed the bodies. They buried them in the family plot in Savannah," Charlie said.

Wes thought it obscene that the only way to refer to his wife and child was in the past tense.

"That's good. Margie would have liked that," he said, and swallowed past the knot in his throat. "Did you go…? To the services, I mean."

"Yes."

"Thank you," Wes said, as the knot continued to tighten. "It's been over a year, and that had been bothering me…not knowing where—" Suddenly he stopped talking and shoved his hands through his hair to keep from hitting the back of the seat with his fist. God, but he hated this feeling of being out of control.

"So tell me about Ally," Charlie said. "She's really different…. From Margie, I mean."

"She makes me feel."

Charlie frowned. "Feel what, buddy?"

Wes looked at Charlie, surprised that he didn't understand.

"Anything…everything. There was a time when I couldn't." Then he changed the subject as they drove past the Monroe property. "That's where she and her family used to live."

The only things left were the concrete foundation and the steps that had led up to the porch. The rest was a pile of charred and smoking embers.

"Damn shame," Charlie said.

A couple of miles later, Wes realized that Uncle Dooley's house was still standing, but only because the walls were concrete and the roof was metal. The vines were all gone, but they would grow back. Ally would be glad to know the little house had survived.

"That's where I was living," Wes said, pointing to the little house.

Charlie smiled. "Sort of looks like a toadstool."

"It belonged to Ally's uncle, Dooley Brown. I'm thinking that he had a pretty good sense of humor."

"How so?" Charlie asked.

"Take a look at the house. What does it remind you of?"

Charlie glanced over his shoulder for one last look as they passed it by.

"Oh…I don't know…sort of like something from a Disney movie, or some miniature silo."

"Dooley Brown was a dwarf."

"You're kidding me."

"No. First two nights I stayed in that house, I kept bumping my chin on my knees when I tried to get out of bed. Everything is normal-size, but lower to the ground."

Charlie just shook his head. "Yeah, I get what you mean about the sense of humor."

At that point, the transmission in the van began to pull as the grade steepened.

"Heck of a long way up here," Charlie said.

"Not far enough," Wes said, as he thought of the evil and destruction Roland Storm had wrought.

When they finally reached the end of the road, it became obvious where the fire had started.

Storm's house was gone, as were the drying sheds and the barn. The field was a mass of charred stalks, with a burned-out tractor and trailer in the middle, like a bad metal sculpture on a plot of destruction.

"Lord…this looks like a war zone," Charlie muttered.

Wes got out without commenting. There was little to be added to the truth. Then he saw Hurley coming and braced himself for bad news.

"Mr. Holden, thank you for coming," Hurley said.

"This is my friend, Colonel Charlie Frame," Wes said, then frowned when he realized the DEA were in regular clothes. "No spook suits?" he asked, referring to the containment clothing the CDC often wore in zones hot with infectious diseases.

"Shero says it's not necessary. His people have only dressed out because they're taking samples all over the place. He also told us not to touch anything, which makes investigations hell."

"Then why am I here?" Wes asked.

Hurley pointed to Shero, who was sitting on the bumper of a van, reading what appeared to be a small book.

"To talk to him."

Wes walked over to the doctor.

"Must be a bestseller," he said.

Christopher Shero looked up, but there was no smile on his face.

"We found this in a metal box in what was left of Storm's lab."

"So what was he doing?"

Shero shook his head, then let the notebook fall shut.

"Ordinarily, I might try being a smart-ass and say he was trying to play God. But that's not exactly the case here."

"What is?" Wes asked.

"I don't quite know what to say," Shero said, then shivered. "My grandmother's favorite saying was 'Playing with fire will get you burned.' I'm not sure whether Storm knew what he was doing or if he created a monster he couldn't control."

Wes was beginning to get a sick feeling that had nothing to do with PTSD.

"For God's sake, Doctor, I'm not big on guessing games."

"And I'm not in the habit of playing them," Shero said. "But the scope of this is almost beyond me.

However, the proof, I guess, is in the pudding, or in this case, his lab notes. From what I can tell, I think he started out trying to grow some kind of high-tech, addictive hybrid plant. Hurley tells me that Storm was a master geneticist, so I'm thinking he was playing around with DNA and it mutated on him. Initially, he writes about the drug as if once used, it would forever hook the user, thereby assuring him of a never-ending market for his crop. But the last dozen pages indicate that something happened he didn't expect. The notes are scattershot, and his writing's messy, like he was distracted or upset. He says that the drug never dissipates from the body. It does all kinds of nasty things before the user dies a rather horrible death."

Wes didn't want to ask, but he had to know. "So how dangerous are we talking?"

"Let's just say it's good that everything up here was burned, or I'd need to be updating my will."

"Christ," Wes said, thinking of Danny and Porter. "What about the crop itself... I mean, before it was dried, or whatever the hell Storm did to it to make it marketable? What about someone who was hired to harvest the crop?"

"That's why you're here," Hurley said.

"Ally's brothers...what can you tell me?" Wes asked.

"If they're not dead already, they will be soon," Shero said.

"Tell me why," Wes said.

"The monster Storm created was more powerful than

even he expected. The worst of the drug was in the sap…the juice in the stalks."

Wes felt sick. "Ally's brothers were hired to harvest the crop."

"Did they wear protective clothing?" Shero asked.

"I don't think so," Wes said. "Remember Ally saying how crazy they acted about their clothing when they came home…not wanting her to touch it, before or after it was cleaned?"

"Then if Storm's notes are correct, there's no hope for them. Even if they survive the fire, which isn't likely, not only will they die, but they'll go mad in the process."

Wes thought of his own flashbacks and knew what it felt like to go mad.

"Mad…as in not knowing who they are…that kind of thing?"

"Well, according to Storm, the lab rats tried to kill one another, but since they were in separate cages, all they managed to do was chew off one another's paws."

Wes flinched, as if he'd just been punched in the gut.

"We've got to find them," Wes said.

"I have search teams out right now," Hurley said. "We should know—" Suddenly, his two-way crackled with static. "Agent Hurley…sir…this is Vernon. You need to come now."

Hurley keyed his two-way. "What's your location?"

"The edge of the field…south of the burned machinery."

"We're on our way."

"Sir…bring the doctor."

"Will do," Hurley said.

"Oh, and sir…hurry. For God's sake, hurry."

It had to be the brothers. Wes bolted past Hurley and started to run.

"Holden! Wait!"

"He isn't the waiting kind," Charlie said, and started after him.

Hurley waved some of his men forward as they hurried to Vernon's aid. Whatever was going on, it had sounded as if Vernon was rattled, and it took a lot to rattle the DEA.

The smell of the fire was still strong in the air. Wes knew it would take weeks, maybe months, and some good soaking rains before the land would even begin to heal. As he reached the field, he saw a group of men on the far side and headed for them at a lope.

He was less than thirty feet away when the group suddenly parted and Wes saw something on the ground between them. It took a few seconds for him to realize it was a man.

"Sweet Jesus," he muttered, and abruptly stopped.

Hurley and his men ran past more slowly, Wes followed. Upon his arrival, all the men in the circle began to talk at once. Wes wanted to look away but was transfixed by the horror.

Suddenly Charlie appeared and grabbed at Wes's arm.

"Son of a— Who is that, and what the hell happened to him?" Charlie asked.

Hurley turned toward Wes. "Is it one of them?"

"It can't be," Wes said.

"Damn it, man…we've got to know one way or the other."

Wes shuddered, then moved a step closer. As he did, the man looked straight up into the sun and then started to scream. When one of the agents reached for him, Shero grabbed his arm.

"Don't touch him," Shero ordered.

"There's so much blood on him, but I can't tell where it's coming from," Vernon said.

"I don't think it's his," Shero said.

"That's Porter Monroe," Wes said.

"Are you sure?" Hurley asked.

"Yes."

"Poor devil," Shero mumbled.

"Why isn't he dead?" Hurley asked.

"Basically, he is. His heart just hasn't stopped beating," Shero said.

Wes squatted down beside Porter's body.

"Don't touch him!" Shero yelled.

Wes flinched, then glared up at the doctor.

"You need to shut the hell up. You don't know what he's hearing or thinking."

"According to Storm's notes, he shouldn't even be alive," Shero said.

Wes pointed at Porter. "But he is, isn't he? Which

means Storm was wrong...at least in part. We're still missing a brother, and I'd like to know what happened to him, too, before I go back to Ally."

Shero glared.

Wes looked back at Porter and kept thinking about the rats in Storm's lab that had chewed off their paws. He'd never seen this much blood on a man who was still alive, and with Danny missing, the thought of where it might have come from was making him sick.

"Porter...can you hear me? It's Wes Holden."

Porter lifted his hand up in front of his face and began slowly moving his fingers, as if he didn't know what they were.

Wes gritted his teeth. "Porter! Where's Danny? We can't find Danny."

Porter blinked slowly. His fingers stopped moving, although his arm was still up in the air.

"Porter, I need to find Danny. Where's Danny?"

"The deer...got Daddy a deer. Venison...likes venison."

Wes wanted to weep with relief. The blood. It must have come from the deer.

"Did Danny go hunting?" Wes asked. "Tell me, Porter. Was Danny with you?"

"Lost," Porter whispered. "Little brother lost." Then his eyes rolled back in his head. Breath rattled at the back of his throat, and then he was gone.

Wes stood as Hurley fired a question at Vernon.

"Where did this man come from?" he asked.

Vernon was trying not to gag. "We just found him here," he said.

Wes was already searching the ground for blood splatters when Hurley realized what he was doing.

"I've got people for that," he said. "You're going to mess up the trail."

"You don't have any people better than Wes," Charlie said. "Or me, for that matter. Uncle Sam trained us well. Let us help."

"Fine, but I'm still in charge, and if I say stop, then somebody better be hitting the brakes."

Charlie strode off after Wes, leaving the rest of them to sort out who was boss and bring up the rear.

As Wes moved, it was easy to see where Porter had come from. There was blood all over the place. Unfortunately for Wes, Porter's trail was as confused as his mind. It appeared that he had stumbled often, fallen repeatedly and doubled back on himself countless times. But Wes didn't think it was to throw anyone off the track. It was nothing more than an echo of the random chaos in his mind.

Charlie caught up with Wes, and without speaking, they spread out and began backtracking along Porter's trail.

As they started down the hill into the woods opposite the path the fire had taken, Charlie suddenly stopped.

"Whoa," he muttered.

"What did you find?" Wes asked.

"Dead raccoon."

"Don't touch it," Wes said. "Remember what Shero told us."

Charlie gave it a wide berth and resumed the search.

A short distance away, Wes came upon a dead deer. Some of the points on the deer's antlers were broken off. He found them embedded in a tree.

As they continued to track, they could hear Hurley and his men coming down behind them. When the agents came upon the dead animals, Wes heard Hurley key up his two-way. The CDC was going to have their work cut out for them now.

"Here," Wes said, pointing toward a path through a thicket. "I've got blood on the brush, and broken branches."

Charlie nodded and shifted his path a bit to the right, as did Wes.

Minutes turned into a half hour and Wes was of the opinion that Porter would not have been physically able to go any farther, when he heard the sound.

He stopped, then held up his fist. Charlie saw the signal to stop and paused, then he heard it, too. He looked at Wes and frowned.

"Bees?"

"Some kind of insects," Wes said. "Sounds like they're swarming."

"We'd better wait," Charlie said. "Remember what you said about all those ants?"

Wes's stomach was already in knots as he turned around and waved Hurley down.

The agents came quickly.

"What?" Hurley asked.

Wes pointed toward the direction from which the sound was coming. "Listen," he said.

At first they heard nothing but the wind in the trees. They'd already noted the absence of birds and seen the dead animals. But it was Vernon who keyed in on it first.

"Bees. Sounds like bees swarming."

"Or flies," Wes added.

Hurley frowned. "Flies don't make a sound like that."

"They do if there are enough of them, and if they're on something dead," Charlie said.

The color faded from Vernon's face as he glanced nervously around.

"Maybe we should wait for CDC," he suggested.

But Charlie was already moving.

He stepped between two bushes that had overgrown a narrow path, then stopped.

"Oh, God," he mumbled, then turned around and threw up.

Wes was right behind him. Whatever he'd been about to say died on his lips. He stood for a moment, trying to take in what was draped over the rock in front of them, then he grabbed Charlie by the arm and dragged him out of the path as Hurley started past.

"Don't," Wes said.

Hurley frowned. "I'm sorry, Holden, but this is my case and I—" Hurley stopped, then slowly began to move backward. "Lord have mercy," he whispered.

"What is it?" Vernon asked. "What did you find?"

Wes wanted to cry, but he knew if he started, he might never stop.

"Porter's deer. I think we found Porter's deer."

He turned to Hurley and the men who were with him, and without raising his voice, gave them a promise they knew he would keep.

"You can put what you have to in your written report, but don't tell Ally. In fact, if any of you ever tell what you've seen here today, I will find you—each and every mother's son of you—and make you sorry for the day you were born."

Hurley wanted to argue. He could have had Wes arrested for what he'd just said, but he knew where it was coming from, and for once, he understood.

"We have no desire for any of this to get out," Hurley said. "Nor will the CDC. There's no way the bodies can be handled by a funeral home, anyway. They'll have to be burned."

"I'm going to go back to Blue Creek, and I'm going to tell Ally that you found the remains of her brothers. Then we're going to the nearest funeral home, where the director is going to produce two nice caskets that will supposedly contain their remains. And we're going to bury those empty caskets down in the cemetery in Blue Creek. Do I make myself clear?"

Hurley nodded.

Without looking to see if Charlie followed, Wes started back the way they'd come. He was sick to his stomach and shaking so hard it was difficult to put one foot in front of the other. He didn't know exactly what he was going to say to Ally, but it damn sure wouldn't be the truth. How could you explain to a sister that one of her brothers had killed and gutted the other, as if he'd just field-dressed a deer?

By the time Wes got back up the mountain, Porter's body had been covered and there was one man standing guard. He nodded to Wes and then looked away.

Wes just kept walking.

When he and Charlie got back to the van, there was a different driver waiting. He introduced himself as Agent Devine.

"We're done here," Wes said. "Take us back."

Charlie was silent getting in. All the way back down the mountain, he kept glancing at Wes, as if expecting him to explode. Finally Wes spoke.

"Quit worrying," he muttered. "I'm not going to self-destruct."

Charlie shuddered, then swiped his hands across his face, as if trying to wipe away the memories of what they'd just seen.

"God… I'm bordering on the act myself. I wouldn't blame you if you did."

Wes's chin jutted angrily.

"I didn't know her brothers long," Wes said. "But I think they were good men. They just got taken in by a man who offered too much money for them to turn down, and it cost them their lives."

"What about that man?" Charlie asked. "What was his name…Stern?"

"Storm. Roland Storm. If we're lucky, his sorry carcass is lying somewhere up on this mountain and turning to dust."

"Are you okay?" Charlie asked. "I mean…did all of this trigger any flashbacks?"

"No."

"What are you going to tell Ally?"

"That I love her. I haven't got a clue as to what I'll say after that."

Twenty

Roland spent the night under the loading dock behind Harold James's feed store. He wouldn't even let himself think about what the fire might have done to his home and kept hoping that something had survived. He didn't give a damn about his hired hands. All he knew was that by now they had to be dead, and if they'd gotten caught in the forest fire, so much the better. That way, no one would ever know that they'd been dying before it happened.

If Wes and Ally had also perished in the fire, then he was home free. He could collect the insurance on his place, take the money and start over somewhere where no one had ever heard of Blue Creek, West Virginia. But he had to get out of this first.

There were blisters on his skin where he'd come too close to the fire, and he knew he needed to see a doctor, but he decided to wait. Until he knew for sure that all the witnesses were dead, he would have to lie low.

He rolled over onto his side and started to crawl out from under the dock when he came face-to-face with a very large cat. When the cat suddenly arched its back and hissed at Roland, he tried to shoo it away. When it hissed at him again, he picked up a small rock and chunked it at the cat. It hit the animal on its side and sent it running, but before he could make his escape, the doors leading to the dock suddenly opened. Cursing beneath his breath, he was stuck until whoever it was moved away.

"Here kitty, kitty, kitty. Scooby…where did you go, boy?"

Roland recognized the voice as belonging to Harold James, the owner of the store, and realized the cat he'd just run off was probably Scooby. Then he heard Harold chuckle.

"There you are, boy. Come on, I've got breakfast for you."

Roland heard the shuffling of feet, the clank of a metal pan being set down, then another man's voice being added to the mix.

"Hey, Harold. I thought I might find you out here."

"Morning, Duane. I was just feeding old Scooby here. Be with you in a minute."

"No hurry, but where's your hired hand?"

"Up on the mountain, I reckon. Someone said the DEA sent for him."

Roland rolled his eyes and mentally cursed. Holden was alive, which probably meant Ally Monroe was, also.

"Are those the men in the big vans?" Duane asked.

"Naw, that's them people from the disease control."

Roland froze. *The CDC? The DEA? What the fuck is going on up there?*

But he knew the answer to his own question. Either Holden or Ally or possibly both of them must have called the government in.

"Have you heard how Gideon is doing?" Duane asked.

"Someone said over to the café this morning that he was still in Intensive Care."

"Darn shame," Duane said.

"I'd probably have me a heart attack, too, if I'd lost my home in that fire and my boys were still missing."

Roland shifted nervously. He'd never meant for any of this to happen, and he hadn't caused the fire, so he wasn't going to shoulder all the blame.

"What about Gideon's girl?" Duane asked. "Her with that crippled foot and all… It's a good thing Gideon came home when he did, or her and your man, Wes, would have burned up with the place."

"Yes, that's what I heard," Harold said.

"Is she still in the hospital, too?" Duane asked.

"I don't think so. I thought I saw Wes driving toward the motel with her early this morning. That's where they're staying till all this gets sorted out. Now, do you want the twenty-five-pound or fifty-pound sacks of chicken feed?"

"Give me a dozen of them twenty-fives," Duane said. "Them fifties are too heavy for me now. I ain't as young as I once was."

Harold laughed. "None of us are," he said, then added, "Just drive your truck around here and I'll load you right up."

"All right," Duane said.

Roland listened until he heard both men's footsteps moving away from the loading dock, then he crawled out from beneath it and slipped into the alley between the buildings.

He stood for a minute while deciding what to do next. It was obvious that strolling over to Kathy's Café and getting some breakfast was out of the question. If Holden had called all those government people, then it stood to reason that Ally would have reported what she knew, too. It made him furious to think that after all he'd endured, he was going to be blamed for this mess. He hadn't intended to create anything as deadly as Triple H. It was just an accident of nature.

His focus now was to get some different clothes and affect a disguise. With all the strangers in town, he should have no trouble getting around without being caught. But as he slipped along the alley, he knew there was one thing yet to do—get rid of Ally Monroe. He didn't want to live the rest of his life knowing that there was a witness to his horrible mistake.

The television in the motel room was on Mute, although the screen still flickered with life. The bucket of ice was slowly melting on the table, and there was an empty pop can and a candy wrapper in the trash beside the bed. The rest of the stuff that Charlie had brought was uneaten and lying at the foot of the bed while she slept.

Suddenly there was a knock at the door, then someone was calling her name.

"Miss Monroe! Miss Monroe!"

She came awake within seconds, but for a moment couldn't think where she was. Then the memories of the past twenty-four hours returned, and she rolled over and sat on the edge of the bed.

"Who's there?"

"Mr. Holden sent me to get you. There's news of your brothers."

Ally gasped, then scrambled out of bed, taking care not to put much weight on her bad ankle as she hobbled to the door and opened it.

Before she could ask any questions of the man at the door, he grabbed her arm and shoved her inside.

"What are—"

"Shut up!" Roland said. "Just shut up!"

Ally gasped. She didn't recognize the man, but she knew that voice. It was Storm.

He sneered. "What? Don't you like my new look? I'm rather partial to it myself," he said, then rubbed a hand over his slick pate. Not only had he cut off his ponytail, but he'd shaved his head, too, stolen a man's shirt and a pair of pants from a clothesline, and snitched a pair of sunglasses from an unlocked car out in the parking lot. In a lineup, he wouldn't have recognized himself.

"What did you do to my brothers?" Ally asked.

He frowned. He'd expected fear and tears, not belligerence.

"Their deaths were an unforeseeable result of their employment."

"No!" Ally wailed. Her legs went weak as she collapsed at the foot of the bed, then began to cry.

Roland cursed. "Shut up!" he said. "Just shut up." He wrapped her hair around his hand.

"No!" Ally screamed, then yanked off his sunglasses and tried to scratch out his eyes as she kicked him between his legs.

In the time that it took for his brain to register the pain, she was already hobbling toward the door. The moment she cleared the doorway, she started to scream.

Roland cupped himself with both hands, stifled a shriek, then dropped to his knees. She was getting away, but he couldn't move, let alone walk. Precious seconds passed before he could stand, but as soon as he could, he stumbled after her.

The drive down from Roland Storm's property had been completely silent. Neither Charlie nor Wes had been in the mood to discuss the horror of what they'd seen. Agent Devine hadn't seen fit to do any talking, either.

Wes was so distracted by thoughts of what he was going to tell Ally that the rattle of the wooden planks on Blue Creek Bridge failed to trigger any response. As they started down Main Street, he took a deep, cleans ing breath. Whatever happened, he and Ally had each other, and that would bring them through, but Charlie had gotten more than he'd bargained for.

"Hey, Charlie."

Charlie cleared his throat. "Yeah?"

"Sorry you got caught up in all of this."

"No need to apologize to me. I have no emotions invested in this town or these people, other than an overwhelming sadness for what's happened. I'm nothing but a witness." He looked at Wes, then shuddered. "Did you feel it up there?"

"Feel what?" Wes asked.

"The Devil."

"Odd that you would say that," Wes said. "Ally said as much."

Suddenly Charlie grabbed the back of the seat and pointed.

"Wes! In the parking lot!"

Wes leaned forward, but his view was blocked. Then Agent Devine pulled forward, and they all saw Ally, stumbling and falling, then crawling across the parking lot. When a stranger suddenly ran out of their motel room after her, Wes felt the world shift. He didn't recognize the man, but there was something oddly familiar about his long, jerky stride.

Then it hit him. It was Storm, and he was after Ally.

"Stop!" he shouted. "For God's sake, stop!"

Devine slammed on the brakes as Wes opened the car door and jumped out. The driver got a brief glimpse of

Wes running between two cars before a tall, bald-headed man tackled Ally Monroe in the parking lot. He shoved the car into Park and got out on the run, with Charlie Frame right behind him.

Ally knew, even as she cleared the sidewalk, that she wasn't going to be able to outrun Storm this time. There was no Wes around to save her, and no trees behind which to hide.

"Help…somebody help me!" she screamed as she stumbled, then fell.

Pain ripped through her as the concrete grated against her skin. She cried out, then just as quickly began scrambling to get up.

Suddenly Storm's hand was around her ankle, pulling her down and dragging her back.

"No…no, God, no!" she said as she began to beg for her life.

This time, Storm dodged her heels as he grabbed her by her hair, yanking her upright. Between one breath and the next, he had her up against his chest and a knife across her throat.

In total despair, Ally began to thrash and moan. She couldn't die, not now, not when she'd just found love.

"Be still or I'll cut you now and forgo the pleasure of a little torture," Roland snarled.

Ally froze.

He laughed, then bit her ear just enough to cause her pain.

"You know, you're just like your freaky little uncle. He meddled where he didn't belong, and it got him killed," Roland said, then pushed the knife a little harder against her skin. "So soft," he muttered. "It won't hurt a bit."

Ally was trying to come to terms with what he'd said about Uncle Doo when everything came undone.

Before Roland could shove the knife in, he saw something from the corner of his eye. Just as suddenly, his body went numb. He could hear Ally screaming as she slid out of his arms, but he could no more have stopped her than he could have saved himself.

In slow motion, his mind registered that the knife he'd been holding was no longer in his hand. There was a moment of panic, then steel was slicing through flesh and bone, but not Ally's. His. His arms felt like rubber, his hands flailing uselessly at his neck as he went down. Cradled by concrete and with the sun in his eyes, he had yet to see who had brought him to this place.

Feelings began to intensify as his pulse echoed in his ears—the precious sound of his life, fading with each beat. The coppery taste of his own blood was on his lips, the scent of Ally Monroe's shampoo as her hair slid through his fingers in his nose, and in his ears an emotionless voice telling him something—something he strained hard to hear.

Then, when he did, his last thought was one of regret. He should have left town. Wes Holden didn't lie. He'd warned him to leave Ally alone.

* * *

Ally didn't know what had happened or that Wes was even there until he picked her up in his arms.

"I've got you, baby…. I've got you. It's over. He can't hurt you again."

Ally began to tremble, then she started to weep.

"They're dead. They're dead. He said my brothers are dead…and oh, Wes…oh, Wes…he killed Uncle Dooley, too."

Wes could hardly grasp what she was saying, but if he could have killed Roland twice, he would have done it right then.

"Oh, baby…I'm sorry…so sorry."

Charlie appeared and grabbed Wes by the arm.

"Get her out of here," Charlie said. "Devine and I have got the scene until the authorities arrive."

Wes quickly carried Ally back into the room, kicking the door shut as he went. He laid her on the bed and then ran into the bathroom for a wet cloth. Moments later he was back and sat down on the bed beside her.

"Ally…honey…let me see your hands."

She sat up. Her fingers were trembling as she felt along her neck, feeling for the cut and the blood, remembering the knife against her throat. Then she put her arms around Wes's neck.

"You saved me," she whispered. "You saved my life."

Wes tossed the wet cloth aside and pulled her into his lap. She was shaking hard—so hard. Every breath was followed by a sob, but she didn't break. She was tough, this woman of his heart.

"Sweetheart, I'm so sorry. If I'd known you were in any danger, I would never have left you alone."

"It's not your fault, it was Storm's. All of this. It was his fault, wasn't it?"

Wes closed his eyes as he held her and tried not to think of what he'd seen up on the mountain.

"Yes."

"My brothers… Did Agent Hurley find them? Storm said they were dead."

Wes said a quick prayer for the lie, then nodded.

"Yes, darling…he found them."

"I need to see them, please."

Unconsciously, he tightened his hold.

"No, honey, no. You don't…you can't…."

"But—"

"Honey…the fire…they just—"

Ally moaned, but she didn't argue. For that, Wes was thankful. He hadn't exactly lied. He'd just led her to believe what she needed to know, so he could keep her from a more horrible truth.

"Oh, Wes, how am I going to tell Daddy?"

"Ally, honey, unless you want to, you'll never have to do anything alone again. I'll be right beside you when it's time."

"Okay."

"Now, let me take a look at your hands."

She leaned back as he held them palms up, then

grabbed the washcloth from the table where he'd tossed it, and began cleaning the grit and gravel from the scrapes.

"Wes?"

"Hmm?"

"Our house…it's gone, isn't it?"

He paused, then looked up.

"Yes, honey, but your uncle Dooley's house is still there."

She tried to smile, but it was hard to come by. She didn't want to go back. She would never be happy on the mountain again.

"What's going to happen to Daddy? To us?"

Wes laid the cloth aside, then cradled her face.

"Wherever we are, your father will be with us."

"I don't know if he will leave this mountain," Ally said.

Wes heard more than concern for her father in her words.

"What do you want?"

"To be with you."

"That's already a done deal, darlin'. What else?"

Her lips were trembling, her eyes swimming with unshed tears.

"I don't think I can be here anymore."

"Do you mean here in Blue Creek?"

She nodded. "Too many bad memories."

God, he knew just what she meant.

"It's all right, baby. I understand."

"So what happens now?" she asked.

There was a long moment of silence as Wes considered his words.

"We do as everyone has done during times such as these. We pick up the pieces that are left of our lives, weep for the dead, and live the best life that we can for those who can no longer live it for themselves."

"Oh, Wes, what a gift you are to my life."

"As you are to mine," he said softly, then added, "So…have you ever been to Montana?"

Ally shook her head slowly.

"What would you think about going there?"

"To live?" she asked.

"Yes."

"If you're there, then I think it would be fine."

"The sky is closer to the ground and the space wider than you can imagine," Wes said.

"Sounds like heaven."

Then there was a knock at the door.

Wes pulled her close, kissing her hard and fast, before going to answer.

The loose ends of their lives had yet to be tied before they could begin to tie knots of their own, but when they began, there would be no more need to look back.

The worst was over.

Colonel John Wesley Holden was no longer missing in action.

Thanks to Ally, he'd found his way home.

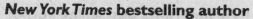

MIRA®

New York Times bestselling author

ERICA SPINDLER

"Spindler's latest moves
fast and takes no prisoners.
An intriguing look into the
twisted mind of someone
for whom murder is simply
a business."

—*Publishers Weekly*
on *Cause for Alarm*

When a friend is found brutally
murdered in her New Orleans
apartment, former homicide
detective Stacy Killian has reason
to believe her death is related to
the cultish fantasy role-playing
game White Rabbit. The game is
dark, violent—and addictive. As
the bodies mount and the game is
taken to the next level, Stacy sees
cryptic notes that foretell the next
victim and no one—no one—is
safe. Because White Rabbit is more
than a game. It's life and death. And
anyone can die before the game is
over…and the killer takes all.

KILLER TAKES ALL

*Available the first week of May 2006
wherever paperback books are sold!*

MES2305